Skeleton Picnic

Books by Michael Norman

The Sam Kincaid Mysteries
The Commission
Silent Witness

The J.D. Books Mysteries
On Deadly Ground
Skeleton Picnic

Skeleton Picnic

A J.D. Books Mystery

Michael Norman

Poisoned Pen Press

Poisoned Pen Press
6962 E. First Ave., Ste. 103
Scottsdale, AZ 85251
www.poisonedpenpress.com
info@poisonedpenpress.com

Printed in the United States of America

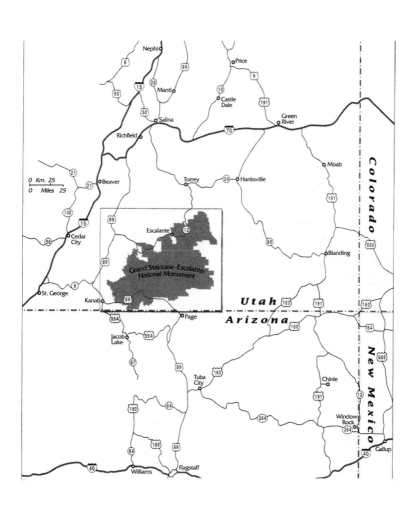

Chapter One

Irritated, Roland Rogers glanced at his watch. The retired Kanab High School teacher was anxious to get under way. Abby, his wife of thirty-seven years, was late. He dialed her cell number at the supermarket.

"Hi, Rolly—can't talk now. We're busy."

"You promised you'd get off early today. We need to get going."

"I tried. They won't let me off."

"If we don't get moving soon, it'll be dark before we find the site."

"I'm too busy to talk, gotta go," said Abby. "I'll get there as soon as I can."

He started to argue, but she disconnected before he could say anything else. He closed the flip phone muttering to himself.

Rolly Rogers hooked the small pop-top trailer to the back of his Ford F-350 pickup. The massive 4 x 4 had almost unlimited towing capacity and had always gotten him through, no matter how difficult the terrain. The Silver Beast, as he liked to call it, looked just the same as when he'd driven it off the showroom floor six years earlier—better in fact. Shiny new chrome wheel covers decorated the tires. Rogers was a man who took good care of his things. Everything neat and tidy and everything in its place was a standard he lived by and had instilled in each of his children.

He had already loaded the off-road vehicle into the truck bed. Now, he only needed to add groceries and several tools for digging, and, of course, wait for Abby to get home.

A third-generation Kane County resident and a lifelong pot hunter, Rogers grew up in a family that collected ancient artifacts from anyplace it could find them—usually that meant public or tribal lands. It was illegal, sure, but everybody did it. As a kid growing up in the fifties and sixties, he recalled outings with family and friends where everybody collected whatever they could find—pot shards, arrowheads, ceremonial blankets, beads, clay pots, baskets, even human bones. His grandfather referred to these weekend adventures as "skeleton picnics." Collecting ancient artifacts was a family tradition in the Rogers household, one that he passed along to his own children as they grew, and an activity that had united the close-knit Mormon community of Kanab during good times and bad.

His personal collection of Fremont and Anasazi antiquities rivaled that of anyone in southern Utah. While he would never admit it, selling valuable artifacts not only raised his standard of living, but also helped pay the cost of sending his children to Brigham Young University.

This trip was the first of the year. Like most serious collectors, Rogers confined his artifacts hunting activities to the spring and fall months to avoid the blistering summer temperatures that turned the arid Colorado Plateau into a high altitude inferno of parched clay, sandstone, and granite.

They left Kanab a couple of hours before dark heading south along State Highway 89A until they crossed the Arizona State line near Fredonia. At Fredonia, they turned west on Highway 389 and followed it to the Paiute Reservation, then further west, deeper into the reservation, until they saw road signs for the Pipe Spring National Monument.

Instead of entering the monument, Rogers turned south on a narrow, washboard dirt road that ran along the banks of the

Colorado River until it eventually dead-ended at a recreation area called Toroweap. Rogers had no intention of going that far south, so he turned east into a remote, sparsely populated area where he and Abby had stumbled upon an Anasazi site the previous fall. In less than a mile, the road disappeared and Rogers found himself slowly picking his way around and through granite boulders, salt and sagebrush, cheat grass, and misshapen sandstone pinnacles and buttes. A large-eared piñon mouse darted in front of the truck, disappearing into a stand of isolated junipers.

"Think anybody discovered our little treasure?"

His wife looked genuinely bored. "I doubt it. It's a pretty remote site, and we're so early in the season that most people haven't started hunting in earnest."

"I hope you're right."

When Rogers felt he could go no further without risking damage to the truck and trailer, he stopped and set up camp not far from where he believed the site was located. He disconnected the trailer and unloaded the off-road vehicle while Abby busied herself unpacking. A cool desert breeze blew vermilion specks of sand into his eyes causing them to tear. In the distance he could see a small cluster of large cottonwood trees and willows, an indication of a creek or other water source nearby.

A whip-tailed lizard scampered through camp disappearing into a rock formation just as Abby emerged from the trailer. The creature startled her and she cried out. "Gosh, I never get used to those little guys."

"What?" he said, glancing up from his GPS.

"Nothing, just a lizard."

Abby studied Rolly as he read coordinates on his GPS while reviewing a detailed map of the area. She loved the man to death, always had. She considered him her own version of Indiana Jones. It was silly, she knew. The thought made her smile.

Abby zipped her fleece vest tight around her neck and shivered involuntarily in the cool evening breeze. She looked skyward and noticed an accumulation of puffy white clouds on the western horizon above jagged rock formations cast in hues of orange and pink in the evening twilight.

"Did you check the weather before we left?" she asked. What worried her was the possibility of rain. The soil was composed of sand and clay. When it rained, the clay adhered to tires, rendering roads impassable. If you had the misfortune of choosing a campsite near a dry wash bed, a sudden downpour could turn an otherwise dry wash into a torrent of raging muddy water, sweeping away anything in its path.

"I did. The forecast calls for clouds, wind, but no rain. We should be fine."

They met while attending Brigham Young University. Rolly had fallen for her almost immediately. The attraction was mutual, and they married at the beginning of his junior year. After graduation, Rolly accepted a teaching job at his high-school alma mater in Kanab, Utah. With a newborn son and Abby at his side, they moved to Kane County and never left.

"You're not thinking of trying to find the site tonight, are you?" she asked.

He didn't look up from the topo map. "Why not?"

"Because it's getting dark, and you know how these places give me the creeps at night."

He looked over at her and shrugged. "Oh, come on, Abby. There's still a few minutes of daylight left, if we get a move on it. Besides, we're supposed to have a full moon tonight, and that'll help us see—might even be a little romantic."

"Romantic, I don't think so—just you, me, and a bunch of dead Indians. No, thanks. I'm tired, and I'd rather wait until morning."

That was his Abby, he thought. In their thirty-seven years together, she always spoke her mind. He admired that quality about her, but he wasn't about to give up.

"Look, I know where we are, and the gravesite can't be more than a few hundred yards from here. Let's just go take a quick look. We won't do any digging until tomorrow morning. I'm anxious to see whether anyone else has disturbed our little find or whether we'll be the first to turn soil."

Abby had learned long ago that Rolly was tenacious when it came to hunting artifacts. Once on the trail of a possible site, he became almost obsessive. "I don't feel like walking," she said.

"I don't either. We'll take the ORV."

Reluctantly, she agreed.

Abby paced nervously while Rolly searched for the keys to the ORV. Scanning the horizon in every direction, she observed giant rock sculptures of every size and dimension. As the evening sky with its fiery orange hues surrendered its final moments of daylight, the setting sun cast the cliff faces and rock walls in awe-inspiring colors of pink, yellow, red-rust, and creamy beige.

Rolly had been right. They discovered the ruin not more than a quarter-mile from camp. Almost immediately they realized the site held great potential. It was an undisturbed surface ruin with a small alcove in one corner. Because they were protected from the elements, alcoves frequently contained a wide array of pristine artifacts.

Rogers could hardly contain himself. He wanted to begin digging immediately. Increasingly nervous, Abby wanted to return to camp and begin excavation the next morning. Twilight had now given way to complete darkness. Large, misshapen granite slabs surrounding the ruin created eerie shapes and shadows that frightened her when cast against the moonlit sky.

"Rolly, I want to get out of here now. Let's go,"

"Patience, my dear, give me another minute. I think I just found a corner wall." He was on his knees, digging straight down using a trowel to scoop away loose sand and dirt.

Abbly glanced into the darkness. "What was that?"

Rogers looked up, momentarily interrupting his digging. "What was what?"

"Shh. I heard something, I'm sure of it. It sounded like a wail or maybe a chant of some kind."

"You're hearing things." He was about to resume digging when he heard something as well, a high-pitched guttural sound coming out of the darkness to the east. Was it animal or human? He wasn't sure. He had never heard anything like it before. Instinctively he reached to his side, cursing when he realized he'd left the nine-millimeter Glock in the truck.

They stood together in the cold darkness feeling vulnerable and afraid, hearing nothing save their own labored breathing and the rustling wind, hoping that whatever they thought they heard they hadn't. Abby was shaking and muttering something incomprehensible, a prayer, he thought.

"What should we do, Rolly? I'm really frightened."

Rogers stood transfixed, watching for any sign of movement from the direction of the sound. "What is that smell?" he said.

"I think it's sage or maybe burning incense."

And then they came out of the darkness, several large black figures running directly at them spread out in a ragged skirmish line. They hardly looked human.

Abby screamed.

Chapter Two

It was noon on Sunday when Bureau of Land Management (BLM) Law Enforcement Ranger J.D. Books woke from a restless night's sleep to a nasty hangover and a throbbing headache he doubted an entire bottle of Advil could relieve. As he reached his mid-thirties he had discovered, much to his dismay, that an evening spent with his face in a bottle exacted a heavy price the next day.

He rolled over, glanced at the clock on his nightstand, and then stumbled into the bathroom. He turned on the cold water and stuck his head under the tap, wondering if he could possibly look as bad as he felt.

He did.

A small group of fellow BLM employees met once a month for a poker party. This one had been hosted at the home of his boss, Monument Manager Alexis Runyon. While her poker-playing acumen was nothing to get excited about, she served pitchers of Margaritas strong enough to bring a mule to its knees. He'd added a generous helping of chips and guacamole, and then gorged himself on spicy beef tacos—a perfect recipe for an extended stay kneeling in front of a commode. He'd gotten home at two in the morning, fifty bucks lighter in the wallet and with a bellyache requiring a fistful of Rolaids.

He limped into the kitchen to fix coffee. The bullet he'd taken in his leg eight months earlier at the hands of a contract killer, while fully healed, had left him with what doctors called "phantom pain." It didn't seem phantom to him. His doctors couldn't readily diagnose the cause, and, therefore couldn't prescribe an effective treatment. All they'd been able to do was tell him to be patient, that the pain would eventually disappear. So he'd learned to cope through physical therapy, lots of physical exercise, and an occasional dose of Ibuprofen on particularly bad days.

He cursed when he reached for the coffee. He had just enough for one carafe and then he'd have to roast. He placed the last of the Guatemalan in the French press, added boiling water, and then waited the requisite five minutes before plunging. Books was fussy when it came to coffee. Years earlier, he had begun roasting his own green coffee beans. Mostly through trial and error, he discovered that he had an affinity for coffee grown at high altitude in countries in Central and South America. He'd never acquired a taste for African beans or the overpriced Hawaiian Kona.

He reached for the phone and dialed Ned Hunsaker's number. He had invited Ned to Sunday breakfast. He now called with an apology and an offer to reschedule.

"Got in a little late this morning, did ya?"

"Yeah. Sorry about breakfast, Ned, a few too many margaritas last night. How did you know I got in so late?"

"Couldn't sleep. I was up reading from midnight until around two-thirty. I heard you when you drove in."

"If you're not busy, come on over. I just made coffee."

Renting the mobile home from Hunsaker had worked out well. The arrangement provided Ned with a little extra retirement income and gave Books an inexpensive place to live while he got his bearings in a community he hadn't lived in for more than a dozen years.

The two men sat in Books' small living room drinking coffee and reading the *Salt Lake Tribune* Hunsaker had brought. Since they both enjoyed reading the Sunday paper, they had made a ritual out of getting together for breakfast.

Books glanced up from the sports section. "I haven't seen much of you the past couple of days. What have you been up to?"

"I've been around." Hunsaker didn't take his eyes from the newspaper. "It seems like I get up in the morning with nothing to do and go to bed at night with only half of it finished."

That brought a smile to Books' face. "That's retirement for you."

Hunsaker had become the father-figure he had longed for but never had. And then Hunsaker's revelation that he, not Bernard Books, was actually J.D.'s biological father had shaken Books to his very core. He had never suspected the love affair between his late mother and Ned Hunsaker, not for a second. Books had opted not to tell Bernie or anyone else for that matter. He didn't see the point.

Books had just toasted bagels when the telephone rang. It was two-thirty in the afternoon. The number on the caller ID looked all-to-familiar. It was Kane County Sheriff Charley Sutter.

"*Hola,*" said Books.

"What's this *hola* shit, J.D.? You go to Mexico for a week?"

"Just practicing."

"Yeah, would you mind practicing on somebody else?"

"You're a cranky old fart today, Charley. What's gotten under your skin?"

Sutter's tone softened. "I got a problem, J.D. Would you mind helping me out with something? It won't take you long."

"*Sí, Sí, Señor* Sutter. What can I do for you?"

"Would you mind taking a drive over to Rolly and Abby Rogers' home and take a look around? They live right near you."

"Sure. Anything wrong?"

"Don't know. We got a call this morning from their daughter who says they didn't show up at church this morning. We went ahead and took a missing persons report. Melissa told one of my deputies they left Friday afternoon on a camping trip and were supposed to come back Saturday night."

"Maybe they decided to stay out another night."

"Possible," said Sutter. "I haven't contacted county search and rescue yet. Figured I'd give it a little more time. See if they turn up."

"Has anybody been by the house?"

"Melissa's husband drove by after church looking for Rolly's truck and their pop-top trailer—nothing there."

"What time was that?"

"Around noon."

"I'll head over there now and call you as soon as I have a look around."

Books remembered Rolly Rogers from his years growing up in Kanab. Rogers had been his U.S. history teacher during his junior year. He had also coached the girls' and boys' cross country teams.

Long-revered members of the small southern Utah town of Kanab, infamous pot hunters Rolly and Abigail Rogers had been looting ancient Anasazi and Fremont Indian sites for decades, stealing artifacts, and, over time, accumulating what some people regarded as one of the most extensive and valuable antiquities collections in all of Kane County. As an elementary school student, Books remembered accompanying his classmates on a science field trip to the Rogers' home to see their vast collection of ancient artifacts. Only later did he understand the significance of the collection and what it meant to be a digger.

As Books dressed he had no way of knowing that a simple request for help from Charley Sutter would not only jeopardize his own life but those of his family.

Chapter Three

Books rolled into the Rogers' circular gravel driveway shortly after three. Ned tagged along. The single-story brick rambler had an attached garage that, at some point, had been converted to living space. A detached garage had been added next to where the original garage once stood. A Tuff Shed sat behind the house off to one side.

They walked to the front door and knocked. Nobody answered. The closed drapes made it impossible to see inside. Ned waited out front while Books walked to the back of the house. He climbed two steps on to a cedar deck that led to a set of French doors. The patio doors served as the home's rear entrance.

One look at the wood door jamb and Books reached for his snub-nose .25 caliber Smith and Wesson revolver. Around the lock, he saw fresh pry marks probably made by a screwdriver. The unlocked door stood slightly ajar. Books pushed it open and listened. The house was quiet.

"Police, anybody here?"

Silence.

He stepped into the home's great room. The kitchen sat off to one side. On the kitchen floor laid a dead cat, a small pool of drying blood around the body. Shit, thought Books.

He moved quickly from room to room, searching the entire house. Books discovered a broken jewelry case in the master bedroom. The contents had been dumped on the bed and the shattered case tossed to the floor.

The converted garage served as an office, complete with a roll-top desk, a computer station, a printer, and file cabinets. The stuffed heads of a five-point mule deer and a pronghorn antelope were mounted on respective walls. Across the room, a glass display case had been smashed and the contents removed. This was the artifacts room, Books thought. Whoever had broken in had come primarily for the antiquities collection, he guessed, and they'd taken it all.

He rejoined Hunsaker out front and used his cell to call the sheriff. "You got a B&E over here, Charley, and a dead cat—better send a deputy and have somebody from the family stop by."

"A dead cat."

"That's what I said. It looks like it's either been shot or knifed. I couldn't tell."

"Was there forced entry?"

"Yup. Somebody went in through the French doors at the back of the house. Nothing very sophisticated. It could have been the work of kids."

Sutter grunted. "All right. I'll send a deputy right over and I'll be along shortly."

Sutter made it to the Rogers' home ahead of his deputy. He nodded at Books and Hunsaker. "I'm startin' to get a bad feeling about this, J.D."

"Maybe the two incidents are unrelated."

"Could be, I suppose. Let's hope so. After your call, I went ahead and notified search and rescue. It'll take a couple of hours for them to mobilize, but they should be able to launch the search before dark."

As he looked around, Books noticed two newspapers lying in the driveway and a UPS parcel lying on the front porch. He walked to the mail box, opened it, and saw mail inside.

"Tell you what, Charley, the Rogers might as well have hung a sign in the front yard saying, 'on vacation—thieves welcome.'"

"Why do you say that?"

"Look around. When you leave town and don't have somebody pick up the mail and newspapers, it becomes a standing invitation for any thief. And the bad guys don't have to be particularly sophisticated to notice, either."

A white Dodge Caravan pulled into the driveway. A plump woman with stringy brown hair in her early thirties got out. She walked up and gave Sutter a weak smile and a warm hug. She smiled at Hunsaker. "Afternoon, Ned."

"Melissa."

"J.D., this is Melissa Esplin, Rolly and Abby's daughter," said Sutter.

Esplin gave him a curt nod but didn't say anything. Books figured his BLM employment probably earned him a less than enthusiastic greeting.

"Ranger Books checked out the house at my request and discovered the break-in. We'd like you to come in with us and take a look around. I'm sorry to have to tell you this, but there's a dead cat lying on the kitchen floor."

"Oh, my gosh, that must be Einstein. Mom and dad have had that cat for over a decade. The thieves must have killed him."

"Afraid so," said Sutter. "I'm going to ask that you don't touch anything. We haven't had time to take pictures or look for prints. I hope you can help us determine what's been taken."

"I'll try."

"I understand your folks left on Friday afternoon," said Books. "Would you happen to know what time?"

"Mom didn't get off work until four o'clock, so sometime after that."

"Any idea where your parents may have gone on their camping trip?"

She regarded Books for a moment and then shook her head. "They never said."

"Anybody go with them?" Books asked.

"They were alone as far as I know."

"Can you think of any places they preferred to go?"

"No place in particular. What is this, Ranger Books, play twenty questions?"

"Not at all," said Books, "but anything you can think of might help us find them."

She didn't reply.

Sheriff Sutter broke the tension. "Well, why don't we go inside and take a look around. We can come back to this afterward."

Books couldn't tell what upset Melissa Esplin the most, the dead cat, the theft of expensive pieces of her mother's silver and turquoise jewelry, or the discovery that the perp had cleaned out the family's valuable antiquities collection.

A Kane County Sheriff's Department patrol vehicle pulled into the circular driveway. A uniformed deputy parked, got out, and came into the house. Sutter introduced his newest and only female deputy, Beth Tanner. She looked to be in her mid-twenties and had that fresh, just-out-of-the-police-academy look. Turns out she had grown up in nearby Cedar City and had taken this job as a means of returning to her southern Utah roots.

With the arrival of Deputy Tanner, Books saw no reason to stay. His presence seemed to irritate Melissa Esplin and the sheriff seemed to have the matter under control.

"I'm out of here, Charley. Let me know if there's anything else I can do."

"Give me a second, would you J.D.? I'll be right along." Sutter directed Deputy Tanner to carry on with the investigation while he followed Books outside.

"Sorry about that little exchange, J.D. There was no reason for Melissa to become defensive with you."

"Don't worry about it, Charley. I'm a Fed and she comes from a family of dedicated pot hunters—no love lost there."

"Still, there's no reason for her to behave that way."

Books shrugged and gave Hunsaker a faint smile. The old man had remained quiet during the exchange, glancing from Sutter to Books and back again at Sutter.

"There is something else you could do for me," said Sutter. "Would you mind sticking around here for a few minutes and helping Tanner? She hasn't been on the job long."

"Sure. Where are you going to be?"

"I need to hook up with county search and rescue. They're gathering at the fire station to organize the search. I'd be happy to drop Ned at home on my way in."

Books glanced at the sky. "Be dark soon, Charley. Your search may have to wait until daylight.

"You're probably right. Maybe that's for the best. If we get lucky, they'll show up by morning and we can skip the whole thing."

"That would be nice."

"But damned unlikely, right?"

"I think so, Charley."

"I'm open for suggestions, J.D."

Books turned to Hunsaker. "What do think, Ned?"

"Since Melissa was no help, it's going to be like looking for a needle in a haystack. That said, here's what I'd do if I were you. I'd concentrate the search around here."

"What makes you say that?" asked Sutter.

"If they didn't leave until sometime Friday evening and planned to return Sunday morning in time for church, they haven't gone very far. My recollection is that old Rolly prefers collecting Anasazi artifacts instead of Fremont Indian antiquities. That tells me he's probably gone somewhere south of Kanab along the Arizona strip. The Four Corners area is too far away for such a short trip."

"Makes sense," said Books.

"Only if they've gone pot hunting," countered Sutter. "What if they haven't?"

"It's possible Charley, but I doubt it," said Books. "It's springtime. The pot hunting season is in full swing for the next several months. Then they'll lay low until fall before going back to work. And Rolly Rogers is one of the busiest pot hunters in the county; always has been."

"I agree, Charley," said Hunsaker. "I've known Melissa all her life and I like her just fine. But let's be honest. She was deliberately vague when J.D. started asking specific questions concerning the whereabouts of her parents. If her folks had gone off visiting friends or family, Melissa would have said so. If they were going to some event someplace, she would have told us. I'm not saying Melissa knows where they are, but I do think she knows they're off somewhere pot hunting."

Hunsaker left with the sheriff. Books re-entered the house to see if he could do anything to help Tanner. He wanted to be available to assist without making her feel threatened or incompetent. Books found Tanner and Melissa Esplin seated in the living room filling out the police report.

"Anything I can help you with, Beth?"

She looked up from the report. "As a matter of fact, there is. Melissa tells me that her folks had the artifacts collection and some of the jewelry appraised and insured. The insurance file contains photographs of everything in the collection. Would you mind taking a look at that while I snap some crime scene photos and dust for latent prints?"

"Sure."

Tanner returned to her patrol car for the crime scene kit and camera while Books accompanied Esplin to the converted office at the back of the house. While Books waited, Esplin removed a small key from the desk and used it to unlock a four-drawer file cabinet in the corner. It took less than a minute for her to locate a file folder marked collectibles. Without speaking, she handed it to Books.

"Let's take a look."

Books opened the folder and laid it on the desk. Inside was an addendum to a home owner's insurance policy and an appraisal document from a Salt Lake City company called Gilbert Fine Art & Appraisal. An insurance policy was issued in December. 2009, following an appraisal completed in November. Several pieces of the silver and turquoise jewelry as well as the antiquities collection appraised for $250,000. All in all, it would make a significant insurance claim.

Books turned to Esplin. "I didn't notice, but does the house have any kind of alarm system?"

She shook her head. "We nagged mom and dad continually about that but they never got around to it."

That revelation surprised Books. The antiquities collection was worth a small fortune.

"The appraisal and insurance policy are fairly recent. Did your folks ever have the collections insured before?"

"Not sure, but I don't think so."

Books hit the mother load when he opened a manila envelope inside the folder. It contained color photographs of the jewelry and the antiquities collection.

The Rogers' collection contained an impressive variety of artifact types including stone hammers and knives, ornate baskets and sandals woven from native fibers such as yucca, willow, and milkweed; intricately designed clay pottery used as pitchers, ladles, jars, and storage containers, some with handles and some not, some pieces textured and some polished smooth; necklaces made of beads, often black or white, with bits of turquoise; animal hide artifacts like moccasins, breechclouts, and robes; and finally, two glass display cases filled with arrowheads and pot shards of every size, color, and configuration.

"The photographs are going to be helpful," said Books. "If everybody did this with their valuables, the recovery rates would be a lot higher. Can we borrow the file temporarily until we can make copies?"

Esplin thought about it for a moment. "I guess, but don't lose it. It's the only record we've got."

"The insurance company and art appraiser probably have copies, but we'll take good care of it and get it back to you sometime tomorrow. With luck, by that time, your parents will be back, and this'll all have been for naught."

As they left the office, Books noticed a small framed photograph of the Rogers couple. The photo looked recent and Books asked if he could borrow it. Esplin nodded.

Books found Tanner up to her elbows in latent print powder. She was about finished and asked Books to meet her outside. Good PR maybe, but often the attempt to find latent prints didn't produce anything useful although it usually left the victim felling better about the police investigation.

"You look good covered in fingerprint powder."

She smiled, "Romantic, isn't it?"

"No, but you wear it so well."

"Must be the CSI effect."

"Must be."

Tanner had piercing green eyes and hair the color of honey that she wore pulled back in a pony tail.

Books handed her the insurance file containing the art appraisal and the photographs. "This ought to increase the likelihood of recovering at least some of the stolen property, and maybe it'll lead you to the perp."

"That'd be nice. I appreciate your help. I've been out of the academy only three months, so I'm pretty new at this."

"Experience is a good teacher, Beth. You'll do fine. So what are you going to do next?"

Tanner looked around. "I thought I'd canvass the neighborhood. See if anybody saw anything."

"That's a good idea, but before you leave, you might want to sit down with Melissa and find out which pieces of fine jewelry in that insurance file are actually missing. We know the entire antiquities collection was taken, but you'll want to be sure about the jewelry."

"I'll do that before I leave. What about Einstein?"

"I'm not sure. You should probably ask Melissa," said Books. "It must've been a damn smart cat."

Tanner suppressed a laugh. "Smart ass."

Books gave her his cell number and told her to call if she needed help with anything else.

Chapter Four

Books rose early the next morning. He filled a travel mug with some Starbucks coffee he used as backup when he ran out of fresh roasted, wolfed down a toasted cinnamon raisin bagel, and headed out. Radio traffic confirmed that Rolly and Abby Rogers were still missing and that county search and rescue had been unable to begin the search until first light.

He had offered to help and Sutter assigned him an area south and west of Kanab in the general vicinity of Hildale, Utah, and Colorado City, Arizona. If it turned out the missing couple was the victim of foul play on BLM land, the BLM would assume jurisdiction in the case.

Books drove in a southwesterly direction across the state line into northern Arizona near the Paiute Indian Reservation. The flat desert landscape contained stands of juniper and scattered sage flanked by towering, copper-colored granite peaks to the north.

He searched as far west as the two polygamist communities before turning north into the National Smithsonian Butte Backway. He stopped at a couple of remote gas stations and showed the picture of the missing couple in the hopes somebody might recall seeing them. Nobody had.

Books backtracked to Colorado City and began searching an area southeast of the town. He periodically reported in using a radio frequency set up exclusively for the search-and-rescue effort. After nearly seven hours, nobody had a clue as to the whereabouts of the missing couple. Members of the search team sounded frustrated.

All that changed at two-thirty in the afternoon when a National Park Service helicopter, flying out of Flagstaff, discovered the Rogers' truck and trailer parked several miles north of the Colorado River on a remote dirt road near Mount Trumbull. The pilot and spotter reported seeing an off-road vehicle parked almost a quarter mile from the campsite. Sadly, there was no sign of Rolly or Abby Rogers at either location.

As Books listened to the radio traffic, he realized the area in question belonged to the BLM. "Ah, shit, here we go again," he muttered to himself. He had hoped the incident had occurred on tribal lands or on land belonging to the state of Arizona so the BLM wouldn't have jurisdiction.

Books was at least thirty minutes away. He needed to get there as quickly as possible to assume control of the crime scene. As a precaution, he instructed the dispatch center to radio the helicopter crew and tell them not to land anywhere close to the camp or excavation site. He didn't want the chopper inadvertently blowing anything of evidentiary value into the next county. Unfortunately, it had happened before. Also, Books contacted ground units approaching the area and advised them not to enter the campsite but to establish a secure perimeter a couple of hundred yards out.

According to the chopper pilot, the site around the off-road vehicle appeared to have undergone recent excavation. Rolly Rogers' truck, trailer, and off-road vehicle, pointed squarely to a pot hunting case. However, a disturbing question remained. Where were Rolly and Abby Rogers?

When Books arrived, he called the Kanab office and asked them to notify the regional field office in Salt Lake City. Personnel higher in the food chain than uniformed rangers typically investigated pot hunting cases. In the distance, he could see the empty campsite and the truck and trailer. The helicopter had set down well out of the way from the throng of searchers and their vehicles.

People from various agencies milled about, seemingly with nobody in charge. He observed staff from the National Park Service, the National Forest Service, Kane County Search and Rescue, as well as officers from two Arizona law enforcement agencies.

A man wearing a Mohave County sheriff's uniform approached Books and extended a hand. "Welcome to Mohave County, J.D. I don't know whether you remember me, but I'm Ralph Meeker, the Mohave County sheriff. We met a couple of months ago at the Arizona Sheriff's Association meeting in Flagstaff."

"Sure do. Nice to see you again, Sheriff."

"Don't mind saying, I'm pleased this little incident is unfolding on BLM land."

"Your good fortune, I guess."

Books regarded Meeker. The man looked to be in his late thirties with thinning black hair turned prematurely gray. His smooth, unlined face would have made him look years younger otherwise.

"If you wouldn't mind," said Books, "maybe you can establish a perimeter around this area while I go over and have a look inside the trailer and at the dig site. I don't want a bunch of people trampling through the area just yet."

"Glad to, but I think I can help you with something else." Meeker motioned toward a uniformed deputy who had been standing in the background by himself. The man appeared to be in his late twenties. Books figured him to be Navajo but he wasn't sure.

"J.D., let me introduce you to Joe Nez—best tracker in the department. I suggest you allow him to accompany you. He might just spot some things you and I would miss." The two men shook hands.

"Glad to have the extra pair of eyes," said Books.

Meeker established a circular perimeter some distance west of where the truck and trailer were parked while Books and Joe

Nez proceeded on foot to the trailer. They had decided to make the entire area, including the dig site, one large crime scene, restricting access only to those who needed entry. Until they could figure out what happened, it made sense to treat the area as a scene involving foul play.

As they approached the trailer, Books and Nez passed the Dodge pickup. A ramp used to unload an all-terrain vehicle stretched from the tailgate to the ground. The truck's doors had been left unlocked with the keys still in the ignition. They moved on to the pop-top trailer. The top had been raised so Books could see through the canvas covered windows. Two sleeping bags were tossed on the beds and an ice chest rested on top of a small dining table. Food, kitchen utensils, and cookware were scattered around the interior. Either the Rogers had hurriedly unpacked, or someone had tossed the trailer.

"Not very tidy," said Books.

Nez nodded. "Notice the digging tools?"

"Yup. It's a family with a long history of digging."

As he checked the campsite, Books noticed Nez studying the ground as he walked slowly out of camp to the east, away from the direction of the dig site.

"It's this way, isn't it, Joe?"

Nez looked in the direction Books pointed and then back at the ground. "Maybe, but the ATV went this way."

On closer examination, Books saw the faintest tire tracks leading off the pot-holed dirt road into an area devoid of any semblance of a trail. They followed the track a couple of hundred yards until it turned south, passing through a sandy wash and then around the base of a pinnacle-shaped rock formation. On the far side of the outcropping, they emerged on a flat plain, where they discovered the remnants of a crumbling stone and mud structure.

Nez stopped and studied the ground near the off-road vehicle. Even to his untrained eye, Books could see faint shoe and boot prints. "What do you make of it?"

"Not sure, but there was a group of them circled around."

"How many?"

"Five, maybe six, counting the missing couple."

"Looks like they ran into some unwanted company," said Books.

"Could be."

Books guessed the size of the L-shaped structure at ten by twelve feet. He didn't know what the room had been used for, religious ceremonies or maybe a burial site. The room, particularly the corners, had been thoroughly excavated.

Deputy Nez remained in the background, outside the structure. As Books moved closer, he saw the skeletal remains of what appeared to have been a small child tossed casually off to one side. The scene gave Books the creeps. Even though he'd grown up in a community where pot hunting was considered socially acceptable, that hadn't been the case in his own family. He wondered how people could desecrate gravesites and toss human remains around like so much unwanted garbage.

Books turned and started to say something but realized that Nez was no longer there. He glanced around and spotted the deputy in full retreat toward the truck and trailer.

Back at the campsite, Books found Charley Sutter engrossed in conversation with the Mohave County sheriff, Ralph Meeker. Deputy Nez was standing off to one side talking quietly to another officer.

Sutter and Books exchanged greetings. "Any sign of them, J.D.?"

Books shook his head. "It looks like a thoroughly excavated burial site, but no sign of the Rogers. It appears they had company. We saw footprints, Nez thought five, maybe six people."

Sutter looked worried. "Any sign of a scuffle or fight?"

"Not sure, but I don't think so. Nez didn't mention it, but he didn't stick around very long either—acted kind of skittish."

"That doesn't surprise me," said Meeker. "Traditionally raised Navajos, like Joe, are real superstitious when it comes to the dead. They believe it's best to leave them alone. Some even think that if you disturb the dead, bad things will happen to you—like sickness, mental illness, that sort of thing."

"Yeah," said Sutter. "In fact, about the only exceptions are Navajos raised in a Christian religion, those who follow the Jesus Road as they call it."

Sutter continued. "What about physical evidence?"

"Somebody left a trowel at the dig site—no idea who it belongs to. And there are a couple of cigarette butts on the ground."

"They're both nonsmokers," observed Sutter, "so that means the cigarettes belong to somebody else. I'm not sure what to make of it, but it sure doesn't feel right."

Sutter told Meeker about the break-in of the Rogers' home and the theft of their valuable antiquities collection, adding, "It might be a coincidence."

"Doesn't seem likely," said Meeker.

"No, not likely," said Sutter. Turning to Books, he said, "What happens now, J.D.?"

"My hands are tied, Charley. BLM procedures require me to protect the scene until I'm relieved by a special agent. We already called the Salt Lake office—haven't heard back from them yet."

"Think they'll send in a forensics team to process the scene?"

"I would think so, but it's up to the agent assigned."

Personnel from the various agencies who had participated in the search left Books, with two Mohave County deputies, to secure the area until BLM reinforcements arrived.

Chapter Five

An hour and a half later, BLM Special Agent Randy Maldonado arrived from St. George. Books didn't know the man personally, but his reputation was impeccable. Maldonado, a fit-looking fifty-something veteran, knew more about grave diggers and pot hunting cases than anybody in federal law enforcement. He had investigated more antiquities cases than anybody in the country. Prosecutors in the U.S. Attorney's Office knew and respected him.

The two men exchanged greetings and shook hands. "On the drive over, I got a call from Sheriff Sutter," said Maldonado. "I didn't get all the details, but he seems to think this case is related to a B&E in Kanab."

"It could be."

"You're not convinced."

"I'm a skeptic by nature."

Maldonado shrugged. "It's the nature of the business, I guess. Anyway, Charley would like to proceed as if the two cases are related."

"All right."

Motioning toward the abandoned campsite, Maldonado said, "Tell me what you've got here."

"The truck and trailer belong to a Kanab couple. Rolly and Abigail Rogers, both dedicated pot hunters. Near as we can tell, they left Kanab late Saturday afternoon on what the family says was supposed to be an overnight camping trip—didn't make it back for Sunday church services, so a daughter reported them missing."

"Camping trip, my ass," said Maldonado. "Rolly's been a known antiquities collector for as long as I've been with the agency—never have made a case against him, though. But pardon my interruption. Please go on."

"On Sunday afternoon I checked their home and discovered the break in. Among other things, their antiquities collection was stolen."

"Any suspects?"

Books shook his head.

"Who found this?" Maldonado pointed at the campsite.

"Chopper unit out of Flagstaff found it early this afternoon. About three hundred yards to the west, we found an ATV parked next to a recently excavated Anasazi burial site. The ATV also belongs to the Rogers couple."

"And they're nowhere to be found?"

"That's right."

"So, for the time being, you've got yourself mixed up in a federal pot-hunting case, a missing person investigation with possible foul play involved, and a good old fashioned B&E with no suspects."

"That's about it."

"Easy enough to understand why Charley thinks the cases are connected—be one hell of a big coincidence for this couple to go missing on a pot-hunting trip at the same time somebody breaks into their house and steals their artifacts collection."

"That's exactly how Charley sees it."

"But you don't."

"It does seem logical. It's just that, at the moment, we don't have a shred of evidence to support that theory. I prefer to wait until I see what the facts tell us."

Maldonado studied him for a moment. "Seems reasonable. Here's what we could do. If you're interested, I can authorize you to investigate the illegal digging case. You can coordinate what you're doing with the sheriff's investigation. I'll be available to answer any questions you might have, and I'll make arrangements to have the crime scene processed. That work?"

"Let's do it."

◇◇◇

Books remained at the crime scene long enough to show Maldonado the path from the Rogers' campsite to the location of the excavated burial site. While Maldonado handled the crime scene, Books decided to canvass the area hoping to find somebody who might have seen something.

An hour later, Books had stopped at several dirt-scrabble ranches in the immediate area. Nobody was home at the first two stops. At a third ranch, an elderly man sitting on his front porch reported seeing nothing unusual. At the last stop, he gave up after the biggest damn dog he had ever seen chased him back to the Tahoe.

Eventually he ran across an elderly man camped by himself off a dirt road about a mile from the Rogers' truck and trailer. The man was seated outside an old Ford pickup truck with an ancient camper mounted on top, drinking a Pabst Blue Ribbon beer and eating Fritos. The rig had more rust on it than the Titanic and the old man didn't look much better.

"Howdy, young fella. Why all the cop cars runnin' around here?"

"We're searching for a missing Kanab couple," said Books. "Found their camp site not far from here, but no sign of them. You see anything that looks suspicious?"

The old man smiled. "You mean besides all the cop cars?" He gazed off into the distance momentarily thinking the matter over. "I did see a big black SUV, Cadillac Escalade, I think, driving past here a couple of times."

"When was that?"

"Yesterday afternoon."

"What made you think it was suspicious?"

"Shiny new black Cadillac Escalade—just seemed out of place, that's all."

"Are you from around here?"

"Nope. I live in Dove Creek—betcha don't know where that is?"

"Bet I do. Dove Creek is in the Four Corners area just across the Utah line in Colorado."

"It surely is."

"Anything else you can remember about the Escalade?"

He thought some more. "Only that all the windows were tinted so you couldn't see inside."

Books extended a hand and introduced himself. "And you would be?"

"Hitch. Eldon Hitch."

"Pleasure to meet you, Mr. Hitch. What brings you way out here?"

"Driving to Mesquite to visit my daughter and son-in-law."

"How long have you been camped here?"

"Got here day before yesterday. I'll be headed out first thing in the morning."

Books wondered, but didn't ask, what Hitch was doing camped in this desolate place. Dove Creek was a community well known for having a significant population of diggers.

"Well, I'll be on my way, then. You travel safe, Mr. Hitch."

"I'll do that, Officer Books. You take care now, hear."

Books handed him a business card. "Appreciate the tip about the Escalade. If you remember anything else or see anything that looks suspicious, I'd sure appreciate a phone call."

"You can count on it."

Books returned to the Tahoe, jotted down the plate number of the truck, and ran the registration. Everything checked out. He'd run a background on Eldon Hitch later.

Chapter Six

It was dark by the time Books returned to Kanab with little to show for the time he'd spent looking for witnesses save the tip about a black Escalade that would probably turn out to be useless. He stopped at his office and found a voice message from Beth Tanner asking him to join her at the Cattle Baron. He stopped at home first and changed out of his uniform.

The Cattle Baron liked to call itself a sports bar, but Books always considered that claim a stretch. The menu consisted of mediocre sandwiches, pizza, beer, and wine. A pool table stood in one corner and a wall-mounted big screen TV hung next to the bar.

The few times he had been in the place, the only sports he'd seen on the television were pro-rodeo events or those high-stakes poker games where most of the players wore mirrored sunglasses as they tried to play head games with their opponents. Worse, the television was often tuned to Fox News, which required him to listen to a boatload of right-wing political tripe. Books didn't much care for politicians, and he didn't care whether they came from the left or right. Unlike most cops, his own political leanings were definitely left of center, something he figured he'd gotten from his parents, both of whom had been active members of the Democratic Party.

As he entered, he observed Tanner shooting a game of pool with a couple of off-duty Kanab City cops he recognized but couldn't put names to. They were sharing a half-empty pitcher of beer that they'd left on the bar along with three beer steins. Between shots, she spotted him and waved him over. Books shook his head and pointed to an empty booth across from the bar where he took a seat. He ordered a pitcher of draft beer from the waitress and waited for Tanner to finish the game.

Beth Tanner looked good in uniform and even better out of it. She filled out a pair of jeans nicely. When she finished the game, she picked up her coat and a half-empty glass of beer and joined Books.

"Not up for a game of pool, huh."

"Not really. Never could play very well."

"Why not?"

"Poor hand-eye coordination, I guess. I discovered the problem when I was in the police academy in Denver. I was number one in my academy class until we headed over to the firing range. I came in dead last and barely scored well enough to qualify."

"The cop who couldn't shoot straight," she said, laughing at him.

"That would be me. What did you want to see me about?"

Tanner reached into her coat and removed a manila envelope.

"I brought you copies of the police reports on the Rogers B&E—everything except the lab reports. Those are going to take a while."

"Appreciate that," said Books. "You work fast. I'll get you copies of mine just as soon as I can find the time to get them written."

"That works. I figured we might as well share information, since Charley wants the two cases worked together."

"That probably makes good sense. My BLM superiors have essentially delegated the pot-hunting case to me for follow up."

"I'm not surprised, given your reputation."

Books wondered what she meant by "reputation."

"Yeah, the way you handled that murder case last year. I was in the academy at the time. Kanab's never seen anything like it—I mean a Las Vegas hit man in town. It doesn't get any cooler than that."

"It didn't strike me as all that cool, since I ended up getting shot."

"I heard. You heal up okay?"

"Just fine, thanks."

For the next hour they drank beer and made small talk about policing and their lives outside of work. Elizabeth Tanner was single. She was the youngest of five children, and the only female. Family influence played a major role in Tanner's decision to enter law enforcement. An uncle and two brothers were cops.

She had grown up in a family that placed a premium on self-reliance and participation in all manner of outdoor sports. She was an avid hunter, backpacker, cross-country skier, and motorcycle racer, dirt bikes mostly. She also considered herself an accomplished, if out of practice, karaoke singer.

They finished the pitcher of beer. Tanner suggested they find a restaurant for dinner. Books asked for a rain check, citing fatigue and the prospect of a long day ahead. The excuses sounded lame, even to him.

Tanner's invitation seemed innocent enough, but Books was wary. His own divorce had been final for less than six months. The closest he had gotten to any member of the opposite sex since his return to Kanab was local attorney Becky Eddins, and that relationship had its ups and downs.

Books found the message light blinking on his ancient answering machine when he got home. He hit the rewind button and listened to messages from Charley Sutter and BLM Special Agent Randy Maldonado. Both men asked for a return call as soon as possible. Books glanced at his watch. It was almost midnight. The calls would have to wait until morning.

The last message was from his father, Bernie, asking him to meet the next morning at seven at a local java joint called Beans & Such. He had invited Books' younger sister Maggie as well. That piqued his interest. He wondered what was on the old man's agenda that required an immediate council of sorts with his two children.

Books' relationship with Bernie had improved marginally in the nine months since his return to Kanab, but he still hadn't completely adjusted to the shocking revelation that Ned Hunsaker was his biological father, not Bernie. The relationship with Bernie was still awkward, distant, and lacking emotional intimacy—not something Books blamed entirely on the old man. A part of him preferred it that way. Books had kept the paternity secret to himself, not sharing it with Bernie, his sister Maggie, or anyone else.

He had no sooner undressed and gone to bed when the telephone rang. He turned on the bedside lamp and picked up. It was Charley Sutter.

"Sorry to bother you so late, J.D. I called earlier, but you were out."

"That's okay, I wasn't asleep. Any news?"

"None. The family is becoming increasingly anxious, and that spells trouble for you."

"How so?"

"They're planning to organize a search party made up mostly of friends, relatives, and a few volunteers. They're chomping at the bit to get out to the campsite and start snooping around."

"It's easy to understand their anxiety."

"Of course it is, but you can't have them running around out there tearing up the crime scene."

"I understand. I'd be happy to talk to them, but I think they're more apt to listen to you."

"You're right. I'll try to talk some sense into them."

"Maldonado left me a message earlier—any idea what he wanted?"

"I haven't talked to him, so I'm not sure," replied Sutter. "Maybe he wants to give you an update on how the crime scene processing went."

"Maybe. What about the Rogers' home. Is it still sealed or has the family had access?"

"We've kept everybody out, family included. I told them we'd let them know when we were finished. Until then, it's a crime scene and off limits to everybody."

"You'd best be sure that Deputy Tanner has done everything inside that house that needs to be done—because the family will undoubtedly want access sooner rather than later."

"I'll look into it, and if anything else needs to be done, I'll send for a CSI unit."

"I'll touch base with Tanner in the morning and make sure she's on the right track."

"Thanks, J.D. She's a good kid but green as grass. Let's talk tomorrow." They disconnected.

Books slept badly that night. He lay awake for a long time going over every theory he could think of that might explain the disappearance of Rolly and Abigail Rogers. Was their disappearance connected to the burglary of their home? So far, there was no evidence linking the disappearance with the burglary. Books, however, doubted the two events were unrelated—too much coincidence.

His police instincts told him that working backwards from the burglary would give him the best chance of discovering the whereabouts of the missing couple.

The hodge-podge of tracks around the dig site made it clear that the Rogers' had been interrupted by a number of unknown subjects. There were no obvious signs of a struggle, but that didn't mean much. Had they been kidnapped? If so, why hadn't the family heard from somebody demanding a ransom?

Books didn't want to imagine the alternative—that the Rogers were taken hostage, led to some remote part of the desert and killed, their bones left to bleach under the hot desert sun. In such expansive and remote terrain, the bodies might never be recovered, particularly if they had been hidden or buried.

As he lay awake, he wondered what had become of the sleepy little ranch community he'd grown up in. By returning to Kanab, he had hoped to escape the grinding poverty and crime of big cities like Denver. Yet, in less than a year as a BLM ranger, he had encountered multiple murders and now the disappearance of a prominent local couple.

Tuesday Morning—Day 5

The phone rang just as Books climbed out of the shower. The caller was his sister, Maggie. "Morning Mags, what's up?"

"You got the message from dad?"

"Sure did. I haven't a clue what this little get-together is about. Do you?"

"No idea. It came out of the clear blue. I'm worried about it, though."

"Hell, sis, maybe he's bringing us together to announce he's marrying a hooker and moving to Las Vegas."

"Not funny, J.D."

"You're right. Sorry. I've been thinking about it. Maybe he's decided to move away from Kanab. You mentioned that he was spending time in Vegas. Let's face it. Kanab isn't a great town if you're a single senior who enjoys female companionship. Vegas, on the other hand…"

"Hadn't thought about that possibility. It makes sense, though."

"I can't think of what else it might be. And who knows, per-haps we're making a big to-do about nothing. Maybe the old man just wants to have breakfast with his kids."

"I don't think so. It's not like him." She sighed. "Well, I guess we're about to find out. See you in a few minutes."

Chapter Seven

By the time Books arrived at Beans & Such, he found Maggie and his father sequestered at a corner table engaged in a quiet conversation. Judging from the empty coffee cups, the meeting had begun without him. Maggie dabbed tears from her eyes with a paper napkin—not a good sign he thought.

The two men exchanged subdued but pleasant greetings before Books turned his attention to his sister. "Mags, what's wrong?"

Teary eyed, she blew her nose into the napkin.

Books turned to his father. "What's going on, Bernie?"

"I got colon cancer, son, stage 3, they tell me."

Books tried to hide his sense of alarm, not wanting it to register on his face. "I'm really sorry to hear that. Who are you seeing?"

"The docs at the University of Utah Hospital."

"When did you find out?"

"About two weeks ago."

"You should have told us right away, dad. Why didn't you?" Maggie's voice held an edge.

"Been putting it off, I guess. I didn't want to burden you kids with my problem. You've got enough to worry about in your own lives without having to fret about mine."

"But, Dad, that's what families do," Maggie said. "If we don't worry about you, who will?"

"She's right, Bernie. What made you think something was wrong in the first place?"

"I haven't been feeling all that well for the last couple of months—not much appetite, weight loss, tired all the time. So I went in to see old Doc Petty. He listened carefully to my list of symptoms, gave me a thorough physical, including a blood test, and then referred me to the hospital for a colonoscopy. The colonoscopy revealed the tumor so Doc Petty referred me to an oncologist acquaintance of his at the Huntsman Cancer Center in Salt Lake City. I've been running back and forth to Salt Lake for the past couple of weeks."

Doc Petty had been the family physician for as long as Books could remember. He'd run a family practice in Kanab for generations. Getting referred by Petty to a specialized cancer treatment center must have scared the old man half to death, thought Books. The experience would scare anyone.

"You mean you've been going to Salt Lake City to see the cancer specialists while you've been telling us you're off in Las Vegas partying." Maggie's irritation was even more evident. Bernie nodded, head down, avoiding eye contact with her.

Books quickly came to his rescue. "Nothing we can do about that, Mags. Best let go of it and figure out how to help D..., Bernie going forward."

Maggie softened. "What happens now, Dad?"

"They got me scheduled for surgery Friday of next week. They're going to cut out part of my colon, sew it back together, and then put me through several weeks of chemotherapy."

They decided Maggie would travel to Salt Lake City with their father prior to the surgery. Books would arrange home health care services after his father returned to Kanab. He would also try to be at the hospital for the surgery if his work schedule permitted. His father's illness couldn't have come at a worse time.

Books left the coffee shop badly shaken and headed for his office. What was he feeling? He wasn't sure—sadness, regret, guilt—perhaps some of each. He never anticipated having to confront a health care crisis in the life of the man who had raised him, nor had he figured to be so upset about the news. But he was.

From his office, Books called Dr. Petty's office where a pleasant sounding female voice asked him to leave a detailed message. He then Googled stage 3, colon cancer, and quickly found the information he sought.

He learned the survival rate for individuals diagnosed with stage 3 colon cancer varied by the location of the tumor as well as the stage it was in. There were five stages of colon cancer. The overall survival rate for people with stage 3 was 62 percent, meaning that nearly two out of three patients were still alive five years after the initial diagnosis. That was good news.

Books turned his attention back to the dual investigations. He carefully perused Deputy Tanner's police report to get a better handle on things she had already done, clues she might have overlooked, and leads she hadn't had time to follow.

Despite all the advances in forensic science, Books still believed that most serious crimes were solved the old-fashioned way, by talking to people. After reading the report, it was clear that while Tanner had interviewed some people, there were many more she hadn't spoken to who might have pertinent information.

He dialed the sheriff's office and discovered that she was off-duty and unavailable. He sorted through his own file until he found her phone numbers. She didn't pick up the home number so he left a message on her cell. Ten minutes later, Tanner stuck her head in his office.

Books glanced up from the notes he was writing in the investigative file. "Working on your days off, huh. That's got to make Charley happy."

Tanner shrugged. "Not much choice, really. The sheriff's feeling a lot of pressure right now, and when Charley feels it, he makes sure the rest of us do as well."

"No rest for the wicked."

"I guess not. Have you had time to read my report?

"I have, Beth, and I think you're moving in the right direction. Keep talking to people—friends, family, coworkers, even enemies if you can find any. In the meantime I'm going to be looking at the Rogers' bank account. I want to find out whether there have been any withdrawals in the last day or two—checks written, ATM withdrawals, that kind of thing."

"You're thinking that the kidnappers might have forced them to get cash."

"Wouldn't be the first time."

"That makes sense."

"I'll also pay a visit to the area pawn shops. Maybe we'll get lucky and find some of the jewelry or items from the antiquities collection. My guess is that whoever broke into the house didn't do it because they wanted to add to their own antiquities collection. They'll want to turn the jewelry and artifacts into quick cash."

"And the easiest way to do that is by selling them at pawn shops."

"Yup. Any idea where the Rogers do their banking?"

Tanner shook her head.

"That's okay. There are only two banks in town, and it's got to be one of them. I'll check it out."

"What about the pawn shops? I'd be glad to help you there."

"Maybe later. For now, why don't you stick with the interviews? We'll touch base later in the day and see where we are."

On his way out of the office, Books ran into his boss, Monument Manager Alexis Runyon. She had heard about the missing couple but didn't have many details. Books filled her in.

"Be sure you keep me in the loop," said Runyon, "in case we start getting calls from the regional office in Salt Lake City."

"Will do. I expect the case will start attracting increased media attention, particularly since they remain missing."

As he climbed into the Tahoe, a smiling Runyon said, "By the way, I really enjoyed taking your money Saturday night. How was your Sunday morning hangover?"

"Substantial. And remember, Alexis, payback's a bitch. Have a nice day."

At his second stop, Books learned that Rolly and Abby Rogers banked at the Kane County Regional Bank in Kanab. Delbert Adams, the bank manager, agreed to dispense with the legal niceties that would have required Books to obtain a court order before accessing bank records.

"Abby and Rolly maintain joint savings and checking accounts here at the bank," said Adams.

"Can you check for recent account activity?"

"Sure. Let me just change screens." Moments later, Books had his answer. "No activity in the savings account for more than two weeks," said Adams. "Not so, I'm afraid, with the checking account. The account shows two recent ATM withdrawals. The first occurred on Saturday night, at 11:54 p.m., for $500.00. The second occurred ten minutes later on Sunday morning, at 12:05 a.m., again for $500. Five-hundred is the maximum any customer can withdraw in a twenty-four hour period."

"Where were these withdrawals made?"

"The Page Community Bank in Page, Arizona," replied Adams.

Books was sure of one thing. Whoever made the withdrawals wanted to get the maximum amount of cash in one visit to the ATM. It wasn't hard to imagine kidnappers forcing a PIN from the terrified couple. Given the timeline, Books concluded that Rolly and Abby Rogers were probably taken soon after their arrival at the dig site. Who abducted them, and why, remained a mystery.

"What would it take to freeze the accounts right now?" asked Books.

Adams made a couple of key strokes and said, "Done. The accounts are frozen. I'll have to notify the family, Melissa since she's local."

Books thanked the bank manager, jumped in the Tahoe, and made the one-hour drive to Page in just over forty-five minutes. He planned to check the pawn shops and make a stop at the Page

Community Bank. He wanted to see the surveillance tapes of the ATM transactions during the time the Rogers' withdrawals had been made.

Page had one pawn shop, and it operated as a combination pawn and payday loan store—the type that preys on the underclass by offering small, short-term loans at exorbitant interest rates.

Books found Page Quick Loan and Pawn in a strip mall one block off the main drag. He was greeted by a heavy-set, middle-aged woman who introduced herself as May Flagg. She looked like a woman who had seen and heard just about all there was to see and hear. The silver ring above the pierced eyebrow, coupled with the multiple body tattoos and copious amounts of makeup, made her look like a carnival performer who might handle snakes and offer tarot readings on the side.

She gave Books the once over. "Never seen feds in here before, only a few local cops. What can I do for you, officer?"

"I'm actually looking for stolen property taken recently from a home in Kanab."

"Never known feds to have any interest in monitoring pawn shops."

"Usually we don't, but this one's a bit complicated."

Books opened a file folder and showed her photographs of the missing artifacts and jewelry. "Have you seen any of these items in the past day or two?"

She glanced at the photos. "Matter of fact, I have. And just this morning, too."

"What time?"

"I open at nine o'clock. I'd say the kid came in around nine-ten, nine-fifteen, maybe."

Books glanced at his watch. "Do you know who he was?"

She shook her head. "Nope. Never seen him before."

"Which items was he trying to sell?"

She pointed to a turquoise squash-blossom necklace and a pair of matching turquoise earrings.

"Describe him for me, would you?"

"Sure. Navajo kid—early twenties, I'd say, dark brown hair, medium height and build."

"Was there anything unusual about him such as scars, tattoos, or body piercings?"

"Nothing I recall."

"I take it you didn't buy," said Books. "How come?"

"Frankly, the kid didn't look like he had a pot to piss in. I been at this a long time, Ranger Books, and, after a while, you develop a sixth sense about this kind of stuff. When I started asking him questions about the origin of the pieces, he picked them up pronto and headed out the door."

"You didn't happen to see a vehicle or get a name, did you?"

"Nothin' on the car. I asked him his name and he said it was Sammy Yazzie, but I wouldn't take that to the bank."

Books gave her his business card, and she promised to call if the suspect returned. From the Tahoe, Books ran the name Sammy Yazzie through NCIC and came up empty. When he accessed DMV records in New Mexico, Arizona, and Utah, he found five individuals with the name Sammy Yazzie. Three had driver's licenses in the state of New Mexico. The other two were licensed in Arizona. Unfortunately, none of the subjects had a birth date that put them into the age group May Flagg had described.

Chapter Eight

The Page Community Bank was located in another strip mall on the other end of town. Books hoped the bank's surveillance tape would provide a good look at whoever had made the ATM withdrawals. He discovered the ATM in a vestibule at the front entrance to the bank. The area was well lit, good for the quality of the tape. He feared he was going to hear the dreaded subpoena word, a potential glitch that would cost him precious time he could ill afford to lose.

Books was ushered into a small, cramped office and introduced to Jennifer DiJulio, the bank manager. DiJulio barely glanced up from a stack of documents she was busily signing and wasted little time on small talk.

"My secretary tells me you're interested in viewing surveillance tape of our ATM transactions. I have privacy concerns about that. Did you happen to bring a subpoena with you?" She continued signing documents as she spoke.

"I only learned about the existence of the tape this morning," said Books, "and time, I'm afraid, is something I have very little of."

"I'm sorry officer, but bank policy…"

Books interrupted. "Lives are at stake here, Jennifer, and the time it would take me to obtain the subpoena you require might mean people are going to die. I really need your help. Can't you dispense, just this once, with bank policy? A bank manager in Kanab just did."

Now he had her full attention. She set her pen down and sat up straighter in her chair. "Do you mind telling me what this is about and why you want to see the tape?"

DeJulio listened attentively as Books filled her in. When he finished, she excused herself and huddled with her secretary. Moments later, she returned.

"Ranger Books, given what you've just told me, I think we have an obligation to cooperate with you. Brenda, my secretary, will arrange for you to view the tape. You can use our conference room. Understand that I won't be able to turn the tape over to you until you get me a subpoena. Would that be satisfactory?"

Books felt relieved. "Absolutely. Thank you very much."

The surveillance tape showed the same individual, a rail-thin, white male, dressed in camouflage military fatigues, making both withdrawals minutes apart. It was impossible to see his face because he wore sunglasses and a round, floppy hat.

Books was disappointed not to see Rolly or Abby Rogers at either the ATM machine or with unknown Navajo male from the pawn shop. He wasn't sure what to make of this new development, but he didn't like it. The investigation had taken a new and worrisome turn. They now had a second suspect and nothing to substantiate whether the Rogerses were still alive.

Books hurried back to Kanab, stopping for a late lunch at the Ranch Inn & Café. The owners, Rusty and Dixie Steed, were fourth-generation Kanab residents who had always treated Books well, despite their general disdain for the federal government. Books had learned that the restaurant, because of its predominant local clientele, was a good place to troll for information.

He took his usual seat at the front counter, nodding a greeting to Rusty, who stood nearby folding paper napkins around silverware. The lunch hour was long over and the restaurant was nearly empty. "Coffee, J.D.?"

"I think just water today, Rusty. I'm dehydrated, and I've already had enough caffeine to float a battleship."

Steed set the glass of water on the counter. "Know what you want to eat?"

"The usual."

"One turkey, bacon, and avocado sandwich coming up."

When Steed returned with his sandwich, Books ate while the two men talked.

"What's the scuttlebutt about the Rogers case?" Books asked.

Steed stopped what he was doing, poured himself a cup of coffee, and sat down on the stool next to Books. "It's what you might expect—shock, anger, sorrow—the full gambit of emotions. And while nobody is saying anything out loud, there's probably a healthy dose of fear among the collectors that maybe they'll be next."

"You think that'll put a damper on the digging?"

"Maybe temporarily, until you guys find out what happened. But in the long run, I doubt it. The serious hunters will probably take more precautions and become increasingly suspicious of anybody approaching them at dig sites."

"What kind of precautions?"

"I'd expect them to become more aggressive, making sure everybody in their party is armed, start posting lookouts so they're not caught by surprise when people approach. It's bound to become more dangerous for folks like you who are out to stop them."

"That's not terribly comforting."

"It wasn't meant to be. Just watch your ass out there."

Good advice, Books thought.

"Collectors can be jealous, competitive types. Did Rolly have anyone he didn't get along with—somebody who might want to do him harm?"

Steed didn't hesitate. "Naw, you're barking up the wrong tree on that one, J.D. Everybody liked Abby and Rolly."

"Well, somebody apparently didn't."

"Trust me. Once this gets sorted out, you'll find that the people responsible were complete strangers to the Rogers."

Books wasn't so sure. "Time will tell. Will you keep me posted if you hear anything?"

"You can count on it. And you know, J.D., you ought to talk to Ned about all this. He's the resident expert on artifacts collecting and grave diggers."

"I didn't know that. I'll talk to him. Thanks, Rusty."

Books hooked up with Beth Tanner at the sheriff's office. Tanner had been busy interviewing friends, family, and coworkers of the missing couple and was up to her neck writing reports.

"Hey, deputy, you're looking a little busy there."

Tanner glanced up from the computer screen and managed a grunt. "They don't tell you about all this report-writing crap in the academy. Each time I interview somebody, I have to document it. It's really boring."

"Welcome to the real world of law enforcement. What have you found out?"

"I spoke with all four of the victim's children as well as two of Rolly's three siblings. Basically, the family seems solid and they all seemed genuinely distraught. The only note of discord I could find concerned a daughter and son-in-law in Salt Lake City who are constantly in financial trouble."

"What's the problem there?"

"They borrow money from Mom and Dad at every turn. There's no way to tell whether the parents are upset, but the other siblings are seriously pissed at what they see as greedy, irresponsible behavior."

"It doesn't seem like we're going to find any family members with motive."

"I don't think so."

"What about the family estate? Is there a will or maybe a trust?"

"There is. The eldest son, who's a bank executive in Provo, is the executor of the family estate. He referred me to a local attorney who prepared both a will and trust. His name is Ed Rollins. I've called him, but so far he hasn't returned my call."

"It sounds like the family angle will turn out to be a bust, but we need to speak to Mr. Rollins anyway. It never hurts to find out which family members stand to gain financially in the event of a death."

"I don't think it will get us anywhere, either, but I'll stay with it."

Books reported on his trip to Page. He told Tanner about the surveillance video from the bank and shared the information about the unknown Navajo man who had attempted to sell the jewelry at the Page pawn shop.

"What do you make of all this, J.D.?"

"I wish I knew. We don't have all the pieces of the puzzle yet. What I do know is that we need to find this Navajo guy, whoever he is. In fact, I think it would be a good idea to get a sketch artist to sit down with the pawn shop proprietor so that we can get something visual into circulation. I'm just not sure where we find a sketch artist in these parts."

"I'll ask Charley. He'll know."

"Okay. In the meantime, there are a couple of more things you can do. First, get a hold of the DA, Virgil Bell, and tell him we're going to need a subpoena for the surveillance tape held by the Page Community Bank. Then check with the local LDS Church bishop and find out if anyone matching the description of our Navajo suspect happens to attend the ward. Also make the same inquiry with the town market where Abby works."

"You're thinking the Navajo man might have been acquainted with the Rogers."

"It's possible."

"Alright. And while I'm at it, I'll get back in touch with Melissa Esplin and see if she knows anything about this Navajo kid."

"Good idea. Now you're thinking like an experienced cop." said Books.

She smiled.

"First thing in the morning, I'll be headed to St. George with a stop at the crime scene for another look around. It turns out Page is a one horse town when it comes to pawn shops. That won't be the case in St. George. I'll catch up with you later in the day."

"What about the guy in the camouflage fatigues. How does he fit into all this?"

"Not sure. It's possible the Navajo and this guy are working together as a team. What really worries me is that the Rogers may have run across a group of militia types—outdoor survivalists who poach and have become adept at living off the land. Some of those boys can be downright dangerous."

"I hope you're wrong about that."

"Me, too, Beth, me, too."

Chapter Nine

Books saw Charley Sutter in the parking lot as he left the sheriff's office. The sheriff was not a happy camper.

"What's up, Charley?"

"The Rogers family is out there running all over hell's creation looking for their folks, the damn fools. They're disorganized, ill-equipped, and mostly without leadership. If they keep at it, I'm sure one of the dumb bastards will end up lost and Mohave County will have to mount a search and rescue operation of their own."

"The good news is that if it happens, it won't be your headache. Did you happen to talk with them about staying away from the crime scene? I plan to be out there again early tomorrow morning."

"I did, but there's really not much I can do. It's not my jurisdiction, and they know it. Unfortunately, local sentiment seems to be laying the blame on my department for not finding Rolly and Abby. It's very frustrating."

Books gave him an update on the investigation and complimented the work of his newest deputy.

"I sensed when we hired her that she'd be a real go-getter," said Sutter. "Glad to hear she's pulling her weight. I'll see what I can do to find you a sketch artist who might be willing to travel to Page and work something up with the pawn store operator."

Books hopped in the Tahoe. "Appreciate that, Charley. I'll keep you posted."

"Please do."

Since his return to Kanab the previous summer, Books had managed to forge a workable, if at times, uneasy relationship with Charley Sutter. This occurred despite the sheriff's constantly having to pay homage to the local political establishment, a constituency so anti-federal government and so far removed from the political mainstream that they made Sarah Palin look like a left-wing liberal. Books was surprised that he and Sutter were able to set their differences aside and focus on getting a job done. But they'd managed it, and Books had developed a grudging admiration for the old sheriff.

It was getting dark by the time Books eased the Tahoe down a gravel road past a sign that read Case Cattle Company. The Triple C brand was well known in the area, because it remained one of the few viable cattle operations in the county and because Doug Case owned it. Case happened to be his sister Maggie's father-in-law. He also owned the local John Deere franchise and chaired the powerful Kane County Commission.

Maggie had invited him and his girlfriend, Rebecca Eddins, to dinner. He had arrived ahead of Becky. From what he could tell, Becky's solo law practice was doing quite well. It was a general practice and she focused primarily on family law—juvenile court, divorce, child custody, that sort of thing. He parked the Tahoe in the gravel circular driveway next to the main ranch house and invited himself in.

"That you, Bobby?" he heard Maggie shout from the kitchen.

"It's me, sis. Where is that lazy brother-in-law of mine, anyway?"

Maggie walked over and gave him a light peck on the cheek. "Who knows? Lately, it seems like he disappears off the planet and I haven't the slightest idea what he's doing or who he's with."

"Well, Mags, you know how boys are. Sometimes we just have to retreat to our caves for a while."

"I guess so. I'm running a little behind. Would you mind setting the table for me?"

"Glad to. Are we eating inside or out?"

Before Maggie could answer, Becky Eddins shouted from the front door. "Outside, I hope. It's going to be a beautiful spring evening."

"Outside it shall be," said Books, "if that's okay with you, sis."

"Absolutely," Maggie answered.

A half-hour later, Books and Maggie sipped cold Miller MGDs outside under the portico while Becky enjoyed a chilled glass of Kendall Jackson Chardonnay. They still hadn't heard anything from Bobby, not so much as a phone call, and Maggie had grown irritated with him. Dinner was almost ready and Books' two young nephews, Chad and Jeff, prowled the kitchen like vultures circling a dead carcass.

"I'm going to go ahead and feed the boys. They'll be happy to eat at the kitchen counter," said Maggie. "We can finish our drinks and then bring our food out here."

"Great," Books said. "What's for dinner? I'm starving."

"Nothing fancy. I've had a pork roast cooking in the crock pot, and Becky brought a loaf of French bread and a scrumptious looking salad."

"Um," said Books. "Beef, it's what's for dinner."

The two women glanced at each other smiling, "You do a poor Sam Elliott impression," said Maggie. "Besides, he's a lot better looking than you are."

"What do you mean? He's an old geezer," protested Books.

"All old geezers should look that good," said Becky.

"I'll drink to that." Maggie raised her glass in a mock salute.

The dinner conversation focused on the status of the ongoing Rogers investigation as well as the revelation that Bernie had been diagnosed with colon cancer. That news shocked Becky, who expressed her sympathy and asked if there was anything she could do. Maggie thanked her but explained that there was little anyone could do for the time being.

After dinner they sat quietly enjoying the last minutes of daylight as the sun disappeared over the western horizon, casting the mountains peaks below in jagged, black shadows. The women had donned sweaters as the gathering darkness brought an evening chill. Becky continued drinking the Chardonnay while Maggie and Books sipped shots of Crown Royal Reserve. The bourbon warmed them. When it was time to leave, Becky wrapped herself around Books in a full body press and whispered in his ear. He returned the hug and told her he'd come by as soon as he had a chance to talk with Maggie. Becky thanked Maggie and left to pick up her young son, Cody, at the home of her parents.

"I don't mean to pry, sis, but I can tell you're upset with Bobby. Can I help with anything?"

"Probably not, but thanks for asking. Frankly, I'm not sure what to think. I don't know what's going on with him lately. He's become increasingly aloof, disappears at times without explanation. I'm beginning to wonder if he's having an affair."

"I doubt that, Mags. An extramarital affair doesn't seem like Bobby's style. Is anything else going on?"

She shrugged in resignation. "The ranch is in trouble financially, but that's nothing new. Things have grown steadily worse since the downturn in the economy."

"If the ranch needs an infusion of cash, can't you go to Bobby's dad? He's still part owner of the ranch, isn't he?"

"Bobby won't even consider it. Things aren't going well for Doug either. He's seen a decline in business at his John Deere franchise. People just aren't buying farm and ranch equipment like they used to."

"I don't know if it's possible, but has Bobby considered going to work for his dad at the store?"

"Not seriously. Doug has already had to RIF several employees. I think Bobby feels that if he had to ask his dad for a job, it would just place an extra burden on the business."

As she walked him to the Tahoe, Books said, "I'm really sorry that you guys are struggling, Mags. If there's anything I can do, please don't hesitate to ask."

Maggie hugged him.

Chapter Ten

Books drove to Becky's thinking not only about the medical condition of his father, Bernie, but adding to his worry list, the money troubles facing his sister and brother-in-law. He arrived just in time to say goodnight to Cody, Becky's seven-year-old son. He and Becky spent the next hour discussing the financial plight facing Maggie and Bobby as well as the community in general.

"I would never have guessed that Bobby and Mags would end up having financial problems," said Books.

"Why not?"

"I don't know—maybe because Bobby's folks have a lot of money. If the ranch floundered, I always assumed that all Bobby would have to do is ask his dad for help."

"Everybody in this economy has been hurt, J.D., some worse than others. I wouldn't assume that all Maggie and Bobby have to do is snap their fingers and Doug will write a check. From the rumors I hear around town, it sounds like his John Deere dealership is in trouble."

"Maggie mentioned that. I didn't want to suggest it, but I wonder if she'll have to look for work away from the ranch. I'm sure she doesn't relish that idea, but it might become necessary. She really enjoys being a stay-at-home mom and raising the boys."

"It's probably not your place to suggest it, but it makes sense."

"How's your father getting along financially?" Neil Eddins was a powerful local rancher and real estate developer who headed an anti-environmental group called the CFW, Citizens for a Free West. Neil wasn't a big fan of J.D.'s and the feeling was mutual.

"Dad's struggling like everybody else. I'm sure he and Boyd are facing some of the same difficulties on the ranch that Bobby and Maggie are. And the real estate business has taken a nose-dive—people wanting to sell but no buyers. They're handling mostly short sales and foreclosures."

"If the big ranchers are having trouble, you can imagine how difficult it must be for the little guys."

It felt good to have someone like Becky to discuss things with. When the conversation finally lapsed, they decided it was time to go to bed.

They showered together. It was easy for Books to slide into Becky's arms and feel her silky warmth pressed firmly against him. He kissed her, enjoying the feeling of her soft lips on his. They made love and then drifted into a deep, uninterrupted sleep.

◇◇◇

Wednesday Morning—Day 6

Books was up early the next morning. He planned to stop at the crime scene, have another look around, and then make the hour and a half drive to St. George in time to catch the area pawn shops when they opened.

The first rays of sunlight bathed the western mountains in shadowy light as Books eased the Tahoe down an almost nonexistent dirt road to where the Rogerses truck and trailer were parked. Orange crime scene tape was stretched across a wide swath of terrain surrounding the camp site. He'd developed the habit, as a robbery/homicide detective in Denver, of revisiting a crime scene alone after the lab technicians had done their work. It sometimes gave him a new and different way of looking at the crime.

A Mohave County sheriff's deputy sat in a patrol vehicle drinking coffee from a thermos. He got out as Books approached and introduced himself.

"Deputy Speers, pleasure to meet you," said Books.

"Likewise."

"Everything quiet?"

"Speers nodded, "I'm bored out of my skull."

"Well, you shouldn't have to do this much longer."

"Things quieted down as soon as it got dark. The Rogers family and their entourage disappeared. Now that it's getting light, they'll probably be back."

"Have you heard anything from Special Agent Maldanado?"

"I think he's finished here," Speers said. "We plan to release the truck and trailer to the family sometime this morning."

Books spent the better part of the next hour rummaging through the truck and trailer looking for anything that the crime scene team might have missed. On foot, he retraced the path the couple's ATV took to the excavation site laboriously searching the ground for any missed clues. The spring morning was deathly quiet, save a cool breeze that gave his arms goose bumps and made his nose run.

He carefully studied the footprints in the sand and clay soil where several unknown subjects had confronted the Rogers couple. His instincts told him that this wasn't a random incident but a well planned crime that had intentionally targeted the victims. But why? Probably, he thought, because somebody familiar with the Rogerses knew about their antiquities collection as well as the fact that Rolly Rogers was a famous, or perhaps infamous, pot hunter. He retraced his steps to the camp site, climbed into the Tahoe, and headed for St. George.

As he rolled into St. George, Books' cell phone rang. It was Randy Maldonado. "I hope you got the word from Sutter about the family search party,"

"I did."

"We've kept them away from the crime scene about as long as we can. Unless you've got something else that needs to be done, I suggest we let the family have the truck, trailer, and ORV."

"Fine with me so long as they understand we might need to produce that stuff in court at some point in the future," said Books.

"We managed to get photos and measurements of the foot-prints Joe Nez discovered. Somebody out there's got damn big feet. One of the boot impressions looks to be a size thirteen or bigger."

"Big feet, little brain," said Books.

"Let's hope so."

"Did the crime scene guys find anything else?"

"Two cigarette butts and a trowel, but I think you saw those. Are you making any progress on the investigation?"

Books told Maldonado what he had learned about the ATM transactions and the Navajo male who had attempted to sell pieces of the stolen jewelry.

"They've been taken, no doubt about that," said Maldonado. "The only question now is, are they alive?"

"I wouldn't bet on it."

"Keep me posted on what's going on. The brass in Salt Lake City is already pestering me for information about the case. I'll keep them off your back as long as I can. Do a good job, Books, and it'll definitely get you noticed at headquarters. Screw it up, and, well, you know."

Books understood but didn't really care about what the brass in Salt Lake City thought. He did, however, promise to keep Maldonado in the loop.

Unsure of the number or nature of the pawn shops in St. George, Books made an unscheduled stop at the local police department. Burglary detective Greg Bell gave him a rundown on each store.

"Look," said Bell, "we've got four pawn shops in town. Two of the four almost never cause us problems. The other two, Red Rock Pawn and Gun and St. George Pawn, receive a lot more of our time and attention."

"How come?"

"The usual. We make unannounced inspections of all pawn shops, and these stores have had a tendency to be a little care-less about their record-keeping. Careless record-keeping is often associated with taking in disproportionate amounts of stolen property."

"I see. Anything else I should know?"

Bell thought for a moment. "Yeah, one thing. Red Rock Pawn and Gun is operated by a guy named Harold Tittlemeyer. Harold's brother, Ernie, is a known fence. He's been busted multiple times for possession and receiving stolen property. Because he's a convicted felon, he can't be on the business license to operate a pawn shop."

"So he hired his brother as a front man."

"Exactly. Harold runs the place, but the money behind the operation comes from Ernie."

"Guess I'll visit those two stores first."

"I would."

Books thanked him and left.

St. George Pawn had a flashing neon sign in the front window that read "quick loans" and "checks cashed." The clerk didn't own the shop but understood the drill whenever police officers came knocking. A perusal of the shop's records revealed nothing remotely similar to the items stolen from the Rogerses' home.

Books hit the mother lode at the next stop, Red Rock Pawn and Gun. Harold Tittlemeyer took a careful look at the photographs of the stolen property. He slowly shook his head. His eyes never left the photos as he muttered, "I had a funny feeling about that kid."

"What kid would that be?" said Books.

"Navajo kid came in here yesterday with some jewelry pieces he claimed had been left to him by his deceased grandmother— not much I could do except take his word for it."

Sure, thought Books. Don't ask too many questions.

It was the same turquoise necklace and matching earrings that the suspect had attempted to sell to May Flagg in Page the previous day.

"I'll need to take the jewelry, and I'd like the identity of the young man who sold it to you. His name wasn't Sammie Yazzie, was it?"

"I don't think so, but let me have a look at the records," said Tittlemeyer. He stepped over to the store's computer and pulled up a spreadsheet.

"There he is. The kid's name was Joe Benally. He had a Utah driver's license with a Kanab address, if I recall correctly."

"You got a look at his driver's license?"

"I think I can do better than that," said Tittlemeyer. "How would you like a copy of the license?" He excused himself and disappeared into an office in the rear of the store emerging moments later with a photocopy of the license.

Books studied the drivers' license carefully. Joseph Benally was a twenty-year-old whose five-foot eleven-inch," 170-pound frame matched the physical description May Flagg had provided. The license showed an address in Kanab.

"How much did you pay for the jewelry?"

"We dickered back and forth, but he finally accepted $150.00 for the neclace and $75.00 for the earrings."

"Can you identify this kid if you were to see him again?"

"You bet I can. Would you do me a favor? Be sure to get us into the court record for $225.00 in restitution."

"Sure." Books wrote a receipt for the jewelry and left the store, anxious to call Sutter and Tanner with the news.

Before returning to Kanab, Books stopped at the remaining St. George pawn shops to see whether Benally had tried to sell additional stolen items to them. He came away empty.

During the return drive, Books spoke with Beth Tanner. She had been conducting interviews with anybody who might have theories about the crime or who might be familiar with the mysterious Navajo youth. Now they would have a name to go with the physical description.

In response to the news about Joe Benally, Tanner said, "That's awesome news, J.D. This is going to make the sheriff happy."

"Now that we've got a suspect, Charley can hold a news conference and tell the press that his department is making progress on the case."

"Have you got any idea where we can find Benally?"

Books gave her the Kanab address on Benally's drivers license.

"Can I go after him or do you want me to wait until you get here?"

"Before you go, run Benally for outstanding warrants and prior record—always a good idea to know what you're walking into. And make sure you've got back-up."

"I'll do it. Anything else?"

"Yeah, call the juvenile court and see if he's got a juvie record."

"Will do."

"And call me as soon as you clear the house."

Books stepped on the Tahoe's accelerator. He probably wouldn't make it back in time to go with Tanner, but he wanted to be as close as possible in case she needed additional help. He hoped that she would heed his advice and not go out to Benally's home by herself.

Books was all too aware that young people in general tended to see themselves as bullet-proof, and rookie cops were no exception. More than a few times during his years in Denver, he'd seen their enthusiasm and gung-ho attitude, get them hurt or killed. He didn't want to see that happen to Tanner.

As he hit the outskirts of Kanab his police radio crackled. It was Tanner informing him that Benally wasn't at the address in question but that she had received several useful leads from the occupant of the home as to his possible whereabouts. Books glanced at his watch. Tanner certainly hadn't wasted any time getting to the address.

They agreed to meet at Books' office and plot their next move.

Chapter Eleven

At BLM headquarters, Books opened the small refrigerator that occupied one corner of his small, cramped office and peered inside. "I've got Coke, Diet Coke, or Arizona Iced Tea—pick your poison."

"What about the Corona I see in there?" said a smiling Tanner.

"Observant one, aren't you? I'm afraid that's an off-duty beverage only."

"Then I guess I'll have to settle for a Diet Coke."

He handed it to her and grabbed a can of iced tea for himself. "Don't keep me in suspense. What did you find at the house?"

Tanner removed a small notebook from her uniform shirt pocket and began turning pages. "It turns out the house belongs to Diane and Bruce Alston. Mr. Alston works for the Utah State Highway Department and Diane is a teacher's aide at the local elementary school. They have three kids and also take in foster children from the State Division of Child and Family Services."

"Go on."

"Benally was a foster child with the Alston family for part of his senior year. Then he got kicked out of school for fighting and smoking pot. Mrs. Alston said he fell apart after that and ran away. He was in and out of detention and several group homes until he turned eighteen, and then the state cut him loose."

"Does he have priors?"

"He does. His juvenile record includes two arrests for possession of alcohol, one for possession of a controlled substance, one for shoplifting, and two for burglary of a vehicle. Since he turned eighteen, he's had one arrest for DUI, as well as citations for driving while suspended and driving without insurance."

"Sounds like a kid carrying a lot of baggage," said Books.

"I think so. According to Mrs. Alston, he comes from an extremely dysfunctional family. His mother and father were both alcoholics. The old man apparently enjoyed beating his wife while the kid watched. The father is currently doing time at the state pen in Gunnison for armed robbery."

"Books shook his head. "It's hard to blame the boy when the most important role model in his life is an alcoholic and a stick-up artist. It's a damn shame."

"Sure is."

"Do we know what the kid's driving?" asked Books. "I ran him through DMV and they couldn't find anything registered to him."

"Mrs. Alston says he drives a rusty old blue Mazda pickup registered to his uncle. The uncle, Howard Benally, lives in a small town on the rez called Many Farms."

"I hope the kid didn't make a run for the rez. When did Mrs. Alston say she last saw him?"

"She says about a month ago. He drops by once in a while and asks for money. They give him food but never cash."

"Does Mrs. Alston have any idea where he's staying?"

"That's gonna be a tough one. She thinks he spends some of his time living out of the truck. His mother has remarried and lives in Escalante. He apparently crashes with her periodically. He's also got a girlfriend in Escalante by the name of Ruthie Todd."

"Navajo or Anglo kid?"

"Anglo. She apparently lives with her parents."

"And what about his mother?"

"Her name is Ruby Grant now. It was Ruby Benally."

Books paused considering their dilemma. They had too many leads to follow and too little time. "Here's what I think we should do. Let's get an arrest warrant charging Benally with one count of possession of stolen property. We've got enough evidence to sustain that charge. We can always add other counts later."

"That makes sense."

"Then we better haul ass to Escalante and hope we find him at his mother's place or with the girlfriend. We gotta locate this kid ASAP. I think he's the key to finding Rolly and Abby Rogers, and the longer it takes, the less chance we'll have of finding them alive. Do you want to write the warrant or would you like me to do it?"

Tanner looked slightly embarrassed. "Would you mind doing it? I've never written one before."

"Nothing to be embarrassed about—not that much to it. We all had to write our first one sometime. But in the interest of saving time, why don't I do this one. I'll go over it with you later, and we'll both go to the judge to get it signed."

"Okay. In the meantime, I'll get over to the high school and the Jubilee Market and see if anybody can help us connect Benally to the Rogers."

"That's important. Anything else I should know about?"

"One thing," said Tanner, again turning pages in her note-book. "I got a call from the family attorney, this Ed Rollins. He confirmed the existence of a will equally dividing the family assets among the five children upon the death of both parents."

"Did you ask him how well the kids get along?"

"I did. He was blunt about it—told me we were barking up the wrong tree if we're pursuing that angle. Apparently, it's a close-knit family, and at the moment, everybody is terribly upset."

"All right. For the moment at least, we'll assume family members aren't involved. Let's focus on Mr. Benally. He's the key to getting answers to some very difficult questions."

Tanner left him to work on the arrest warrant. Something about the case had been bothering him, and until now, Books hadn't been able to figure out what it was. He understood enough about pot hunting to know that Kane County was not the epicenter of ancient Fremont and Anasazi culture. That distinction belonged further east in a geographical area referred to as Four Corners—the point at which the borders of New Mexico, Colorado, Utah, and Arizona came together.

It was in that area where grave digging and pot hunting cases proliferated.

Books wanted to find out whether law enforcement agencies in the Four Corners region had any recent cases involving pot hunters who had been accosted or had mysteriously disappeared. The difficulty was he wasn't sure who to contact. He called Charley Sutter.

"Worth lookin' into, if you ask me," said Sutter. "I don't have a lot of contacts over there, but I do know the chief of police in Cortez, Colorado—guy by the name of Ray Mendez. Give him a call. He can probably help you out."

Chief Mendez would have to wait. Books had an arrest warrant to write.

An hour later, a beaming Tanner thundered into Books' office with good news.

Books glanced up from his computer screen. "What's up?"

"I made our connection between the victims and Benally."

That piqued his interest. "Tell me about it."

"You'd asked me to check with the LDS Church. I struck out with them so I headed over to the high school. It turns out that Benally was a student both his junior and senior year in two of Rolly's classes. The guidance counselor told me that Rolly took a liking to the boy and really tried to help him."

"Interesting."

"Get this. Rolly took him home one day after school and introduced him to Abby. She helped him get a job bagging groceries at the Jubilee Market."

"There it is, the high school and the grocery store. Plus, if the kid spent any time around their home, he might well have seen the artifacts collection."

"It would probably be a hell of a temptation for a kid with a drug problem," added Tanner.

"For sure. So I assume you stopped at the Jubilee Market."

"I did. I picked up a copy of the kid's job application. The store owner, Hank Allen, told me Benally lasted less than two months on the job. They canned him for missing shifts without notifying anybody and for constantly being late on days he did work."

"No big surprise—dopers don't typically make reliable employees. What address do you have on the job app?"

"He used his foster family's address."

The phone interrupted their conversation. The caller was Charley Sutter.

"Afternoon, J.D. I wanted to give you a heads-up on something I just learned. Apparently, the Rogers never go on a pot hunting trip, excuse me, a camping trip without taking a firearm. We've got a missing nine-millimeter Glock."

"How do we know that?"

"The family told us. After we returned the camper, they turned it inside out looking for the weapon. It wasn't there."

"What about the house?"

"Not there, either."

"The implication is that whoever abducted the couple now has possession of their Glock," said Books.

"Exactly. Better assume that whoever kidnapped them is probably armed."

"Appreciate the heads-up. I'll go ahead and get the weapon entered into NCIC."

Chapter Twelve

Ten minutes later, Books and Tanner sat outside the office of district court judge Homer Wilkins waiting while he finished a calendar of arraignments in his courtroom. The wait annoyed Books. In Denver, this didn't happen. When you needed a warrant, you headed straight for your favorite judge. If she was busy, you walked down the hall to the chambers of another judge. But this wasn't Denver. This was Kanab, and it was a one-judge town. If the judge was busy, you sat on your keester until he became available.

Tanner carefully read the affidavit and then asked Books several questions.

"It looks like the document contains two different parts, the affidavit and the arrest warrant itself. Am I right?"

"You are. The warrant is mostly boilerplate language where we fill in the blanks as to the charge and the identity of the accused. The judge likely won't pay much attention to it, but he will carefully read the affidavit."

"That's the specific information that supports the request for a warrant, right?"

"Exactly. We call it a probable cause statement. The legal standard under the Fourth Amendment to obtain an arrest or search warrant is probable cause."

"So if the judge doesn't think there's enough evidence, he'll refuse to sign the warrant."

"You got it."

Thirty minutes later, they were out of the courthouse with a warrant. The 120-mile drive to Escalante took just under two hours. They traveled for long periods without speaking, which was perfectly fine with Books. The silence gave him time to decompress and absorb the sheer beauty of the Escalante River as it snaked its way along the canyon floor. Navajo sandstone formations, replete with vivid colors and muted tones, were visible all along the route. In places, he could see the desert coming alive with the arrival of spring—an ocean of yellow-flowering snakeweed and the occasional prickly pear cactus with its bright pink blossoms.

Despite its breathtaking beauty, Books also understood that it was a hostile arid land whose overwhelming size and remoteness made you feel small and insignificant, where a careless step or sheer ignorance might prove fatal. Yet there was something about this land that drew you in making it part of you—a part of your soul.

When they reached the west end of town, Tanner asked, "How do you want to play this?"

"Why don't we do a drive-by of his girlfriend and his mother's homes to look for the kid's pickup? If it's not there, we can always knock on doors."

The houses were on opposite ends of town. Ruthie Todd, Benally's girlfriend, lived with her parents on the west side of town in an A-frame style log home. A detached two-car garage connected the house to a covered breezeway. A white Ford Explorer was parked in the garage, and smoke belched from a cinder block chimney at one end of the house. There was no sign of the Mazda pickup.

"Let's try the other house," said Books. "We'll come back here if we strike out at his mom's place."

Books headed down Main Street to the other side of town. He turned north on to a gravel side street that quickly gave way to a pothole-filled dirt road. Variety hardly described the homes nestled side-by-side along these streets. There were old, two-story brick homes, probably built in the early 1950s, sitting beside newer, stucco models. A handful of trailers and mobile homes had been tossed in for good measure.

Ruby Benally, now Ruby Grant, lived at the end of one of these streets in a single story brick rambler that sat behind a chain link fence. Books honed in on the Beware of Dog sign attached to the gate. A rusted out Dodge Dart was parked under a carport at one end of the house.

"Damn," said Books. "No sign of the truck."

As he passed the house, Tanner said, "Hold up a minute, J.D." She was turned in her seat looking back at the home. "There it is there's the Mazda. It's hidden behind the house."

Books grunted. "Nice spot. Damn near missed it, didn't we?"

"That, I think, was the intent."

Books parked around the corner. "I'll take the warrant with me and go to the front door. You get out here and hustle around in back in case Junior decides to rabbit on us."

Tanner got out of the Tahoe. "Give me a couple of minutes."

"Will do. And Tanner, did you notice that big cottonwood tree in the back yard?"

"Yeah."

"Plant your butt behind it and stay there. It's the only decent cover around. Don't stand in the open."

Tanner frowned. "Expecting trouble?"

"Always. Good thing to remember, too. It might save your life some day."

Books waited until Tanner had moved into position and then parked the Tahoe in the gravel driveway next to the house. He grabbed the warrant from the visor above the driver's seat and walked to the front door, ever alert for sound or movement from inside. He wasn't sure, but he thought he saw the drapes covering the living room window move ever so slightly. He felt naked and exposed. He hoped that whoever awaited him on the other side of the front door wouldn't greet him by shoving a gun in his face.

He heard muffled voices inside. He knocked, and moments later, the front door slowly opened. Books was greeted by a heavyset woman in her late forties. "Yes," she said.

"Ruby Grant."

"Yes. What do you want?"

"I'm looking for your son, Joe. It's important that I talk to him." He didn't mention the warrant.

"He's not here now. What do you want to see Joey about?" Books ignored the question. "Where is Joey, Mrs. Grant?"

"I don't know. He comes and goes. Look, why don't you come back later after my husband gets home from work. I'm by myself and this isn't a good time for me."

Books held up the warrant. "Mrs. Grant, I've got a warrant for your son's arrest, and I'm going to have a look around the house."

She shook her head and started to close the door. Books blocked the move with his foot. He brushed past her saying, "Sorry, Mrs. Grant, but I don't think you're alone. I heard voices, and Joey's truck is parked behind the house."

As Books moved past her, he heard retreating footsteps in the hallway, followed by the sound of the back door opening and slamming shut. He grabbed his service revolver and ran to the back door in pursuit. He opened it just in time to see Tanner launch herself from behind the cottonwood tree and tackle a fleeing Joe Benally. He never saw her, and when they collided, Books heard an audible grunt from the kid, as the air was forced from his lungs. When Books reached the pair, Tanner was already straddling a face-down Benally clamping handcuffs to his wrists.

They pulled Benally to his feet. "Have you ever considered auditioning for the Green Bay Packers?" asked Books, smiling.

"Not lately. Why?"

"Because that tackle you just made would make any NFL linebacker proud."

"It was nothing really," she replied, "just an old rugby move."

"I didn't know you played rugby."

"There's a lot of things you don't know about me, J.D. Come on, Junior, let's go." With that, she marched Benally to the Tahoe while Books spoke with Ruby Grant.

Books explained the nature of the criminal charge against her son. He didn't tell her about the connection of the stolen property the kid had sold to the pawn shop, to the abduction of Rolly and Abby Rogers. He asked for permission to search Benally's bedroom. The search revealed a hash pipe, Zig-Zag papers, and trace amounts of what Books' suspected was marijuana. As he left the bedroom, he noticed a folded scrap of paper lying on a nightstand next to the bed. The slip contained a hand-written Kanab phone number. Books pocketed the slip, confiscated the drug paraphernalia, and rejoined Tanner outside.

"Find anything?" asked Tanner.

"Yeah. From his bedroom, drug paraphernalia and trace amounts of marijuana. Did you find anything when you searched him?"

"Two hundred in cash and about a half-ounce of pot."

"Good. You can never have too many charges. By the way, that was a nice bust, Tanner."

She smiled, "Thanks. It was a piece of cake. The kid was so busy looking over his shoulder to see where you were, he never saw me. Are we ready to go?"

"Sure. Did you happen to advise Benally of his Miranda rights?"

"Not yet, but I will."

"Don't bother," said Books. "We'll advise him after we get back to Kanab. In the meantime, let's see if he says anything on the drive back."

"Isn't that illegal?"

"No. It's an old trick, really. You give the suspect the opportunity to blurt out something incriminating during the ride to the station. If he does, it's admissible, whether or not he's received the Miranda warnings. The courts refer to it as volunteered or spontaneous statements. The catch is that the spontaneous statement has to be given voluntarily—not a product of our questioning him. We'll do the Miranda schtick once we get him booked."

"It may not be illegal, but it sure sounds unethical."

"Illegal it's not; unethical, maybe. I won't lose any sleep over it, I can promise you that. Bad guys have plenty of rights. I don't mind using whatever tricks and tools are available, so long as we play by the rules."

Chapter Thirteen

The return to Kanab was uneventful. Joe Benally hardly said a word despite Books' clumsy attempt to get him talking about his family. When that didn't work, he turned to the subject of school. Again, it was mostly a one-way conversation. Finally, everybody settled into a long period of silence.

By the time they arrived at the sheriff's office, it was dark. They had called Sheriff Sutter, and he was there to greet them in the booking area of the jail. Tanner placed Benally in a holding cell while Books spoke with the sheriff.

"Damned happy we got somebody in custody," said Sutter. "The political heat was starting to get downright uncomfortable."

"This should take some of the heat off. You ought to schedule a press conference for tomorrow morning."

"I plan to—first thing. Have you questioned him yet?"

"Not yet. I'll do that now, although I'm not sure how far we'll get. The kid's awfully tightlipped. Maybe it's his personality, maybe it's cultural. I'm not sure. He didn't have shit to say on the way in—and he had two hours to think about it."

"Well, let's get after it. Maybe you'll have better luck with him here. Want me to sit in with you?"

"Do you know the kid?"

"No."

"Then I'd rather conduct the interrogation with Tanner. Maybe she can mother him into opening up and talking to us."

"However you want to play it is okay with me."

Before they started, Books asked Tanner to see if Benally wanted anything—food, coffee, pop, anything that might make him amenable to talking.

"He says he's starving," said Tanner. "Wants coffee and a burger. I'll be right back." Ten minutes later, Tanner appeared with a McDonald's coffee and a Big Mac.

After he was processed, a jail deputy delivered Benally to an interrogation room adjacent to the booking area. After he ate, Tanner activated the video camera, and the interrogation proceeded. Books walked Benally through the Miranda warnings. He agreed to waive his rights and answer questions without the assistance of defense counsel—always a dumb idea, Books thought.

Books began the interrogation by avoiding any reference to Rolly and Abby Rogers. That would come later. Instead, he began with several innocuous questions designed to put Benally at ease. "Are you employed, Joey?"

"No."

"Where were you last employed?"

"I worked a few months ago at the Jubilee Market."

"So you've been unemployed for a while."

"Yeah."

"When we arrested you today, Deputy Tanner found two hundred in cash in your pockets. Where did you get that money?"

"I don't know—saved it, I guess."

"Maybe I can help refresh your memory. Were you in St. George on Monday?"

"Um, I'm not sure."

"You're not sure. Look, Joey, you either were or were not in St. George on Monday. Which is it?"

"Okay, I was there, so what?"

"While you were in St. George, did you sell several pieces of jewelry at a local pawn shop?"

Tanner placed photographs of the stolen jewelry in front of him. "This jewelry," she said.

"What if I did?"

"How much did the pawn shop pay you?"

"I ain't sure. A hundred bucks, I think."

"How about two-hundred-twenty-five. Does that seem right?"

"I guess so."

"How did you come into possession of the jewelry?

The old fashioned way, thought Books. He stole it.

The kid was fidgeting in his chair and beads of perspiration had begun to form on his forehead. "A guy sold it to me."

"A guy sold it to you. What guy?"

"I don't know—never told me his name."

"Are you in the habit of buying jewelry from complete strangers?"

"He wasn't a complete stranger. I met him at City Park in a pickup basketball game. Besides, he was selling it real cheap— what can I say?"

"You can start by telling us the truth," countered Books. "The story you're telling us is just so much bullshit, and you know it."

Benally shrugged, "It's the truth."

"Okay, so you paid two hundred twenty-five dollars for the jewelry."

"If you say so."

"Since you're unemployed, where did you get the cash?"

The question caught Benally off-guard. "Stole it from my step-dad," he finally said.

"Bet that'll endear you to him." Glancing at Tanner, Books said, "Make a note to check that out with his step-father."

Books abruptly changed the direction of the interrogation. "Are you acquainted with Rolly and Abby Rogers?"

The question hit Benally like a fist to the solar plexus. He broke eye contact with Books and stared at the floor. The silence between them grew making Benally even more uncomfortable. "Well?"

"Their names sound familiar."

"I would hope so. You took high school classes from Rolly and you worked with Abby at the Jubilee market. Isn't that true?"

"Yeah."

"Isn't it also true that you broke into the Rogers' home, cleaned out their artifacts collection, stole their jewelry, and then sold the jewelry to the pawn shop in St. George?"

"I don't know nothin' about that."

"Sure you do. Have you ever been to the Rogers home?"

"No. I don't even know where they live."

"That's strange," said Books, "because your fingerprints were found plastered all over the inside of their home. How do you explain that?"

Benally looked thoroughly defeated, but he stubbornly held his ground. "Like I said before, I don't know nothin about any B & E."

Books wondered if he had pushed Benally too hard. "Look, Joe, you're not in juvenile court any longer, where you'll end up getting an ass-chewing from the judge, a fine, and some community service. You're looking at enough felonies to put you behind bars for a long stretch. Are you prepared to do that kind of time?"

"I don't want to."

"Maybe you won't have to. Tell us the truth now, and Tanner and I will put in a good word on your behalf with the prosecutor, help get you a reduced sentence."

Benally's voice was barely audible when he finally spoke. "If I do cooperate, what will happen to me?"

"Ultimately, that'll be up to the judge, but I promise you, we'll try to help."

"I'll think about it, but I want to talk to my lawyer first."

Books' heart sank realizing the interview was over. He decided to give it one last try. "Look, Joe, the Rogerses were abducted five days ago. The best chance we have of finding them alive is if we locate them soon. There's no more time to waste. Will you help us?"

"Like I said, I gotta think about it and talk to my lawyer first."

"Then this interview is over, and our offer to help you is withdrawn." Books stood and walked to the door, hoping the kid would call him back. He didn't.

Tanner followed Books into an adjacent room where Charley Sutter had been observing the interrogation. "You lied to him, J.D.," Tanner said. "Why did you do that?"

Books sighed, "Because I can, and I thought it might help to break him down."

"But that's illegal, and even if it isn't, it's morally wrong."

Books was in no mood to spar with Tanner. "It's not illegal, Beth, and frankly, even if it was, I don't give a damn. Every hour that passes, the chances of finding the Rogerses alive decline. I'd have stood on the back of his neck if I thought it would make him talk."

Sutter had been observing this exchange with a bemused expression on his face. "I must say, J.D., you did press the kid pretty hard. Don't get me wrong, I'm glad you did. I just wish you'd have gotten results."

"Well, I think it was just awful," sputtered Tanner.

"And I'm going home." With that, Books got up and left the room.

Chapter Fourteen

It was nearly midnight when Books got home. He was cranky, hungry, and tired. He slapped a grilled cheese sandwich into a fry pan, pulled a bottle of Coors Lite from the refrigerator, and gulped it down while he waited for the sandwich to cook. Minutes later, he had kicked off his boots and settled into his living room recliner.

From the chair, he saw the blinking red light on his answering machine. The message was from his sister, Maggie, who reported that she and Bernie had arrived safely in Salt Lake City and that Bernie was scheduled to undergo a variety of medical tests the next day. The surgery was still scheduled for Friday, although the exact time had not been determined.

"Call me sometime tomorrow afternoon," said Maggie. "I should be able to tell you when the surgery is scheduled. Do you think you'll be able to make it?"

As Books polished off a second beer, he thought it very unlikely that he would be able to disconnect from the investigation in time to make his father's surgery. But he decided to see what Thursday brought. Clear thinking, after a good night's sleep, might change his mind. When his head hit the pillow, he was out in seconds.

◇◇◇

Thursday Morning—Day 6

Books awoke the next morning to the smell of freshly brewed coffee and bacon waffling through the trailer. He stumbled out of bed and poked his head into the kitchen to find Ned Hunsaker standing over the gas stove, spatula in hand. "About to come and get you," he smiled.

"Smells great, I'll be right along."

During breakfast, Books had a chance to pick Hunsaker's brain about the pot hunting trade.

"You never told me that you're considered the resident expert on the illicit artifacts trade."

"Don't know who told you that, but it's really not the case."

"Rusty Steed mentioned it."

"Hmm. I've read a little about it, and God knows, I spend enough time wandering through the desert wilderness, but that hardly qualifies me as an expert. I'm a librarian by training, not an archeologist."

"So what's your theory on what happened to Rolly and Abby Rogers?"

Ned finished chewing a bite of omelet and washed it down with a mouthful of coffee. "Hard to know, J.D. The desert can be a cruel mother. More than a few souls have ventured out there never to be seen again—not always tenderfeet, either."

"You really think that's what happened to them?"

"Naw, I think they're victims of foul play."

"Do you think it's possible they were waylaid by local collectors, people who know them?"

"It's possible, but I doubt it," said Hunsaker. "Diggers are a diverse lot. You've got mom-and-pop types, but you've also got larger and better funded commercial collectors. It's a murky business, hard to know exactly who the bad guys are."

"What do you mean?"

"Illicit collectors can be just about anybody. It might be your neighbor, somebody you attend church with. Museum curators, antiquities dealer, hell, even trained archeologists have been caught collecting illegally. And it's all complicated by the fact that there is a legal antiquities trade."

"Like collectibles that were found prior to laws being passed as well as items bought and sold from private collections."

"Yup. Even the antiquities dealers will tell you that they have no idea whether half the stuff they take in is legal or illegal."

"Interesting information, but you didn't answer my question, Ned. What do you think happened to the Rogers couple?"

"My guess is they had the misfortune of running into a commercial operation. These guys can be pretty sophisticated. Sometimes they use back-hoes with the teeth missing—that reduces the damage to the artifacts. They come in on ATVs, by air, or on foot, and they move quickly from site to site.

"And they're often armed to the teeth."

"Oh, I think you can depend on that. And in the business you're in, J.D., never forget that meth addicts are very much a part of the pot hunting culture, and they're a dangerous bunch. You need to be damn careful out there."

"Sound wisdom."

Ned paused while he buttered a piece of toast. "Was it a promising dig site?"

"I wouldn't know a promising site from one that isn't. The immediate area looked like it had been thoroughly excavated, though, and I saw the skeletal remains of a baby."

Ned shook his head and sighed. "Sadly, dead babies tend to make for prime finds. Infants were often buried in cradle boards or woven blankets along with other artifacts. It wouldn't be uncommon to pull ten grand worth of collectibles out of a single baby's grave."

"Sounds perverted as hell to me."

"Maybe so, but diggers don't see it that way."

"So how big is the market for ancient artifacts?"

"One thing pothunters share in common is that they dig because there's demand," said Hunsaker. "Pots that sold in the 1960s for twenty, thirty bucks are now worth thousands, maybe even tens of thousands. An article I read recently estimated the international sale of illegal artifacts is a four- to eight-billion-dollar a year business, and it's not going away anytime soon."

Sutter had scheduled a news conference at nine o'clock to discuss the arrest of Joe Benally. The sheriff had asked Books to attend to field questions the sheriff either couldn't or didn't want to answer. Sutter's goal was simple. He wanted to quiet the locals who had grown restless as the days had passed and the Rogers remained missing. Books glanced at his watch. It was eight o'clock when he parked the Tahoe at BLM headquarters, giving him just enough time to check a couple of leads.

The first order of business was the telephone number he'd found in Benally's bedroom. It looked like a Kanab number. Books used a telephone reverse directory and made an interesting discovery. The number belonged to a local business, Red Rock Touring. He knew little about the company other than advertisements he'd seen in tourist brochures promoting guided hikes, jeep, and helicopter tours. Books wondered why Benally had a piece of paper with that number written on it.

Next, he ran the name of Eldon Hitch through NCIC and the Utah Bureau of Criminal Identification database. His record was clean despite Dove Creek, Colorado's reputation as being a haven for pot hunters. There was another way for Books to run a background check on Hitch. He placed a call to the office of Cortez, Colorado, Police Chief, Ray Mendez.

"Your reputation precedes you, Ranger Books. I think you've got police agencies from all over the Southwest hunting for that missing couple."

Books wondered what Mendez meant by the comment that "his reputation had preceded him," but he ignored it. "We need all the help we can get."

"What can I do for you today?"

"A couple of things, actually. Have you ever heard of a guy who lives in Dove Creek by the name of Eldon Hitch?"

"Sure have," replied Mendez. "Eldon's an old codger who's a fixture around Dove Creek. He's a pot hunter—has been all his life, but that doesn't make him unique, since half the people in that town are collectors. What makes you ask?"

Books explained that he'd found Hitch camped in a remote area near the site of the Rogers' kidnapping.

"Seems a little odd," said Mendez, "but it's probably just a coincidence. If you're thinking Eldon is somehow involved in the abduction, I think you're wasting your time. He's an innocent old guy who wouldn't have the means or the heart to get involved in anything like that."

"Appreciate your opinion. Frankly, the old boy didn't strike me as the type either. Are you aware of any recent cases, similar to ours, in the Four Corners area where hikers or pot hunters have simply disappeared without a trace?"

Mendez thought for a minute. "Come to think of it, yeah, I think we have had a couple of disappearances over the past two or three years that we attributed to people heading off into remote areas, getting lost, and never being found. That said, we've never attributed any of those cases to foul play."

"Can you get me the files?"

Mendez ignored the question. "You think there might be a connection to your case?"

"I don't know, but it has occurred to me that mom-and-pop operators might make for easy pickings."

"Damn, never thought about that possibility. To answer your previous question, yeah, I can get you the case files, but I've got another suggestion. I'd like you to call Sergeant Dan Walker. He's with the Durango Police Department."

"And how can Sergeant Walker help me?"

"Dan supervises a special unit called the Four Corners Task Force. The task force is made up of police officers from various agencies in the area."

Books had never heard of this unit. "So what exactly do they do?

"They're an intelligence sharing group that conducts joint investigations on everything from drug trafficking to cases involving the illegal antiquities trade. Dan would be a better person to talk to than me, and he can get you the files you're interested in."

Books took the number, thanked Mendez for his assistance, and sprinted to the Tahoe. If he hurried, he would just make it in time for Sheriff Sutter's news conference.

Chapter Fifteen

Books arrived moments before the press conference. He was surprised at the number of media outlets represented. There was more interest in the case than he had previously believed. Sheriff Sutter was standing in the hallway outside the training room engaged in an animated discussion with his jail commander. When Sutter spotted Books, he motioned him over. Books assumed the discussion had something to do with the impending news conference, but he was in for a surprise.

"I just learned something you're going to find quite interesting," said Sutter. "And, frankly, I'm not sure what to make of it."

"And what would that be?"

"Joe Benally was just arraigned in district court and…"

"Don't tell me the judge released him on his own recognizance," countered Books.

"No, it wasn't that. It seems that Mr. Benally has been assigned defense counsel."

"Nothing unusual about that."

"In this instance, I'm afraid there is—since his lawyer is Becky Eddins."

The expression on Books' face went from shock to one of disbelief. "You can't be serious. She can't do that—talk about a conflict of interest."

"That's what the DA tried to argue, but Judge Wilkins didn't buy it. Evidently, the kid's mother called Becky and requested that she represent the boy. Becky sat down with them before the hearing and explained the nature of her relationship with you, figuring that would be the end of it."

"But it wasn't."

"No, it wasn't. They marched into court and laid the whole scenario out for Judge Wilkins. Apparently, the judge thoroughly explained the situation to Benally a second time and did everything he could to convince the kid that this wasn't a good idea."

"All to no avail, I suppose," said Books. "I think Becky has represented Benally in the past during some of his juvenile court cases."

"If there's a history, that might explain their insistence on Becky representing him again," said Sutter. "In any event, Benally and his mother reiterated their desire for Becky to defend the boy and the court went along."

"The DA ought to appeal that decision."

"He could, but I'm not sure he's going to. Benally signed a written waiver indicating that he understood the nature of the relationship between you and Becky, and, despite that, he still wanted her to represent him."

"Well, it is what it is," said Books. "We'll just have to deal with it. One of my former colleagues from Denver P.D. robbery/homicide found himself in a relationship with an attorney who worked for the public defender's office."

"What happened?"

"They've been together for eight years, married for seven."

The beginnings of a slight smile played at the corners of Charley Sutter's mouth as though an idea was beginning to take shape. "Perhaps, J.D., you can turn this into an advantage for us. Since you're cozy with Becky, maybe you can coax her into getting Benally to talk to us—worth a try, don't you think?"

"We need the kid's cooperation, that's for sure, but if you're thinking my relationship with her will translate into an automatic offer of full cooperation, I wouldn't bet on it. Becky Eddins takes her advocacy role very seriously. It's going to cost us something. I'm just not sure what."

Sutter headed off to what turned out to be a routine press conference. He answered a few questions about Joe Benally but carefully skirted all questions about the evidence gathered as well as possible motives for the crime. Afterward, as Books left the building, Lamont Christensen, the editor of the local *Kane County Citizen,* approached. Books moved quickly hoping he could avoid Christensen, but the man fell in step beside him. The newspaper had been openly critical of Books during the recent murder investigation of environmental activist David Greenbriar, and there was no love lost between the two men.

"What's up, Lamont?"

"Looks like you've put yourself square in the middle of another controversy."

Books glanced at Christensen but continued walking. "Afraid I don't know what you're talking about."

"Sure you do."

"Suppose you enlighten me."

"Last year you were ready to throw an upstanding member of the community under the bus for a murder he didn't commit, and now you're up to your neck in a pot-hunting case involving a local couple revered by this community."

"I don't see your point."

"Let me draw it with a crayon for you, then. You're prepared to besmirch the reputation of Rolly and Abby Rogers over their involvement in an activity that most of us see as our God-given right—an integral part of our local culture and history."

"Geez, Lamont, don't you ever give it a rest? We're trying to do our job, and in this instance, that happens to be saving the lives of two people we believe are the victims of foul play. That the Rogers are beloved members of the community who also happen to be avid antiquities collectors seems beside the point."

"Oh, but that is the point, Books. Now you've got another high-profile case where you get to put pot-hunting in the spotlight while scoring points with the press and your BLM bosses in Salt Lake City—never mind what happens to the Rogerses."

Books stopped and faced Christensen, "Look, you little weasel. I don't give a shit what you think of me personally, but for you to assert that I'm interested in garnering kudos from the media and impressing my superiors while a missing couple may be lying out there dead or dying is pure rubbish. Why don't you say what's really got your tail in a knot?"

"And, what might that be?" said Christensen.

"You're pissed because the sheriff no longer calls and leaks sensitive information about an ongoing case to that rag you call a newspaper. And you blame me for that."

"What if I do? It's true, isn't it?"

"I can't help it that you're in the First Amendment business—the public's right to know and all that happy horseshit. That's your business. But somebody has to be concerned about catching the bad guys and not jeopardizing the case before it gets to court by giving too much information to suspects who might be reading the stuff you're printing. And that's my business."

Christensen smiled as he clicked off a small tape recorder he removed from his jacket pocket. "I assume I can quote you on that."

"You can quote any damn thing you want, Lamont, and, while you're at it, you can also kiss my ass. Why don't you print that, too?"

Chapter Sixteen

Books found Ned Hunsaker planting vegetables in a small garden behind his house. He was on his knees and barely glanced up as Books approached. "Morning, J.D. What brings you around this time of the morning?"

"I've got a question for you, Ned. What do you know about a local business called Red Rock Touring?"

Hunsaker stopped what he was doing, sat back on his heels and took a big drink of water from a plastic bottle. "Twelve, thirteen years ago, right about the time you left Kanab, a guy by the name of George Gentry moved here from Albuquerque and opened Red Rock Touring. I never thought he'd make it, but he sure fooled me."

"What do you mean?"

"Tourism in the late 1990s wasn't what it is today. I just didn't think there was enough business to support a company operating seasonally and catering exclusively to vacationers."

"What do you know about Mr. Gentry?"

"Not much—used to say hello when I'd run into him in town, but that's about it. He was retired when he moved here. BLM, I think. He ran the business with his son, Brett. They worked it together until the old man retired five or so years ago. Brett took over, and the business has continued to prosper."

"Is the father still alive?"

"Yeah, as far as I know. I heard he developed dementia and the family moved him to an assisted living facility in St. George."

"Is there a Mrs. Gentry?"

"Brett's married, but I'm not sure about the old man. One time I heard he was a widower, but then someone else told me he got divorced shortly before he retired. Why all the interest in Red Rock Touring?"

"Just chasing what I think is probably another dead-end lead. It's probably nothing."

Books drove to the sheriff's office, met Beth Tanner, and the two of them went looking for Charley Sutter. They found him in the department lunch room drinking a can of Diet Coke while munching a bag of potato chips and eating a peanut butter sandwich. With a suspect in custody, and the press conference behind him, Sutter looked like a happy man.

"Don't look so happy, Charley. At the moment, the only thing we've got is a suspect sitting in your jail who we can't talk to. He's probably involved up to his eye-balls in the disappearance of Rolly and Abby Rogers, and all we can charge him with is a single count of possession of stolen property and misdemeanor possession of pot."

"So figure it out."

"I can't tell you how good that makes me feel considering, that at the moment, we don't have any leads. We'll see how happy you are this time next week if we're still at a standstill."

"How about the physical evidence? Getting anywhere with that?" asked Sutter. "And have you spoken with Becky about interviewing her client?

"No and no. It's too soon to know anything about the evidence and Becky was only appointed this morning."

Tanner added, "The crime lab should have some results later today on the latent prints I lifted at the Rogers' home. I shipped them a copy of Benally's prints and they're running the comparison now."

"That might tie up the burglary beef, but it doesn't get us any closer to finding the Rogers," said Books.

"Charley, what do you know about Red Rock Touring and Brett Gentry?"

"The old man was a damned good businessman if you ask me, a visionary of sorts."

"In what way?"

"Red Rock Touring took off financially right from the get-go. How old George knew it would work is beyond me. It's been a very successful local business for a lot of years."

"What did George do for a living prior to opening Red Rock Touring?"

"He's a retired BLM archeologist—thought you probably knew that."

Books shook his head. "What about his son, Brett?"

Sutter's expression became quizzical. "Why all the questions?"

"When we arrested Benally yesterday, I found a slip of paper in his bedroom with a phone number on it. The phone number was listed to Red Rock Touring."

"That's strange. Was there anything else on the note besides the phone number?"

"Nothing."

When the impromptu meeting ended, Sutter looked noticeably more uneasy. Books had seen cases like this before when all the leads evaporated, leaving detectives with nothing but a cold case. This one was starting to feel like that.

◇◇◇

Books knew a strategy that had served him well in prior cases. With few options remaining, he decided to shake the tree and see what happened.

Red Rock Touring was located in a nondescript stucco building along State Highway 89 on the east end of Kanab. As Books parked the Tahoe, he noticed a half-dozen all-terrain vehicles parked in a row fronting the highway. A rail-thin middle-aged woman with bleached blonde hair greeted him as he entered the lobby.

"Good afternoon," she said, extending her hand. "I'm Emily Gentry. How can I help you, Officer....?"

"Books, J.D. Books."

"Of course, Officer Books, I should have known. What brings you by today?"

"I'm looking for your husband."

"I'm sorry, but he's not here at the moment. Can I help you with something?"

Books ignored the question. "Can you tell me when you expect him to return?"

"He's in St. George playing golf with a couple of his buddies. I expect him back sometime this evening. Now if you'll tell me what you want, I'm sure I can help you."

"Perhaps you can, Mrs. Gentry, but I'd rather wait until your husband gets back so that I have to say it only once."

"Say what only once? What are you talking about?"

"Your company has come up in our investigation of the Rogers couple. And that's all I'm going to say until I can sit down with both you and your husband." With that, he walked out of the office leaving Gentry stammering in mid-sentence. He smiled to himself as he climbed into the Tahoe believing that he'd accomplished what he intended—he'd shaken the tree.

Books found a text message from Maggie: "Surgery at 9 a.m. R U coming?"

Books hit the reply button and wrote, "Doubtful. Call U later."

As he headed for BLM headquarters, Books received a radio call that would change the course of the investigation as well as alter the lives of his own family.

Chapter Seventeen

Tanner was waiting for Books in the sheriff's department parking lot. She jumped in the Tahoe, and they sped south out of Kanab, across the state line into Arizona, and then headed west on State Highway 389.

"What's going on?" asked Tanner.

"Dispatch relayed a call from the Paiute Tribal Police telling us they've arrested a digger they apparently caught red-handed plundering an Anasazi burial site."

"And you think it might be connected to the Rogers case?"

"Don't know, but it's worth checking out. From what I can tell, this site isn't too far from where Rolly and Abby disappeared."

"Is it on Paiute land?"

"Nope. It's further south, not quite to Toroweap and just east of Mt. Trumbull."

They rode on in silence, Books hoping that whatever they were about to learn might give them their first tangible break in the case. Instead, what he discovered shocked him.

Partially concealed behind a stand of juniper pine was an all-too-familiar white Chevrolet Silverado pickup bearing Utah license plates. Seated on a near-by rock, hands cuffed behind his back, sat his brother-in-law, Bobby Case.

"Holy shit."

"What?"

"I know this guy. He's my brother-in-law."

"Whoa, J.D. How do you want to handle this?"

"Just like we'd handle any other case, I suppose. We find out what happened, and, if there's evidence a crime was committed, Bobby goes to jail."

"Are you sure?"

"I don't see another choice. Do you?"

Four armed Native American men milled about the scene. Each was driving an all-terrain vehicle and nobody was in uniform. "Careful here," he told Tanner, as he got out of the Tahoe. "I have no idea who these guys are."

"Jesus, J.D. Am I glad to see you," said Bobby Case. "These assholes….."

"Shut up, Bobby," replied Books. "You'll have a chance to explain yourself in a minute." Case looked surprised but refrained from saying anything further.

One of the men approached Books. "You know this man?"

"Unfortunately, I do. This is Deputy Beth Tanner from the Kane County Sheriff's Office and I'm Ranger J.D. Books. Who might you be?"

"I'm Sergeant Albert Tom, Paiute Tribal Police." The man didn't smile or extend a hand.

"And your colleagues. Are they also tribal police?"

"These two are reserve officers with the Paiute Tribal Police and the one standing by the suspect is with the Navaho Tribal Police."

"And what were the four of you doing out here in the first place?"

"Hunting for grave robbers just like this one," replied Tom.

Pointing at his brother-in-law, Books asked, "How did you happen to come upon this guy?"

"Somebody called tribal headquarters and reported that an Anglo was out here digging. We came in as close as we could on ATVs and walked in from there. Guy was so busy he didn't hear us until we were right on top of him. Easy bust."

"And the four of you just happened to be out here on your ATVs and decided to help out," Books said.

"Something like that, yeah."

Books didn't like what he was hearing. It didn't make sense. Who were these guys and what were they really doing out here? They were patrolling on BLM land well away from the Paiute Reservation. They had no jurisdiction off-reservation, so any time they detained someone it was the equivalent of a citizen's arrest.

He glanced around the site. Shovels, trowels and other tools used by pot hunters were scattered about indicating recent digging. Several cracked and broken clay pots were lying together next to a shallow hole in the ground. From all appearances, it looked like Bobby had been caught red-handed scavenging the site for relics.

Books tried a more direct approach. "Sergeant Tom, there's something I'm not understanding. Are the four of you part of some tribal police unit responsible for protecting sacred burial sites? And if you are, what are you doing patrolling off tribal land?"

Tom studied Books for a long moment before replying. Books couldn't tell whether the look was hostile or merely contemplative. "We are all members of a multitribal organization dedicated to stopping the desecration of sacred Native American sites and returning stolen antiquities to their tribes of origin. And while tribal police authorities are aware of our existence, we are not a part of any specialized unit or agency."

"Look, I have no problem with what you're doing," said Books. "In fact, I think it's admirable. I am, however, concerned about your authority to act when you're off tribal lands as you are this morning."

"Usually we confine our patrols to reservation lands unless we receive a report of an in-progress crime like this one. Then we respond regardless of whether the incident is on tribal or BLM land."

As Books tried to absorb what Sergeant Tom had just told him, Tanner, who had been quietly listening to the exchange, pulled him aside.

"I think we've got a pretty good idea about what happened. If it's okay with you, I'm going to have a look in Bobby's truck."

"Do that while I finish up here."

Books returned to Sergeant Tom. "We're going to need written statements from you describing what happened. How can we get in touch?"

Tom produced a tattered business card with an address and phone number for the Paiute Tribal Police Department. On the reverse side, he wrote another number. "That's my cell number. We'll prepare written reports and have them available for you ASAP."

"Great. I appreciate that. I am going to need the names and contact information for each of your fellow officers."

Tom nodded. "I'll get that for you. What happens to Mr. Case now?"

"He's about to be arrested for illegally digging on federal land. As to whether charges are going to be filed, that'll be up to federal prosecutors."

Tanner interrupted. "J.D., could you come over here please." She was searching the extended cab of Case's pickup.

He walked to the truck and looked over Tanner's shoulder. "What have you got?"

Tanner stepped aside. "I haven't moved anything. Take a look in the back. Anything look familiar?"

Books groaned, "Just when you think it can't get any worse, it does. Bobby's in deep shit."

"You want to talk with him or do you want me to do it?"

"I probably shouldn't. He's family and that puts me in a major conflict of interest. You advise him and see if he'll give you a statement. I'll finish up with the tribal police and then go to work on the crime scene."

After the tribal officers left, Books retrieved a crime scene kit from a storage compartment in the rear of the Tahoe. Tanner had moved Bobby Case into the Tahoe's front seat and had begun questioning him. Moments later, Books looked up and saw Tanner walking toward him.

"Sorry, J.D. Afraid it's a no-go. He says he'll only talk to you. What do you want me to do?"

"Leave him in the truck. He can wait. Let's finish up with the crime scene, impound the truck, and transport him back to Kanab. We'll talk to him there."

They spent the next hour carefully photographing the dig site and gathering physical evidence. They waited until a tow truck arrived to impound Case's truck before returning to Kanab.

Awkward hardly described the drive back to town. An angry and sullen looking Bobby Case sat next to Books in the front passenger seat of the Tahoe staring out the side window at nothing, while Tanner sat behind him. Nobody said a word leaving Books to ponder not only the extent of his brother-in-law's involvement in the illicit pot hunting trade, but also whether that involvement might include kidnapping and murder.

Chapter Eighteen

"What next?" said a visibly upset Charley Sutter as he paced back and forth in front of his desk, perspiration stains decorating the armpits of his uniform. "As if this mess wasn't complicated enough, now we've got the son of the most powerful politician in Kane County caught in the act of pot hunting and in possession of artifacts belonging to Rolly and Abby Rogers. How much worse can it get?" It was a rhetorical question Books thought, and one Beth Tanner should have left alone.

"Don't forget that Bobby Case happens to be J.D.'s brother-in-law," said Tanner.

"Thank you for that enlightening bit of information, Deputy Tanner," snapped Sutter.

Books sat next to Tanner on a weather-beaten, black leather couch facing the sheriff's desk, arms folded across his chest as Sutter continued his rant.

"Nothing like having the chairman of the county commission seriously pissed off at me with department budget hearings scheduled to begin in two weeks. I can probably kiss goodbye my budget request for replacement patrol vehicles and two new deputies."

Books agreed with that assessment but had sufficient common sense not to say it. "Look on the bright side Charley. You can do what everybody else around here does—blame the federal government."

"Somehow, that's not very comforting, J.D. By the way, congratulations for pissing off Lamont Christensen this morning—just what we needed right now, an ass-reaming in the local newspaper. But that'll have to be your problem. You can bet he couldn't wait to get on the phone to your boss and tell her you suggested he go piss up a rope."

Sutter was right about that, Books thought. "I didn't exactly tell him to go piss up a rope."

Sutter stopped pacing and sat down at his desk. "I know what you told him. Now let's get down to business. These artifacts you found in the back of Bobby's truck, you're sure they came from Rolly's collection?"

"Positive," said Tanner. "We matched them to the photographs we have of the collection."

"Get Melissa Esplin down here right away and have her take a look at them. I want somebody from the family to be absolutely sure before we go off half-cocked trying to tie Bobby Case to the Rogers fiasco."

"I'll get right on it, Sheriff," said Tanner.

"See that you do. Has Bobby had anything to say about any of this?"

"Nope. I Mirandized him before we brought him in, and he told me the only person he'd talk to was J.D."

"That opportunity may be long gone, Charley," countered Books. "I think when I showed up, Bobby figured I'd fix things and he wouldn't end up arrested."

Sutter paused, thinking about what Books had just said. "Suppose you don't arrest him today. Suppose we release him and you tell him that federal prosecutors will review the matter and decide whether to bring criminal charges."

"Are you out of your mind, Charley?" snapped Books. "Are you forgetting this is no longer simply an illegal digging case? God knows I wish it wasn't true, but Bobby had in his possession antiquities belonging to a couple who most likely are dead."

"We don't know that for sure," countered Sutter.

Books shook his head, wondering if the sheriff really believed that or was suffering from a serious case of self-delusion. Either way, Sutter's proposal might help him politically but would leave Books in an untenable position with his BLM supervisors.

"Think what you're asking me to do, Charley. BLM policy is clear on this. I'm required to arrest him, family member or not, and book him into the Washington County Jail in St. George. A federal magistrate imposes bail, and when it's paid, he's back on the street. Imagine how it would look if I agreed to ignore the policy and released a family member pending review of the case by a prosecutor. How would I explain it? Never mind what Lamont Christensen would say about it."

Sutter took that in listening thoughtfully. A voice on the office intercom broke the silence. "Sheriff, Doug Case is on line two—says it's urgent."

"Shit," said Sutter. "Somebody must have leaked it because we haven't let Bobby near a telephone."

"It didn't come from us," said Books.

"Good afternoon, Doug. How can I help you?" A blast of sound echoed from the receiver.

"Yes, sir. I'm afraid he was."

Books and Tanner glanced at each other. The decimal level, courtesy of Doug Case, was definitely elevated, and Sutter looked like a man dancing on hot coals. Mercifully, the call lasted less than two minutes. When it was over, Sutter leaned back in his leather chair and placed his worn cowboy boots on the desk. He looked completely defeated.

"He'll be here in a matter of minutes, and he's not happy."

No kidding, thought Books. He eased his six-foot-three inch frame off the sofa, "Stall him for a few minutes, Charley. I'm going try to get a statement from Bobby."

"You really think that's a good idea?"

"Maybe not, but I'm doing it anyway."

Books met Bobby Case in an interview room next to the booking area of the jail. "It's about time," said Case. "How long do I have to stay here?"

"Bobby, you're in a mountain of trouble. I hope you can help me sort it out. Deputy Tanner advised you of your rights. Is that correct?"

"Yes."

"Do you have any questions about them?'

"Is this really necessary, J.D.?"

"I'm afraid it is."

"Then, no, I don't have any questions."

"Look, Bobby, I'm not going to waste time. Let's cut to the chase. I'm more concerned about the relics we found in your truck. Those antiquities came directly from the home of Rolly and Abby Rogers, and I guess I don't have to tell you that they've gone missing. Where did you get that stuff?"

"Wait a minute. If you're insinuating I had something to do with whatever has happened to the Rogers, that's a boldface lie."

"Okay. Then answer my question. Where did you get those relics?"

"I bought 'em, okay? From a Navajo kid—I don't know his name."

Joe Benally, thought *Books.*

"If you don't know who this kid is, how did you meet him?"

"Through a third party, and I ain't gonna tell you who."

"Shit, Bobby. I need that name."

"Well, I ain't givin' it to you. He's a friend of mine and I'm not going to get him involved."

"Would you recognize the Navajo kid if I showed you a picture?"

"Yeah, I think so."

Books dug through his file and produced a mug shot of Joe Benally. "Is this the guy?"

Case hardly glanced at the picture. "Yeah, that's him."

There was a rap on the door. "J.D., I need to see you for a moment." When Books stepped into the hall, Tanner told him that an angry Doug Case was in the jail lobby demanding to see his son immediately.

"Stall him for another minute. Tell him I'll be right out to talk with him."

"Make it quick. He's making a scene in the lobby that's giving Charley fits."

Books nodded and returned to the interview room. "Look me in the eye, brother, and tell me you had nothing to do with whatever's happened to Rolly and Abby Rogers."

Bobby leaned forward in his chair, tears in his eyes. "I swear, J.D., I don't know nothing about what happened to them, and if I'd had any idea those pots and baskets came from their house, I never would have bought them. You got to believe me."

"All right, Bobby, I've got one last question. Why the hell were you out there digging in the first place? You know it's illegal."

He wiped tears from his cheeks before answering. "For the money, J.D., I did it for the money. We're gonna lose the ranch if something doesn't change soon. I'm sure of it."

Books found Doug Case and Charley Sutter in the sheriff's conference room looking equally agitated.

"There had better be a damn good explanation for what's going on here, J.D.," said Case.

"It probably won't make you happy," said Books, "but let me tell you what we know."

Books spent the next ten minutes summarizing for Doug Case the events of the past several hours. Case listened intently and without interruption, something Books read as a positive sign. To Books' irritation, the sheriff interrupted periodically, placing his own spin on the day's events. By the time he had finished, Case had calmed down significantly and sounded more like the smooth politician Books had long admired.

"I want you both to know," said Case, "that I have no problem philosophically with the idea of people pot-hunting. It's been a part of the local culture for as long as I can remember. That said there's been no tradition of pot-hunting in my family. I didn't do it, and I never encouraged my kids to."

"That's why it makes no sense to me that Bobby would get mixed up in something like this," said Sutter.

"What happens now?" asked Case.

For purely political reasons, the sheriff wanted Bobby Case released immediately and with as little fanfare as possible. Books understood this. He explained to Doug Case the federal government's protocol in cases like this one.

Glancing from Sutter to Books, Case said, "And you're telling me that you're unable to make an exception. Surely, there must be something we can do."

The "something" Case referred to turned out to be a courtesy booking at the Kane County Jail. Books phoned the Federal Magistrate's Office in St. George and received permission for Bobby to be booked and released from the jail in Kanab, averting the eighty-three mile drive to St. George. One hour later, Case walked out of the Kane County Jail accompanied by his father. He had been fingerprinted and photographed, and his family had posted $2,500 cash bail.

Chapter Nineteen

Books left the sheriff's department minutes after the release of his brother-in-law. When he arrived at his office, he found three voice messages. Two were marked urgent. The first was from his boss, Monument Manager Alexis Runyon. "Call me ASAP, J.D. I have a message from Lamont Christensen asking me to return his call. He went on a rant about you. I'd like your version of events before I talk to him."

Sutter had been correct, thought Books. It hadn't taken Christensen long to make the call. He'd acted like an idiot with the newspaper editor, and Christensen was going to have some fun at Books' expense. He dialed Runyon's extension, hoping he'd get lucky and find her out of the office. She didn't answer, and he left a lengthy message explaining his side of things and offering a lame apology for his behavior.

The second message had come from Becky Eddins. To her credit, Eddins understood the importance of her new client, Joe Benally, in resolving the disappearance of the Rogers. She sounded all business and suggested a meeting in her office. She asked that District Attorney Virgil Bell attend. Books suspected they were about to find out the price Eddins would exact in exchange for her client's cooperation. A deal was in the works. He could smell it.

The other message came from Sergeant Dan Walker of the Four Corners Task Force offering the assistance of his unit. Books was anxious to talk to Walker for a couple of reasons. He wanted information on any cases similar to the Rogers disappearance in the Four Corners area. Equally important, he wanted any intelligence the task force had about the mysterious group of Native American cops who patrolled federal lands in search of artifact looters. That call, however, would have to wait.

District Attorney Virgil Bell finished a misdemeanor arraignment calendar and hurried from the courtroom to join Books in the reception area outside Becky Eddins' office. She kept them waiting about ten minutes before opening the door and motioning them in. They sat at a rectangular oak conference table, empty except for a yellow legal- sized note pad.

She got right down to business. "What are you prepared to offer my client in return for his cooperation?"

"Depends on how much he knows and how deeply he's involved in the whole mess," replied Bell.

"He knows a lot, and unless you're about to break the case wide open on your own, I think you're going to need his help."

In a moment of awkward silence, Books and Bell glanced at each other. Their look of desperation was all the opening Eddins needed.

"I thought as much. Here is what I'm prepared to take to Mr. Benally for his consideration. He pleads guilty to one third-degree felony count of possession of stolen property and that's it. He's not to be charged with any additional offenses, state or federal, and I'll want the plea agreement in writing. In return, he tells you everything he knows about the burglary, the stolen artifacts, and the disappearance of the Rogerses."

"Depending on what he knows, he might also have to be a witness for the prosecution," said Bell. "That has to be part of any deal."

"Agreed," replied Eddins.

Bell sat quietly mulling over the offer from Eddins. Then he said, "Would you excuse us for a moment, Becky? I'd like a minute with Ranger Books."

"Sure. I'll be out in the reception area. Give me a shout when you're ready." She left.

"Well, what do you think?"

"You're the DA. It's gonna have to be your call. Negotiating plea deals isn't in my job description. Tanner and I pretty well have Benally wrapped up on the possession of stolen property and burglary charges, but as you know, we're nowhere close to finding out what happened to Rolly and Abby."

Bell leaned back in his chair, biting his lower lip, a nervous habit Books had seen before when the man was under pressure. "It's one thing to cut a deal with a thief but quite another to do it with someone who's involved in a kidnapping and maybe even murder."

"Happened every day in Denver. Besides, we don't know for sure whether he's involved in the disappearance or not."

"What's the likelihood he isn't?"

"Point taken."

They called Eddins back into the office. Bell had made his decision. "Here's what I'm prepared to offer. At the appropriate time, your client pleads guilty to one count of second-degree burglary, and I'll move to dismiss the possession of stolen property charge."

"Wait a minute," said Eddins, "he hasn't even been charged with burglary."

"He's about to be," countered Bell. "I just learned this afternoon in a phone call with the sheriff's office that your client's fingerprints were found at the Rogers home."

Bell continued. "The people would further stipulate that no additional state charges would be brought against Mr. Benally in exchange for his full and complete cooperation. He must agree to become a prosecution witness should we require his testimony. If we find that your client has deliberately withheld information or lied to us, the deal is off."

"What about federal charges?" asked Eddins.

"I have no control over that. The U.S. Attorney's Office will have to make that decision."

"Not good enough. I'm not going to allow my client to plead on state charges unless I have assurances from federal prosecutors that they intend to honor our agreement. If you can straighten that out, I'll take your offer to Mr. Benally."

Books admired her grit. She'd driven Bell into a corner and was playing hardball. "Look, let's not allow the deal to go up in flames over the possibility of federal charges. I'll call my people and see if we can get something worked out. It might be necessary for everybody to participate in a conference call in order to finalize the details."

Both lawyers agreed. Books, however, wasn't finished. "Becky, I don't need to tell you how important time is right now. If we're going to do this, it's imperative I interview Benally as soon as possible."

"I understand completely and you have my sympathy, J.D. However, I can't grant you access to Mr. Benally until this matter with the U.S. Attorney's Office is cleared up. Take care of that detail, and I'll go immediately to the jail and present him your offer."

The meeting ended. Bell headed back to his office, leaving Books and Eddins alone. "Tough day," said Eddins, reaching across the table and placing her hand on top of his.

"You don't know the half of it. Tell me something, Becky, why did you choose to get mixed up in this case? Benally would have qualified for a public defender and you know it."

"I tried not to, but in the end, I guess I felt it was my obligation. He really wanted me to defend him and so did his family. In his own twisted way, I think Joe Benally sees me as not just his attorney but as a maternal figure as well. He doesn't trust people, men in particular, but he's always trusted me going all the way back to his juvenile court days."

"I assume you realize if the Rogerses turn up dead and your client's got blood on his hands, it's not going to be pleasant for you as his defense attorney. This is not some low-level drug case or juvenile court matter that nobody cares about. This is a high-profile kidnapping and possible murder case. You could end up being an outcast in your own hometown. Have you thought about that?"

"Of course I have, but because it is a high-profile case, it can do wonders for my legal career. I've never had a case like this, where the media hangs on your every word. I could never afford to buy this kind of publicity."

"Just as long as you understand that all that publicity may come with a steep price."

"I'm sorry you're upset with me, J.D., but I'm only doing my job."

She hesitated. Then, "Are we okay?"

Books didn't feel he could even tell her about the arrest of his brother-in-law, since there was now a direct tie to her client. "I'm not angry with you but it sure puts a strain on things. Starting now, we'd be wise to keep our distance for a while, until the case is resolved—conflict of interest and all that good stuff."

She looked surprised but recovered quickly. "I think you're right. Some distance between us now seems like a prudent thing to do."

Back in the Tahoe, Books grabbed his cell phone and saw he had a call from Red Rock Touring. The message was from Brett Gentry. Gentry wanted to meet as soon as possible. The man sounded anxious and Books liked that. Red Rock Touring would be his next stop as soon as he sorted out this mess with the U.S. Attorney's Office. He needed help, so he called Special Agent Randy Maldonado.

Books filled Maldonado in on recent events, including the arrest and release of his brother-in-law from the Kane County Jail, as well as the tentative plea deal Virgil Bell had worked out with Becky Eddins.

"If I understand you correctly, J.D., this Eddins woman wants assurances that the federal government won't hammer her client with new charges after he pleads to the state offense. Is that it?"

"Exactly."

"And this Eddins woman is your girlfriend?"

"We've dated. That's on hold for now."

"The whole thing sounds like it's getting very messy."

Talk about an understatement, thought Books.

"What do you think the likelihood is that federal prosecutors will go along with the deal?"

"Not sure, but I know exactly who to call. Stay near your cell phone and I'll call you back. The guy I need to reach in the prosecutor's office is Wayne Chance. I've worked with him on several occasions. He's got the most experience handling pot hunting cases. I think he'll go along, but you can never be sure."

They disconnected. Books glanced at his watch. It was late in the afternoon. The U.S. Attorney's Office might be closed for the day. What then? The trail to Rolly and Abby Rogers was growing colder by the hour. He could ill afford to lose another day.

As Books parked the Tahoe in front of Red Rock Touring, his cell phone chirped. He glanced quickly at the caller ID, figuring that it was probably Maldonado returning his call. It wasn't. The caller was Alexis Runyon. He wanted to avoid what he suspected would be an unpleasant conversation for as long as he could. He ignored the call.

Brett Gentry was a squat, muscular man in his mid-forties who had the upper body of a weight lifter and thick legs that looked like railroad ties. He extended a large beefy hand that Books wished he didn't have to shake. He was certain he'd heard the crush of bone and cartilage as Gentry tightened the vice-like grip. Books had never understood people who insisted that you could tell something about the character and personality of a person from a handshake. The softest and gentlest handshake Books had ever experienced belonged to a concert pianist who wielded a straight-edge razor with the skill of a surgeon as he slashed the throats and faces of more than a dozen Denver-area prostitutes.

Books took a seat in a leather chair in Gentry's office. "How was your golf game?"

Gentry seemed taken aback by the question. "Ah, not so good—couldn't putt worth a damn. You know how that goes."

"Sure do. By the way, I hope my visit earlier today didn't upset your wife."

"As a matter of fact, it did."

Books lied. "I'm sorry to hear that."

Gentry ignored the lame apology. "I was shocked to hear that the name of our business had somehow come up in your investigation. I'd like to know how."

"As a matter of fact, it has. You probably heard that we arrested a man in connection with the burglary of the Rogers' home."

"Some Navajo guy, right?"

"That's right."

"Figured as much—shiftless bunch, if you ask me."

Books ignored the comment. "When we picked him up, I found a slip of paper in his bedroom with the phone number to Red Rock Touring on it. I wondered if you could explain that."

"I have no idea. To the best of my recollection, I've never heard of this Benally kid."

"You're sure he didn't work for you in the business or perhaps doing odd jobs around your home?"

"I don't think so. I'm sure I would remember."

Books stood to leave. "Then I think we're finished for now. Appreciate your time and sorry I upset your wife."

"Don't worry about it. I'm sure she'll get over it. And you let me know if there's anything we can do to help. We didn't know Abby and Rolly very well, but this is a small town, and we're all concerned. We'd like nothing better than to see you catch the people responsible for their disappearance."

Books thanked him and left, relieved that Gentry hadn't offered to shake hands a second time. As he maneuvered the Tahoe through the Red Rock Touring company parking lot, Emily Gentry pulled in and gave him a friendly smile and wave. She was driving a black Cadillac Escalade with tinted windows. That was the description of the suspicious-looking vehicle that the old man, Eldon Hitch, had described to Books that day when he was camped near the site where the Rogers had gone missing.

Like most good cops, Books had developed well-honed instincts when it came to people, and Brett Gentry made him feel uneasy. Gentry's expressed concern for the welfare of the Rogers struck Books as disingenuous and well rehearsed. His reference to the couple in the past tense, and his remark about catching the "people" responsible, implying multiple suspects, also hadn't gone unnoticed. Yet his biggest gaffe was lying about not knowing Benally's name. Initially, all he could recall was "some Navajo guy." Moments later, the name Benally popped out of his mouth like it was a name he'd known all along. And now the black Escalade. Sure, it could be a coincidence, but black Cadillac Escalades were not all that common in Kane County.

While he hadn't yet connected all the dots, Books was convinced that Brett Gentry and his Red Rock Touring company were somehow involved.

Chapter Twenty

Books returned to his office to find an irritated Alexis Runyon sitting at his desk. "I guess this is the only way I get to talk with you. Hang out in your office until you finally show up."

"I've been a little busy."

"I believe it. Now tell me about your encounter with Lamont Christensen."

She listened without interruption as Books laid out the incident for her, offering another half-hearted apology.

"Save the apology. Lamont's an egotistical, self-important asshole, and everybody knows it. Well, almost everybody."

Books' relief was premature, because Runyon wasn't finished. "Of course, we both know you have a tendency to act like a bull in a china shop. Tact and diplomacy aren't your strong suit."

"There's more."

She gestured for him to continue. Books explained Becky Eddins entrance into the case as Joe Benally's defense lawyer, as well as the arrest of his brother-in-law, Bobby Case.

"Yikes. That won't do much for family harmony."

"Tell me about it. I can't even bring myself to call my sister to tell her. She's in Salt Lake City with Bernie. He's scheduled for cancer surgery tomorrow morning."

"Better she hear it from you, J.D., than somebody else. So man up and call her. You might already be too late."

"You're right. I'll do it right away."

"Good. Now I'm thirsty. You gotta a beer?"

The question caught him off-guard. "Well, no, but we could go out..."

"Don't lie to me, Books. If you think you can smuggle beer into this building without me finding out, think again. Now, are you gonna give me a beer, or do I have to get it myself?"

"I think it might be against the law to bring alcoholic beverages into a federal building," Books said lamely.

Runyon stared at him but didn't reply.

Embarrassed, he opened his small refrigerator and glanced inside. "Coors Lite or Corona?"

Books hated making the call, but after he'd fortified himself with a couple of beers and sent Runyon on her way, he dialed his sister's cell.

"Hi, J.D." The upbeat tone of her voice suggested that she hadn't heard the news.

"Hey, sis. How's dear old dad?"

"Actually, he's doing pretty well considering. His spirits are high, and he's talking about making a full recovery. They ran some tests and did his blood work today. Surgery is scheduled for eight o'clock in the morning. Are you going to be able to make it?"

"That's partly why I called. Unfortunately, I won't be able to. Things are heating up, and I just can't get away. I feel bad, but I'm afraid it can't be avoided."

"It's okay. Dad is doing fine and I can stay with him until it's time to bring him home.

"How long will that be?"

"They're telling us a three-night stay if everything goes the way they expect."

"Have you heard from Bobby today?"

"Not a word. Why?"

Books paused.

"J.D. Is there something you're not telling me?"

"Yeah, there is, Mags."

"Well, spit it out. What's going on?"

"Bobby was arrested today."

"What! What for?"

"Tribal police caught him red-handed pot-hunting on BLM land. I got called to the scene having no idea who they had in custody. When I got there, I realized it was Bobby…"

"You arrested Bobby?"

"I had to, Mags, I'm really sorry. I wish there had been something else I could have done."

"This is just awful. His parents are going to feel so hurt and humiliated."

"I know. I met with Doug this afternoon, and, considering the circumstances, he seemed to be handling things pretty well. Don't worry about the boys. Doug posted his bail and drove Bobby home."

There was a brief lull in the conversation before Maggie continued. "Was he alone?"

"He was by himself."

"I can't believe he'd do something so stupid. What made him do it?"

"He did it for the money, Mags. He said he needed the income. He's worried about family finances and maybe even losing the ranch."

"That could happen, and maybe it will now."

"I'm really sorry, Mags. I wish there was something I could say or do to make it go away."

"Not your fault, J.D. I guess that explains why he's been gone so much lately. I was getting worried that maybe he had a girlfriend on the side—small comfort."

"Maggie, there's something else."

"I'm listening," she said, anxiety in her voice.

"When we arrested him, we found some antiquities in the cab of his truck."

"So what. That's what he was arrested for, pot hunting, wasn't it?"

"Yeah, except the stuff in his truck didn't come from the site he was excavating. It came from the collection of Rolly and Abby Rogers. It was part of the collection that was stolen in the burglary of their home."

"Oh, my God. Are you telling me you think that Bobby is somehow mixed up in the disappearance of Rolly and Abby?"

"I'm not sure, but I don't think so. Bobby says he bought the stuff from the Navajo kid we arrested yesterday. I haven't been able to confirm that yet, but I'll take Bobby at his word."

"I wonder how Bobby met this Navajo man you're talking about?"

"That's what I'd like to know. He says a friend introduced him, but he refuses to tell me who this friend is."

"You have to believe him, J.D. I know Bobby, and I know he would never harm the Rogers or anyone else. It's just not in his DNA. He's been a great father to your nephews and a good husband to me."

"I know that, sis."

"I'll try to get you the name of the person who introduced him to the Navajo. He'll talk to me or I'll wring his scrawny neck."

"Getting me that name would be helpful, sis. Thanks."

They fell silent. Then, "Can I give you a piece of advice, Mags?"

"Sure."

"I know you're terribly upset right now, and I don't blame you. But so is Bobby. If you talk with him tonight, try to avoid saying a lot of angry things that you might regret later, you know, once you've had a chance to think things through."

"That's probably good advice. Right now I just feel like strangling the guy."

"I know, but that won't help. Wait until you've calmed down and then have the conversation. You can always strangle him later."

"Not a bad idea. Listen, J.D., I'd better go. I'm trying to get Dad to eat something for dinner even though he doesn't have much appetite. He can't eat anything after midnight."

"Okay. Call or text me when he comes out of surgery. And Mags, hang in there. I wish I could be more helpful."

After the call, Books sat at his desk pondering what it might mean to his family if his faith in his brother-in-law's integrity turned out to be misplaced. What if Bobby was involved in the Rogers case? At the moment, all he had was Bobby's word that he'd purchased the artifacts from Joe Benally. What if that was a lie? And who was the mystery man Bobby refused to identify who had introduced him to Joe Benally?

As he prepared to leave the office, Books wondered why he hadn't heard from Special Agent Randy Maldonado. It probably meant that Maldonado had been unable to reach Wayne Chance in the U.S. Attorney's Office. Time was the enemy, and Books knew it.

He walked to the Tahoe feeling totally discouraged. His relationship with Becky was strained and now on hold. He'd made an ass of himself in an exchange with the local newspaper editor. He'd been forced to arrest his own brother-in-law. His father was facing serious cancer surgery the next morning, and he felt guilty because he couldn't be there. And, he was no closer to solving the case despite having a suspect in custody who he knew was withholding valuable information because of all the legal niceties required by being lawyered up. If that wasn't enough, the leg that had taken the bullet several months earlier ached like hell.

Books drove home, changed out of his uniform, downed a handful of Ibuprofen, and returned to town. He parked in front of the Cattle Baron. The place was nearly empty. He took a seat at the bar and ordered a Coors Lite. The bartender returned and placed the beer and a frosty stein in front of him. "That'll be $2.50, or I can run you a tab."

He was in no mood to get sloppy drunk. "Cash." The bartender took his money and returned to the other end of the bar where he resumed reading a newspaper.

Books glanced around the bar. A young couple sat together in a corner booth with a half-empty pitcher in front of them while they played smash mouth. At the other end of the bar an old man, with several days of unshaven stubble on his face in a dirty John Deere ball cap, sat talking to himself while he nursed a beer. Willie Nelson crooned Texas country on the juke box while the big screen television featured a soundless Dodgers–Braves baseball game.

Books lost track of the time as he sat there replaying the day's events. *Could anything else have gone wrong?*, he wondered. Later, he vaguely recalled the bartender telling him that he was about to lock up and that it was time to go home. As he fumbled in his wallet for a tip, he felt a hand on his arm.

"Hope you're not figuring on driving home tonight, Ranger Books."

Books glanced to his left and found Beth Tanner standing next to him. He felt so tired.

"Sorry, J.D., I know this has been a tough day. Let's get you out of here." Tanner walked him out of the bar and into her SUV. He dozed off almost immediately.

Chapter Twenty-one

Friday Morning—Day 8

Books awoke the next morning to sunlight streaming through the living room window of Beth Tanner's apartment. He had been asleep on her couch, his shirt and pants folded neatly at his feet. His mouth tasted sour and he had a headache. He looked around and saw Tanner in the kitchen. Her hair was wet and she was wearing a pink terrycloth bathrobe that hit her mid-thigh.

"Where the hell am I?"

"You're at my place. And relax, I promise I didn't take advantage of you last night."

"What time is it, anyway?"

"Time to get up and get your butt moving. I'll fix us toast and coffee while you take a shower. I left a towel in the bathroom for you."

"Thanks."

Books stood under the steaming hot shower for a long time allowing the warmth of the water to soak into his skin and clear his head. As he dressed, the smell of freshly brewed coffee filled the air. He found Tanner in the small kitchen buttering toast and nursing her own first cup of the day. She filled a mug for him and set it on the counter. Next to the coffee sat a bottle aspirin and a large glass of water.

Tanner saw him looking at the aspirin. "Just in case you need it."

"Appreciate that."

"I assume you take it black."

"Is there any other way?"

"Not for coffee purists, I suppose, but I don't count myself among the coffee elites. For me, it's flavored creamer and plenty of sugar—a liquid candy bar."

Books drank the glass of water with two aspirins. "About last night, uh….."

"What about last night?"

"Well, uh, I wouldn't want you thinking that I'm the kind of guy who goes off on a bender every time things get a little tough."

She looked at him for a long moment. "Why do you care what I think, J.D.?"

The question caught him completely off-guard. "Um, well, professional image, I guess."

"Listen, J.D. If you think I see you as some kind of knight in shining armor or as John Wayne, you can forget that. As far as I'm concerned, what happened last night was a cop under a lot of stress who crashed—I've got no problem with that—pushed myself too hard on a few occasions."

"Fair enough."

"And as far as you sleeping here, it probably wasn't such a great idea. It was a spur of the moment decision on my part, and my place was a lot closer than yours. I can assure you, nothing happened between us. I know you're with Becky Eddins and if you need me to be your alibi, I'll swear on a stack of bibles that you worked late on the case."

"And why would you do that for me?"

"That's what partners are for, isn't it?"

Books continued to sip the hot brew. He was already starting to feel better. "Um, a very good cup."

"Glad you like it."

"I'd guess a medium roast and probably Starbucks."

"How did you know that?"

"Oh, many years of roasting and participating in coffee tastings gives you a nose for it." He broke into a broad grin. "Actually, your Starbucks package is lying on the counter behind you next to the fridge."

"You dog."

"Among my former colleagues in Denver P.D. robbery/homicide, I was dubbed the coffee Nazi. I wore the label proudly. I started roasting my own beans purely as a defensive measure. Most of what they call coffee in the typical police department isn't worth crap. It's usually cheap coffee to begin with, and after it's been brewed and left on burn for a few hours, well, you know."

"You get used to it, I guess, but I have to agree with you."

"How did you find me last night?"

"It really wasn't all that difficult. Let's call it the power of deductive reasoning. I knew you'd had a lousy day so I dropped by your house to cheer you up. I saw the Tahoe but not your pickup. So, I figured a bar, and since Kanab is a one-horse town, I drove past the Cattle Baron, and there you were."

"I'm embarrassed. Thanks for pulling me out of there.

"Not a problem. So, what's on tap for today?"

Books told her about the plea deal negotiated between Becky Eddins and Virgil Bell.

"So we're on hold pending what?" asked Tanner.

"Pending approval of the plea agreement with the U.S. Attorney's Office. Becky won't allow us to talk to Benally until she's been assured that her client won't end up facing federal charges."

"Can't really blame her for that."

"I suppose not. There is something you can do, if you don't mind."

"Name it."

"I'll give you the names of those Native American cops we ran into yesterday. Call tribal headquarters, both Paiute and Navajo, and find out who these guys are and anything else you can learn about them."

"Is what they're doing even legal?"

"Good question. I'm not sure," replied Books. "If they confined their operation to tribal lands, it's perfectly legal. When they detain somebody off tribal lands like they did yesterday, I'm not so sure. It might be something the FBI would be interested in knowing about."

"If they're off reservation, how could it be legal? They're out of their jurisdiction, unless they're making a citizen's arrest."

"Beats me."

"Are you worried these guys might be some kind of vigilante group capable of harming people?"

"You're full of good questions, Beth. I just don't know, but we shouldn't rule it out until we learn more about them. Maybe they're some kind of militant Native American group much like the American Indian Movement was several decades ago? Maybe you can find out."

Although Books didn't know it, the investigation was about to take an unusual and deadly turn.

Chapter Twenty-two

Books hurried home, changed into his uniform, and made it into the office just ahead of nine o'clock. He hoped to find a message from somebody informing him that the plea agreement had been approved and that he was clear to interrogate Benally. No such luck. There were no messages, not from Bell, Maldonado, nor Becky Eddins.

There was little else he could do except wait. He pulled a legal pad from his desk and began preparing questions that he intended to ask Benally. He might get only one opportunity and he would need to make the most of it.

When the phone calls came, they came in rapid succession. The first was from Virgil Bell.

"Good news, J.D. I just wanted to let you know that we got everything worked out with the U.S. Attorney's Office on the plea agreement."

"Glad to hear it." It took long enough, he thought.

"Becky should be on her way over to the jail to go over the details of the offer with Benally. I told her the offer was good until three o'clock this afternoon. After that, the deal comes off the table."

"That puts a little pressure on them," said Books. "It's a damn good offer and they ought to jump on it."

"I agree, and we should hear something very soon. If I were you, I'd be ready to get over to the jail as soon as you get the call from Eddins. And by the way, she intends to sit in on the interrogation. I hope that doesn't cramp your style too much."

"I'd prefer that she not, but I can live with it. I'm ready to go just as soon as I hear from her."

"Let me know how things go," said Bell.

The men disconnected.

Randy Maldonado called next. "Good morning, J.D. I've got some news I think will be of interest to you. You may have heard already, but the U.S. Attorney's Office bought off on the state plea agreement."

"I just heard—got a call from the D.A.'s office. I'm waiting for a call from Benally's attorney giving us the green-light for the interrogation."

"Yeah, Benally's lawyer, that's something else we need to talk about."

Books was sure this wasn't going to be good. "What about her?"

"Uh, this is a little awkward, but when headquarters got wind of what was going on down there, I got a phone call."

"And."

"They smell at least the appearance of a conflict of interest with you in charge of the investigation and your girlfriend representing one of the suspects. And frankly, J.D., had I known things were going to shake out the way they have, I wouldn't have placed you in charge of the case."

It was impossible for Books to argue with the logic of what Maldonado was saying. "So what happens now?"

"I'll be joining you as soon as I can clear up a couple of things here in Salt Lake. This in no way reflects negatively on the way you've handled the investigation, and that sentiment is shared all the way to the top. I'll head the investigation from now on but in name only. As far as I'm concerned, you're still the guy calling the shots."

"Fair enough. When can I expect you?"

"Sometime this evening. Why don't we get together for dinner and you can bring me up to speed on things?"

"Sounds good. Anything else?"

"Yeah, there is one more thing. And this is simply an FYI. Headquarters received an anonymous phone call this morning from some guy who accused you of showing favoritism yesterday in the handling of the pot-hunting case involving your brother-in-law."

"You're just full of good news this morning, Randy."

"Hold your applause. No need to thank me," he said, laughing.

Books didn't see the humor.

"Actually, I do have some good news, some very good news in fact."

"You won't be offended if I continue to withhold my applause until I've heard you out?"

"I don't blame you. Late yesterday afternoon, we received lab results on some of the evidence I submitted from the crime scene. They've identified the make and model of the boot print found at the dig site. It's a Columbia Mountaineer high-top hiking boot, size thirteen. It has to be at least two years old since that was the last year the boot was manufactured."

"Size thirteen, huh. We knew the dude had big feet."

"We got no computer hits on the fingerprints we lifted from inside the Rogers' trailer. It probably means that the prints we lifted belong to our victims—no real surprise there."

"Or, the prints might belong to a suspect who hasn't served in the military and doesn't have a prior criminal record," countered Books.

"That's possible."

"What about the cigarette butts?"

"Negative on the fingerprints, and I haven't heard anything from the DNA lab yet. They're so far behind that it takes a long time to get test results. I'll call them today and see if I can prod them along."

"Anything else?"

"Yes, and it's also good news. Remember the trowel we found at the dig site?"

"I do."

"We got an AFIS hit from a right thumbprint. It belongs to a guy named James Earl Buck."

"And who exactly is James Earl Buck?"

"Mr. Buck is a former U.S. Army sergeant, honorably discharged in 2007. He served for six years as a paratrooper with the 86th Airborne Division. He's also got a minor criminal history, nothing particularly serious."

"Interesting. That's an elite unit."

"Sure is."

"We need to find out everything we can about Buck, including where and how to find him," said Books.

"I'd say the sooner the better."

Books took the information Maldonado had on Buck and promised to get started.

He had no sooner disconnected with Maldonado when the phone rang again. This time the caller was Becky Eddins.

"Morning, Becky. When can I come see your client?"

"We have a problem, J.D."

"What do you mean?"

"Joe Benally was bailed out of jail about an hour ago." Books glanced at his watch. It was now ten o'clock.

"What the hell are you talking about? Who bailed him out?"

"I don't know. I just called his mother and she didn't do it."

"No surprise there," said Books. "There's no way she could have come up with twenty grand. I doubt she'd even be able to come up with the cash necessary to hire a bail bondsman."

Bail bond companies typically charged a nonrefundable fee of ten percent of the bail amount. In this instance, that someone would have had to come up with two thousand cash, money they would never see again. The bond company would then post the full bail amount with the court clerk's office. The company would get its money back so long as the defendant showed up for court proceedings.

"Whoever posted the bond didn't use a bail bond company," said Eddins.

"Really."

"Jail records show that the twenty thousand was paid in cash via a money order."

"Who paid it?"

"Jail personnel didn't have a name. I'm on my way over to the district court clerk's office right now to find that out."

"And you haven't heard anything from Benally?"

"Not a word."

"I'll meet you there in five."

He grabbed his jacket and the keys to the Tahoe and hurried to the parking lot. In the law enforcement business, Books expected to be thrown curve balls from time to time, but this one surprised him. Who, other than family, would have the money and the interest to bail the kid out of jail? The answer gave him chills.

Eddins had made it to the court clerk's office ahead of Books. She was standing at the counter reading from a legal size file when Books arrived. Wilma Harris, the assistant court clerk, stood nearby and appeared visibly upset.

"I hope I didn't do anything wrong," she said. "I followed all the procedures including obtaining a picture form of identification. I don't know what else I could have done."

"You didn't do anything wrong, Wilma," said Eddins.

Books was reading the file over Eddins' shoulder. "Looks like a Utah driver's license was used for identification. The guy's name is Earl Shumway, and this shows an address in Moab, Utah," said Eddins. "Who do you suppose this guy Shumway is, anyway?"

"No idea, but I'll bet we're going to find the driver's license is a forgery and there is no Earl Shumway."

"It sure looked legitimate to me, the driver's license, I mean," piped in Harris.

Eddins ignored her. "What makes you say that, J.D.?"

"Somebody wants him out of jail for a reason, and the only reason I can think of is that Benally might start singing like Lady Gaga."

"If you're right, that means he's in real danger."

"Quite possibly. If whoever bailed him out did so to keep him quiet, the best way to ensure his silence would be to kill him."

"You can't be serious," said Eddins.

"As long as he's alive, he's a threat to whoever kidnapped the Rogerses. He probably knows enough to put some people away for a very long time."

"What should we do?"

"Find him and fast."

"How do you suggest we do that?"

"I've got a couple of ideas."

Books called the jail and obtained a physical and clothing description for Joe Benally. He then provided that information to the regional dispatch center and had the on-duty dispatcher broadcast an attempt-to-locate on Benally. Books asked to be notified immediately if Benally was stopped.

"There's something you can do, Becky."

"I think I should get back to my office in case he shows up there."

"I agree. When you get there, call Benally's girlfriend, Ruthie Todd. Explain the situation and try to enlist her help. And while you're at it, stay in touch with Benally's mother. If you need me, call my cell."

If Benally was on foot, and Books hoped he was, it made sense that he would call his mother or his girlfriend for help. If he was picked up by whoever posted his bail, the chances of finding him were slim. What Books really hoped was that Benally had the good judgment to call his attorney and inform her that he was out of jail. Unfortunately, guys like Joe Benally rarely demonstrated good judgment.

Books obtained a detailed physical description of Earl Shumway, the mysterious man who posted the bail, He decided to drive north out of Kanab in the same direction Benally would have gone if he were hitchhiking home. Several miles north, he gave up and returned to Kanab.

He had just reached the outskirts of town when he heard the radio call dispatching a Kanab patrol car to a hit-and-run car-pedestrian accident on 100 East Street adjacent to the city park. An awful thought occurred to Books. He hoped he was wrong, but he turned on the Tahoe's emergency lights and raced to the accident scene. In route, he radioed dispatch seeking information on the suspect vehicle. He was told to stand by. Moments later, the dispatcher broadcast a BOLO for an older, black or dark blue Ford Explorer, driven by a lone white male a witness had observed speeding south on 100 East, away from the accident scene.

Books arrived simultaneously with the first Kanab patrol car in time to see the body of Joe Benally sprawled on the gravel shoulder of the road. He wasn't moving. Books could see that he was bleeding profusely from the head, and that his right leg was bent backward at an awkward angle. The femur protruded from the leg revealing a compound fracture. He called dispatch again, this time requesting an ambulance.

Chapter Twenty-three

Within minutes, the area was crawling with police cars from several agencies including the Kanab Police Department, the Kane County Sheriff's Office, and the Utah Highway Patrol. Fortunately, the Kanab Hospital was located a stone's throw from city park. An ambulance arrived almost immediately. Books looked around and realized there was nothing he could do for Joe Benally. He overheard one of the paramedics say that Benally's vital signs were stable. It was all in the hands of the gods.

Books decided to retrace the route traveled by the suspect until he reached the intersection with U.S. Highway 89. Then he decided to play a hunch. Anybody who was brazen enough to intentionally engage in a hit-and-run in broad daylight would be smart enough to have an escape plan, he reasoned. It seemed unlikely that the suspect would leave Kanab by any of the three state highway routes. Those were lightly traveled two-lane roads where he would easily be spotted. Books began cruising commercial parking lots looking for an abandoned suspect vehicle.

If his hunch was correct, the perp would have either had someone pick him up, or he would have stashed a getaway car somewhere nearby and dumped the Explorer.

He checked the parking lots of Glazier's Family Market, Ace Hardware, McDonalds, and the Chevron station without success. Then he cruised several blocks south of town and turned around at the local Pizza Hut. Again, he came up empty. Back in the center of town, Books turned east on to U.S. Highway 89 and drove slowly to the east end of town, checking side streets and parking lots along the route.

He was about to give up when his eye caught a dark colored SUV parked on a dead-end street next to the cemetery. He wasn't sure this vehicle was a Ford Explorer. He made a U-turn on 89 and drove slowly past the vehicle. A closer look confirmed that it was an Explorer, but was it the right one? He didn't notice any obvious front-end damage.

Books parked the Tahoe and radioed the dispatcher with his location and the SUV's license plate number. He drew his service revolver and cautiously approached the passenger side of the vehicle on full alert for anyone who might be hiding inside. Satisfied that the Explorer was unoccupied, Books placed his hand on top of the hood and found the engine was still warm. The grill and hood showed minor damage on the front passenger side. A closer examination revealed what Books believed to be bits of clothing fabric and several strands of dark brown hair.

Books felt confident that he had found the hit-and-run vehicle. Evidence technicians would be able to determine whether the clothing fabric and hair matched samples they would take from Joe Benally. Unless he was mistaken, Books thought it highly unlikely that the suspect would have had the time to wipe the vehicle down. That should provide a treasure trove of latent fingerprints and other evidence that might lead them to a suspect.

A Kanab Police Department patrol car pulled in behind him, and Charley Sutter followed in an unmarked sheriff's department car. Sutter and Kanab Police Chief George Spencer got out of their vehicles and walked over to the Explorer.

"How's the kid doing?" Books asked.

Spencer shrugged. "He was alive when they got him to the hospital. That's all I know."

"I heard they're running tests," added Sutter.

"I don't know how you found this thing, but nice work," said Spencer.

Books glanced over his shoulder at the Explorer. "Luck, mostly. I engaged in a little guesswork and followed my nose."

"Glad you did," said Spencer. "The vehicle's a steal out of Big Water. The owner reported it missing yesterday afternoon."

Books nodded.

"I thought the court slapped such an unusually high number on Benally that he'd never make bail," said Sutter. "Twenty grand is a lot for somebody charged with possession of stolen property."

"The bail was set high because the judge was aware of Benally's possible connection to the disappearance of the Rogers," said Books. "But you're right, Charley, nobody thought for a minute that he'd make bail."

"So how did he get out?" asked Spencer.

"Guy by the name of Earl Shumway walked into the court clerk's office this morning and presented a money order for twenty grand," said Books.

"Earl Shumway?" said Sutter.

Books said, "You know this Shumway?"

"Couldn't be the same guy," replied Sutter. "The Earl Shumway I'm thinking of was an infamous pot hunter from over Moab way. But hell, he's been dead for years or at least he's supposed to be dead."

"What do you mean "supposed to be?" asked Spencer.

"Well, old Earl came from a family of grave robbers—always bragged the feds would never catch him. But they did. In fact, it was Randy Maldonado who finally got him. He went off to federal prison for a few years, got out, went back to Moab, and to hear people tell it, went right back to digging. After a while, he disappeared, and then reports surfaced that he'd gotten sick and died. But rumors have persisted for years that he didn't really die and is still out there somewhere."

"How old would he be if he was still alive?" asked Books.

Sutter paused. "Oh, hell, I don't know. He'd probably have to be mid-to-late seventies by now."

"I think we can assume this character isn't the Earl Shumway you're talking about. Wilma Harris described our guy as somewhere in his early thirties."

"Maybe the perp was just trying to be funny," said Sutter.

"Maybe," said Books.

"Well, it's not—funny, I mean," added Spencer.

Books' cell phone rang. He glanced at the number and realized that Beth Tanner was trying to reach him.

"Hey, Beth. What's up?"

"I'm hearing scuttlebutt. What's going on out there?"

Books filled her in.

When he finished, Tanner said, "What can I do to help?"

Books gave her the name and Utah driver's license number used to post Benally's bail.

"Get a hold of DMV and find out whatever you can about that driver's license number. I'm guessing it's a phony, but they ought to be able to tell us. Also, ask if anyone by the name of Earl Shumway holds a Utah driver's license."

"I'll get right on it."

Books turned his attention back to Sutter and Spencer. "Look, fellas, I need to get over to the hospital. Can you get somebody over here to handle the impound?"

"I'll take care of it myself," said Spencer."

"Better get this rig indoors pronto," said Books, glancing nervously at the darkening clouds rolling in from the southwest, "Supposed to rain today. Get the lab boys here as soon as possible. My gut tells me we're going to get plenty of physical evidence off this Explorer."

"Anything else?" said Spencer.

"Yeah, there is and it's important. From the moment Benally comes out of surgery, assuming he survives, he's got to have protection 24/7. That means nobody gets in to see him other than his immediate family, Becky Eddins, his lawyer, your investigating officer, and me."

"You really think somebody might try to off him in the hospital?" said Spencer.

"Look, somebody was serious enough to shell out twenty grand to get him out of jail and then failed to kill him on the first attempt. Why wouldn't they try again?"

"Put like that, it has a ring of desperation to it," said Sutter.

"It's tough for us," replied Spencer. "I just don't' have the manpower, but we'll figure something out."

"I'll help you with it, George" said Sutter. "Might have to authorize some overtime, but I'll find somebody willing to pull some of the shifts."

Books left the two men with the Explorer and headed over to the hospital. He wanted to talk to the witness who had called in the hit-and-run and see what he could find out about Benally's medical condition.

When he entered the hospital lobby, Books observed a uniformed Kanab police officer seated on a couch taking information from Benally's mother, who was dabbing tears from her eyes with a tissue. Becky Eddins was standing off to one side talking to someone on her cell phone. She gave him a slight nod and continued talking.

As soon as the patrol officer finished with Benally's mother, he strode over to Books, extended his hand, and introduced himself. "Ranger Books, I'm Officer Ed Harris. Thanks for the help out there this morning."

Books shook his hand. "Sure. How's Benally doing?"

Harris shrugged, "Haven't heard anything. As far as I know, he's still in surgery."

"The kid looked pretty banged up, that's for sure. Did he happen to say anything to you?"

"Nah, not really. He was in and out of it—mumbled some gibberish that didn't make any sense."

"What about his clothes, do you have them?"

Harris looked embarrassed. "Damn, I forgot about the clothes. Let me run over to the emergency room. That's where they brought him in. I'm sure they'll have them."

"When you go over," said Books, "be sure you find out who removed his clothing. The clothes are evidence and we'll need to maintain a proper chain of custody."

Harris nodded.

Becky Eddins got off the phone and walked over to the two men. "Officer Harris mentioned that you found the SUV that struck Joey."

"We think so. It was stolen yesterday afternoon from Big Water."

"Do you think it was stolen for the express purpose of killing him?"

"Hard to say." This was a discussion Books didn't want to have with Eddins. They were on opposite sides of this one.

"Would you excuse us for a minute, Becky? I need a couple of more minutes with Officer Harris."

"Certainly." She stepped away.

Books turned back to Harris. "I heard you've got a witness."

"Sure do, and a good one, I think."

"What did he have to say?"

Harris looked at his crime scene notes. "Our witness had just returned a couple of library books and was leaving the parking lot when it happened. He got a good look at the suspect vehicle but couldn't help us much with the driver."

"Any chance he could identify the driver if he saw him again?"

Harris shook his head. "The only thing Mr. Simmons seemed sure of was that the suspect was a white male, wearing camouflage clothing including a round, wide-brimmed hat which made it impossible to get a look at his face."

Books recalled the bank's surveillance tape of the two ATM withdrawals. The suspect had been wearing camouflage clothing and a round, wide-brimmed hat.

"Anything else, Ed?"

"That's about it. You want his name and contact information?"

"I do. Thanks."

When they finished, Harris excused himself and headed off to the hospital emergency room to retrieve Benally's clothing.

Eddins was sitting on the couch in the hospital lobby with Benally's mother, Ruby Grant, engaged in a hushed conversation. As Books approached, Eddins motioned him away.

Grant shot Books an angry look that suggested she believed he was responsible for the near fatal assault on her son. And maybe he was. Books moved away from the pair and stood by the sliding doors at the entrance to the hospital until Eddins approached.

"How is Mrs. Grant holding up?"

"About as well as can be expected under the circumstances. What happens now?"

"I've arranged with Chief Spencer and Sheriff Sutter for round-the-clock protection of your client once he gets out of surgery."

"I'm relieved to hear that. I'll pass it along to Ruby. It might make her feel a little better. Tell me something. If they really wanted him dead, why use a car? Why not just shoot him?"

"I don't know. Criminals don't always make smart decisions. Maybe they thought a car accident would look less suspicious than a shooting. Look, it's imperative I talk with your client just as soon as he comes around."

"That's not going to happen, J.D. Nothing has changed as far as I'm concerned. "You can't have access to my client until I've had time to present the DA's plea offer to him. And I won't do that until his doctors tell me he's cogent enough to understand what we're talking about. Until then, you'll have to stay away."

"Jesus, Becky. Don't you understand? The sooner he talks to me, the better his chances are of staying alive. Once he talks, we'll have a better chance of finding the perps before they try to kill him again."

"Don't patronize me, J.D. Of course, I understand. But I've got a job to do just like you do. And I will not jeopardize his legal case until he's competent enough to understand what it means if he accepts the prosecutor's offer. Are we clear?"

"Crystal." Books walked away.

Chapter Twenty-four

Back in the Tahoe, Books couldn't help but notice the abrupt change in the weather. The wind coming out of the northwest had gained strength and turned colder. Thunderheads had formed over the mountains and black cumulus clouds blanketed the sky. A light rain had begun to fall. Like other locals, Books understood that the Grand Staircase Escalante National Monument could be a cruel mistress. He hoped the tourists hiking and four-wheeling in the monument were paying attention.

Recently, a pair of newlyweds from Delaware had been hiking a slot canyon, oblivious to the changing weather, when a sudden flash flood roared down the canyon and swept them away. The woman survived the ordeal. Her husband didn't. From her hospital bed, she had cried that the flood occurred without warning, leaving them no time to escape to higher ground. Books didn't have the heart to tell her the signs were all there, but they simply hadn't paid attention.

He found a voice message from his sister, asking him to call. The news was good. Bernie was out of surgery, the doctors telling her that the cancer hadn't spread to other organs. It was, however, necessary to remove more than a foot of his colon. Their father would remain hospitalized for several days, followed by several weeks of chemotherapy treatment.

Books was elated. He felt an overwhelming sense of relief that Bernie's prospects appeared good, and guilt that he hadn't been at his father's bedside throughout the ordeal. He returned Maggie's call and they spoke briefly. Bernie was in recovery and would remain there for a while longer. They agreed to talk again later that night.

◇◇◇

Books knew that he had held back with Eddins. They now had a lead they hadn't had prior to the fingerprint identification of James Earl Buck. If they could find him, the entire operation might fall apart and the cooperation of Joe Benally would be unnecessary. If that were the case, Books would urge District Attorney Virgil Bell to withdraw the plea offer. That would anger Eddins, and she would undoubtedly view the action as retribution for not quickly accepting the deal and making Benally available for interrogation.

From the onset, he had wondered whether the plea agreement was overly generous, particularly if it turned out Benally was up to his eyeballs in the disappearance of Abby and Rolly Rogers. From experience Books had learned that overly generous plea deals in high-visibility, violent crime cases had a way of coming back to bite the major players on their backside. Should that happen, public anger would be directed at Virgil Bell and Charley Sutter.

With the interrogation of Benally at least temporarily on hold, Books turned his attention to finding Buck. The trowel inadvertently left at the dig site had provided their only strong lead in the case. Apprehending him was now of paramount importance.

He had just parked the Tahoe at Escobars when he received a radio call asking him to return to the hospital to see Officer Harris. So much for lunch, he thought. He was starving. He hadn't eaten anything all day except for the toast and coffee he'd had at Tanner's apartment.

"What's up, Ed?" said Books, as he approached Harris in the hospital lobby. The officer was busy placing individual items of Benally's clothing in separate bags and attaching signed evidence tags to each.

"I think I found something here you're going to want to see."

"What is it?"

"It's a note I found in Benally's pants pocket."

"Did you handle it?"

He cringed, "Sorry. I guess I wasn't thinking. As soon as I realized that it might be important, I grabbed a pair of latex gloves."

A little late, thought Books. "What does the note say?"

"I'll let you read it." Using a pair of tweezers, Harris carefully removed the note from a small, plastic zip-lock baggie. The handwritten note read:

Joey,

We posted your bail as soon as we heard you got busted. Don't worry about nothin. I got us a ride. Meet me at City Park as soon as you get out. We'll get out of town, chill out a while, and maybe cook us up some meth.

Books studied the unsigned note. It had to have been written by someone trusted and known to Benally. But how was the note delivered? That was puzzling. One thing seemed clear. The note provided incontrovertible proof of a conspiracy to murder Joe Benally out of fear he might turn state's evidence.

"Thanks for the call, Ed. I'm gonna take the note with me. I can arrange to have it examined for latent prints quicker than you can."

"But what about my prints?"

"Not to worry—we'll arrange to get a copy of your fingerprints from the city for elimination purposes."

Books left the hospital and headed straight for the Kane County Public Works garage, where the stolen Explorer had been moved. He asked to have the note examined before techs began the laborious job of processing the Explorer. Maybe they'd get lucky and find latent prints belonging to someone other than Harris.

Books returned to Escobar's for lunch. He was joined by Tanner, who had been busy looking into the background of Earl Shumway, the man who had posted Benally's bail. She was also conducting background investigations of the four Native American cops who had arrested Bobby Case.

"How are you doing?" she asked, sliding into the booth.

"What a day."

"I gotta say, Books, you attract trouble like flies to a cow pie."

He laughed. "It's not by design, I can tell you that. What have you been up to?"

"Just like you thought, J.D., the license is a fake. DMV has no driver's license record for anyone named Earl Shumway—probably just somebody's warped sense of humor."

"No, Beth, it's more than that. It's also clever and arrogant—makes me think whoever did it is overconfident and toying with us. Let's hope his inflated sense of self-confidence leads him to make mistakes. What about the tribal cops?"

"I'll tell you this much. Tribal police are not the easiest folks to get information from."

"I'm not surprised."

"I started by calling Paiute tribal police headquarters. I was told that Sergeant Albert Tom is a patrol supervisor, been with the department for almost nine years, and is well respected internally. Eric Bow and Benjamin Youngbear are reserve officers; both are in good standing. Each hopes to secure a fulltime position whenever the opportunity presents itself."

"Bow and Youngbear are going to have a lot less training and experience than Tom."

"Yeah, but probably a lot more time for chasing diggers."

"True. Who gave you this information?"

She looked at her notes. "A captain in charge of personnel and training."

Books nodded.

"Things got a little fuzzier when I called the Navajo tribal police in Window Rock."

"How so?"

"I got passed around several times before my call landed in the office of a sergeant by the name of Miriam Curley. Curley was at least willing to discuss the existence of this group, whereas others I spoke to seemed deliberately vague."

"What does Sergeant Curley do for the department?"

"She runs an office that coordinates various tribal research projects and works to obtain federal grants to help fund the studies."

"Go on."

"Here it gets a little interesting. Curley told me that Ronald Yazzie, the fourth cop and the only Navajo, is no longer a member of the tribal police. He was terminated for cause almost a year ago."

"Interesting. Did she say why?"

Tanner shook her head, "Nope, she cited privacy concerns."

"That's good information, Beth, but there are some other things I'd like to know."

"For instance?"

"For instance, does this group have a name? How are they funded? Do they receive any kind of official recognition from the tribes? How are they organized and do they have a leader? How many members do they have?"

"I can answer some of those questions." Tanner went back to her notebook. "Here it is. Curley told me that the group is called the Society for the Preservation of the Ancients, or SPA for short. Her impression is that the group is made up mostly of Navajo, although she wasn't surprised when I told her about the Paiutes we encountered.

"Anyway, she said the head of the SPA is a man by the name of Rodney Begay."

"Okay. And just who is Rodney Begay?"

"Curley described Begay as a reclusive Navajo lawyer who lives in Sedona. Apparently, he's quite wealthy and supports a variety of Native American causes."

"Has Curley ever met him?"

"No. This is all second-hand information. Curley seemed to think that few people have direct access to Begay; that he's protected by a small inner circle."

Books knew that Sedona was anything but the low-rent district. The town catered to an affluent crowd whose interest in the arts rivaled that of Taos, Scottsdale, or Santa Fe. He'd been there a few times as a kid on family vacations. He recalled the long drives from Kanab down through Page, Arizona, across the stunning, but desolate Painted Desert, and on to Flagstaff and Sedona.

"I'd like you to gather as much information about this guy as you can find," said Books. "Run him through every on-line site that you can think of. Find out where he grew up, where he went to law school, and where he practices law. In the meantime, I'll call Dan Walker with the Four Corners Task Force and see whether his group has any intell on the SPA or Rodney Begay."

"Okay. I'll get right on it."

Chapter Twenty-five

From his office Books began piecing together information about the SPA and James Earl Buck. He dialed the phone number of the Four Corners Task Force. Walker answered on the first ring.

"Chief Mendez tells me you're up to your neck with a pot-hunting case linked to a missing couple from Kanab," said Walker.

Books gave him a brief rundown on the Rogers investigation. "I wanted to find out whether you've had any similar cases in the Four Corners area."

"After I spoke with Chief Mendez and read a newspaper account of your investigation, I went back five years into our records looking for unsolved similar cases. What I found surprised me."

"How so?"

"Well, the records show a total of seven cases during the five-year period where one or more persons went missing and were never seen or heard from again. In one instance, a group of university archeology students, lead by a professor, stumbled upon the skeletal remains of one of the missing victims."

"How did you determine that those skeletal remains were part of the seven cases?"

"The detectives used information they'd gathered from the families of the missing people and determined that this particular victim went missing near where his remains were found. Ultimately they used the guy's dental records to make the match."

"Did the remains show any signs of foul play—bullet wounds, blunt object trauma, that sort of thing?"

"That's a problem. I don't know. The case report doesn't reflect anything of that sort, but none of these investigations has ever been classified as anything other than missing persons cases."

"In other words, nobody thought to examine the remains for foul play."

"That's right. But you've got to remember that people go missing in the desert all the time. Most either walk out under their own power or are found by search and rescue. Only a small percentage disappears permanently."

"You mentioned that something in the records surprised you," said Books. What was it?"

"When I looked for cases where the missing subjects were known or suspected diggers, two things jumped out at me. The first was that I had four such cases, five if we count yours."

"And the other?"

"Each of these cases occurred relatively recently—during the past two and a half years."

"Where did they occur—any geographic pattern?"

"No, not really. They were scattered all over the Four Corners area. In fact, your case is the only one I can find that didn't occur in the Four Corners region."

"Which could mean they're absolutely unrelated."

"Very possible. There's one other difference. None of our cases included a burglary of the victim's residence."

"Even so, if it's all right with you, I'd like to have a look at those case files."

"I'll save you the trouble. We'll review each of these cases and see whether there's anything that might have been overlooked— anything that might indicate foul play. What concerns me is the possibility, however remote, that we might have a gang of rogue pot hunters who are not only engaged in illegal collecting, but who also prey on rival diggers."

"My thoughts exactly," said Books. "And if your concerns are correct, that might explain what happened to our missing couple."

"I've called a special meeting with my staff tomorrow morning ," said Walker. "I'll go over all of this and we'll get to work."

Books shifted gears and described the troubling incident that he and Tanner encountered the previous day with the tribal members who had arrested his brother-in-law.

"And you believe that these four Native American men belong to some group that patrols tribal lands looking for pot hunters?"

"I know it sounds a little weird, but I'd like to know if your Task Force has any intel on this group."

"I've never heard of any group calling itself the Society for the Preservation of the Ancients or the SPA, but I'll sure look into it. One member of our team, George Tso, is a Navajo tribal police officer. I'll ask him to check it out."

"I've got one last question for you. Have you guys had any contact with a man by the name of James Earl Buck?"

"I'll check. Who is he, anyway?"

Books explained the fingerprint that had been lifted from the trowel at the site where the Rogers couple had been digging.

"So this guy's one of your suspects along with the Navajo kid you were telling me about."

"Yup."

Walker put Books on hold while he ran a check on Buck. Moments later, he was back. "We don't have anything in our records on him, but when I ran his name through the database at the Colorado Bureau of Investigation, they show he's got priors from the Grand Junction Police Department."

"When and for what?"

"Let's see. 2008, domestic violence, 2009, assault and battery, 2009 again, this time in Durango for hit and run auto—all misdemeanors."

"Is he on probation?"

"Could be, but I can't confirm it from this record. I'll have to make a call and get back to you. Hold on a moment and let me check one more thing."

Books waited. "Mr. Buck's got a suspended Colorado driver's license showing a Cortez post office box for an address. I'll scan it and send it to you in an email."

The men disconnected with Walker promising to recontact Books as soon as he had further information.

Books leaned back in his office chair and planted his size elevens on the top corner of his desk. Slowly, a picture of James Earl Buck was starting to take shape. For starters, he had probably been a damn good soldier. He'd risen through the ranks to a leadership position in the U.S. Army's prestigious 86th Airborne Division, no small feat in itself. His scrapes with the law seem to have begun after his discharge in 2007. Books wondered what might have triggered the onslaught of arrests, maybe post-traumatic stress disorder, or drug abuse. From the information he'd collected so far, it was impossible to tell.

As Books prepared to leave the office, his phone rang. The caller identified herself as a probation and parole agent with the Utah Department of Corrections. Her name was Roslyn Jones and she was James Buck's probation officer. Jones explained that Sergeant Dan Walker of the Four Corners Task Force had asked her to call him.

"So he is on probation," said Books. "I'm surprised he's in Utah. I thought he was living in Colorado."

"He is on probation, and he was residing in Colorado until recently," replied Jones. "His offenses occurred in Colorado, but he compacted last year to Utah. He lives in Blanding in an old house he and his younger brother inherited from their late mother."

Blanding, thought Books, the heart of Four Corners pot hunting.

"By compacting you mean he got permission from the Colorado court to move to Utah and you lucky folks get the privilege of babysitting him."

"That's about it. All states belong to the Interstate Compact. That means that an offender like Mr. Buck is adjudicated in one state but decides he wants to live in another. In the case of Mr. Buck, that would be Utah. The offender applies, and if permission is granted, he's allowed to move to another state. Utah provides complimentary community supervision of Mr. Buck for Colorado."

"I see. And if Buck screws up in Utah, you ship him back to Colorado authorities."

"That's how it works. Now how can I help you? Is James in some kind of trouble?"

"He could be. At the moment I'd call him a person of interest in a federal antiquities investigation and an aggravated kidnapping case that occurred this past week along a stretch of the Arizona strip."

"Can't say I'm surprised, given the family history."

"What do you mean?"

"Mr. Buck comes from a military family, albeit a dysfunctional one. When the boys were young, the family moved frequently following their father's base assignments. His father served in the Army for thirteen years until he was drummed out for a variety of criminal offenses—nasty-tempered guy, from what the record suggests."

"What became of the father?"

"Good question. The mother divorced him and took the boys back to her home town in Blanding. The father pretty much dropped out of sight. He's been busted twice by Colorado Fish and Game for poaching, and he hasn't filed federal or state income tax forms for years."

"The old man sounds like a wonderful role model."

"That's part of James' problem. Instead of looking at him like the creep he is, James, unfortunately, sees him as some kind of modern-day mountain man who lives off the land and fights the good fight against an oppressive government."

"You'd better give me any information you have on the father," said Books. "For all I know, he could be involved in this thing right along with James."

"I'm afraid I don't have much on the father. His name is Earl Wilson Buck. People call him Willy. He's fifty with a DOB of 3-11-61."

"That's okay. I can do the rest."

Anything else I can help you with?"

"If you can reach James, I'd sure like to talk to him."

"I think I can help you with that. He's in violation of his probation agreement if he's committed any new offenses. And in fact, if he leaves the state of Utah at any time without my written permission, that's a violation as well. We can either prosecute him here for new offenses or simply return him to Colorado."

"How often do you see him?"

"Once a month by appointment."

And where do you meet?"

"Usually we meet here in the Moab office, but once in a while, I visit him at his home in Blanding."

"When's his next appointment?"

Jones looked in her planner. "Here in my office, at nine a.m., one week from today."

"Hmm. I don't have a week to spare. How about employment? Where does he work?"

"I'm afraid that's gonna be a problem. He works sporadically as a day laborer—mostly seems to be getting by on unemployment checks and food stamps. The best bet would be to catch him at home."

"Can you help me with that?"

"Sure, if you tell me how you want to play it. If I spook him, he might run."

"What do you suggest?"

She thought about that. "Here's what we can do. I'll call him and feed him a bullshit story that we are altering the conditions of his probation agreement by loosening some restrictions. He'll like that. I'll tell him that he must come to my office immediately to sign the new probation contract. When he gets here, you'll be waiting."

"I like how you think, Agent Jones."

Before they disconnected, they agreed that she would notify Books the moment the appointment was set, and that Books would be ready to leave for Moab at a moment's notice.

Chapter Twenty-six

While Books finished with Agent Jones, he received an incoming call from Randy Maldonado. Maldonado left a message cancelling their scheduled dinner and explaining that he had been delayed in Salt Lake City and wouldn't make it to Kanab until the following day.

One less complication, thought Books.

Books drove to the hospital to check on the condition of Joe Benally. He learned that Benally's surgery had gone well, and that he had just been moved from intensive care to a regular hospital bed. A uniformed Kanab police officer sat outside the door reading a magazine while Benally's mother remained at his bedside. Books stopped at the nurse's station and was told that doctors expected Benally to sleep for several more hours. That meant his best hope for an interview would likely be sometime the next morning.

As he left the hospital, his cell chirped. The caller was Greg Jasper, a fingerprint technician who had processed the stolen Ford Explorer and the note found in Joe Benally's pants pocket.

"What have you got for me, Greg?"

"On the note, I found latent prints as we expected from Joe Benally and Officer Harris. I also found a third set of prints but, unfortunately, they don't match James Earl Buck."

"Whose prints are they?"

"Wish I knew. When I ran them through the AFIS, I didn't get a match."

Damn, thought Books. He had been confident the prints would have come back to Buck. If they weren't his, whose were they? They couldn't belong to Earl Buck. His prints would have yielded an AFIS match, since he had both a military and criminal history. An ugly thought entered Books' head one he hadn't thought about until now.

"Greg, I've got another individual whose prints I'd like you to look at."

"Sure. Who is it?"

"The man's name is Robert Douglas Case. He was just arrested for pot-hunting. You'll find a copy of his prints at the Kane County Sheriff's Department."

Books saw no reason to explain to Jasper his relationship with Bobby.

"I'll get right on it for you. Now as for the Explorer, I'm afraid that's a bit more complicated."

"What do you mean?"

"I've identified several sets of prints both in and outside the Explorer. Chances are good that some of them belong to the family from whom the vehicle was stolen. Several of them came back as a match to James Buck. But I also got a hit on somebody named Earl Buck. Does that name ring a bell?"

"Sure does," replied Books. "Earl is James Buck's father."

"I figured he had to be family. If you like, I'll go ahead and compare the latents I lifted from the SUV to the prints of Robert Case. Maybe some of the prints are his."

Books doubted that but told him to go ahead.

A few minutes later, Books turned the Tahoe down a gravel road leading to the Case cattle ranch. He hadn't spoken to Bobby since his release from jail the previous day, and with Maggie still in Salt Lake with their father, he was worried about Bobby and his two nephews. Much to his surprise, he found Maggie's Subaru parked in the driveway in front of the house.

He knocked before poking his head inside and shouting, "Anybody home?"

"In here," said Maggie.

She and Bobby were seated across from one another on leather couches. There was no sign of the boys, and tension in the room was so thick you could have cut it with a knife. Bobby glanced up, tears in his eyes, nodded, but said nothing.

"I can see this isn't a good time," said Books. "Sorry for the interruption. I can touch base with you sometime tomorrow."

"That would probably be better," replied Maggie. She got off the couch and walked him outside to his truck.

"Sorry I didn't call you to let you know I was coming. I was so upset when you called, I just had to come home and get this sorted out."

"Don't blame you a bit, sis. How about the boys? I didn't see them."

"Not to worry. When I decided to come home, I made arrangements with Grandma and Grandpa Case to pick up the boys and keep them overnight."

"Anything I can do to help?"

"Yeah, you can take Bobby out to the barn and pound some sense into that thick skull of his."

"Besides that."

"I don't think so. His dad had him surrounded with lawyers the minute he got out of jail. He isn't saying much, not even to me."

"I don't suppose he'd talk to me. I really need to know the name of the individual who introduced him to Benally. So far, he's refused to give up that person. My detective nose tells me that whoever this individual is may hold the key to resolving this mess."

"Let me ask him. I'm sure he won't talk to you—lawyers orders."

Books changed the subject. "How's Bernie?"

"Dad's doing great—improving by the hour."

"He always was a tough old bird, gotta give him that. I'll call him first thing in the morning. I feel awful that I couldn't make the surgery, sis. I can't thank you enough for taking such good care of him."

"You're welcome. I think a call from you would bolster his spirits."

"How long will he stay in the hospital?"

"For at least another two or three days. If he continues to improve, I'd guess he'll be ready to come home early next week.

"That's good."

"They want to work with him, get him back on his feet and put him through his paces."

"Doesn't sound like much fun."

"I'm sure it isn't, but he'll improve a lot faster that way."

"You're right. They don't just let you lie around in a hospital bed these days."

Books gave her a hug and promised to contact her the next day.

Chapter Twenty-seven

Books wasn't particularly hungry but he wanted to talk with Rusty Steed, the owner of the Ranch Inn & Café. When he walked in, Rusty wasn't there, but Ned Hunsaker was seated at the counter drinking coffee, eating a slice of apple pie à la mode, and reading a copy of the *New York Times*.

"Stuff'll clog your arteries and kill you, Ned."

Hunsaker looked at Books over the top of his reading glasses unimpressed and grunted. "When you get to be my age, son, you can eat pretty much any damn thing you want. For a hunk of Dixie's homemade apple pie, I'll take my chances on the clogged arteries."

The "Dixie" Hunsaker was referring to was Dixie Steed, Rusty's wife of more years than Book could remember.

"Where's Rusty?"

"Had to run next door and give something to Dixie. He'll be right back. Grab yourself a cup of coffee. Rusty won't mind. I'd offer to share this last piece of apple pie, but I wouldn't want to do anything that might clog your arteries."

Books smiled. "You got me on that one."

"I think there might be one piece of cherry pie left," said Hunsaker.

"Feeling a little guilty, Ned?"

"Not even slightly. In fact, if you don't grab that last piece, I might just eat it myself."

"It's all yours. I'll pass on the cherry pie."

Books poured himself a cup of coffee and took a seat at the counter next to Ned.

"Suit yourself. How's your investigation going?"

"Not very good, I'm afraid. The Rogerses have been missing for seven days without a single sighting or any word from them. It's hard to remain optimistic after that many days."

"I see your point."

Rusty emerged from the kitchen. "Well, look what the wind blew in. I see you already got yourself a cup of coffee. Can I get you anything else?"

Books shook his head. "Coffee'll do, and maybe some information."

Steed arched his eyebrows. "What sort of information?"

"How often does Bobby come around?"

"As in your brother-in-law, Bobby?"

"One and the same."

"Hmm. I see him some, breakfast usually, lunch once in a while."

"Who's he hang out with?"

"Family mostly, but occasionally he comes in with the Harper kid or Ed Mason's boy—can't remember his name."

"Dwight," Hunsaker chimed in.

"Yeah. Dwight Mason."

"I know the Masons and the Harpers," said Books. "Bobby grew up with those guys. Can you think of anybody else?"

Steed thought for a minute. "Not that I recall. Why do you ask?"

"No particular reason—just an idea and probably a dumb one."

The nagging worry Books hadn't been able to dismiss was that the individual who introduced Benally to his brother-in-law might be Brett Gentry.

So much for that idea, thought Books. He felt relieved.

Steed walked down to the other end of the counter where he began clearing away dirty dishes.

Books' sense of relief was short-lived. A moment later, Steed turned and said, "Come to think of it, I have seen him in here a couple of times with Brett Gentry from Red Rock Touring."

"Recently?"

"Yeah. The past few months."

For a second, that exchange brought Hunsaker's head up from whatever he was reading in the newspaper. He glanced from Books to Steed, but didn't say anything.

"Did you happen to overhear what they talked about, Rusty?"

Steed frowned. "No, J.D. I'm not in the habit of eavesdropping on my customer's private conversations. I assumed he might be planning to do some guiding for Red Rock Touring this season."

"Sorry. I had to ask."

"Is this personal, or does it have something to do with your investigation?"

"It's business and, like I said, it's probably nothing," said Books, hoping he was right.

So far, there was almost no evidence linking Brett Gentry to the Rogers case. All Books really had was Gentry's phone number on the slip of paper found in Benally's bedroom and the fact that a wacky old pot hunter had claimed to have seen a black Cadillac Escalade with tinted windows driving in the area where the Rogers went missing.

Hunsaker closed his newspaper and motioned toward Books' coffee cup. "Want a refill?"

"Sure."

Hunsaker filled Books' cup and topped off his own before returning to his seat. "I can't help but feel you're worried that Bobby may be up to his eyeballs in this thing."

"I don't want to believe it. My sister doesn't believe it. And I'm sure Bobby's folks wouldn't believe it either, not for a skinny minute. But Bobby refuses to identify the person he claims introduced him to Joe Benally."

Maybe he's just trying to protect a friend."

"That's what he says."

"Of course, he could be lying about that. What if nobody introduced him to Benally. Have you thought about that possibility?" asked Hunsaker.

"I have. I suppose he could have invented that story. But if he did, where did he obtain the artifacts we found in his truck?"

Both men paused. "Not a particularly pleasant thought, is it?" continued Books.

"No, it's not."

"He had to have gotten those relics from somebody."

"What's he going to be charged with?"

"Up to federal prosecutors, but I'm sure he'll be charged with a violation of the Archeological Resources and Protection Act for illegally digging artifacts on federal land. It's hard to say what Virgil Bell might decide to do. I'm sure he realizes he could bring state charges against Bobby for possession of stolen property."

"That seems like a no-brainer," replied Hunsaker.

"Maybe, but you know local politics. As the chairman of the Kane County Commission, Doug Case controls Bell's budget in the prosecutor's office. You can bet that Virgil will think very carefully before filing state charges against Bobby."

"True, but it sure doesn't make it right."

"Right has nothing to do with it. Doug Case has a lot of political clout in this community and you can bet that he'll use every bit of leverage he's got when it comes to protecting his family."

Hunsaker finished his pie and both men drank their coffee.

"Present case aside," said Books, "the more I learn about the illegal antiquities trade, the less confidence I have in the ability of the federal government to do much about it."

"Like I've said to you before, it's a murky, complicated business. For starters, you and your colleagues are badly outnumbered. There's too much land to patrol and not enough cops. About the only good thing you got going is that the center of the illegal antiquities trade is a good deal east of us. The Four Corners area is one giant graveyard. Hell, I read an estimate recently that San Juan County alone contains a hundred thousand abandoned settlements and over a half million graves."

"When grave diggers are caught, they almost never end up in prison," Books said. "It's difficult to take the problem seriously when prosecutors and judges don't."

"It's the truth. The federal courts need to make an example out of some of those buggers. The risk/reward factor clearly favors the diggers. Add to that the fact that families pass the pot-hunting tradition down from generation to generation, plus poverty and unemployment probably contribute as well," said Hunsaker.

Books thought about his brother-in-law—grave digging to supplement the family budget.

"How's the Benally boy doing?" asked Hunsaker.

"Out of intensive care, so he seems to be improving. We've got police protection on him round-the-clock in case they go after him again."

"You really think they might?"

"It's hard to say, but why take the chance. It was a pretty brazen attack. That tells me these guys are pretty desperate. And Benally could turn out to be an important prosecution witness, assuming he decides to cooperate.

"Desperate men will do desperate things."

"If he wasn't ready to talk before, it's hard to imagine he won't be ready now," said Books.

The men parted company and Books returned to his office. He still had time to get a couple things done before calling it a day.

Earlier in the afternoon, Books had run a criminal back-ground check on Brett Gentry hoping to find a set of fingerprints on the man. That, however, had turned out to be an exercise in futility. Gentry had no criminal history that Books could find. But there was one thing he hadn't tried.

Books dialed the office of the Utah Department of Public Safety in Salt Lake City. By statute, the Department was required to administer the state's concealed weapon permit program. The law mandated that all concealed weapons permit appli-cants submit a copy of their fingerprints to the state in order to facilitate a background check.

Books had a feeling that Gentry was the kind of man who might enjoy packing heat. And he was right. Within minutes, a Public Safety Department supervisor confirmed that Gentry had been issued a concealed weapons permit in 2009 and had renewed the permit each year since. A few minutes later the same Public Safety supervisor had scanned the prints and emailed them to Books.

The second task was a bit more labor-intensive. Armed with what he believed was an accurate physical description of the man who had posted Benally's bail, Books set about preparing a photo lineup. An hour later, he sat in the living room of assistant court clerk, Wilma Harris.

Harris was nervous as she sat on the couch next to her husband who gently patted her hand. Books wondered if she was going to hyperventilate.

"Relax, Wilma. There's nothing to be afraid of," Books explained. "I'm going to show you a series of photographs one at a time, and I want you to point out the individual who posted Benally's bail if that persons' picture is among the photographs I show you. Do you understand?"

"Yes," she replied, hesitantly.

They moved from the living room to the dining room table where the light was better.

"I want you to take as much time as you need. Look carefully at each photograph and don't make a selection until I have shown you all of them. Okay?"

She nodded.

She studied each photograph intently. After Books had laid all eight on the dining room table, Harris pointed confidently to a photo of Earl Buck.

"That's him."

"Are you sure?"

"Positive."

Books headed home. As he climbed out of the Tahoe, his cell chirped. The caller was fingerprint examiner Greg Jasper.

"Bad news, J.D. The prints belonging to Mr. Case don't match the latents I found on either the note or the Ford Explorer."

Books felt an immediate sense of relief.

"Sorry to pester you again, Greg, but I've got another set of prints I'd like you to look at."

"Sure. Give me the information."

Chapter Twenty-eight

Saturday Morning—Day 9

Early the next morning, Books called the University of Utah Hospital and was immediately connected to his father's room. The phone rang for a long time and he was about to hang up when Bernie finally answered. His voice sounded weak and raspy.

"Morning Bernie, did I wake you?"

"Don't I wish. I hardly slept a wink last night—just couldn't get comfortable."

"Sorry to hear that. Maggie said you came through the surgery just fine and that you'll be out of there in no time."

"I sure hope so. Is something wrong with Maggie or the boys? She sure left here in a hurry, and I could tell she was upset about something."

"Not to worry. The boys are fine and so is Maggie. You just concentrate on getting well." Books saw no reason to upset Bernie further by telling him that his son-in-law had been arrested for pot hunting. That would come later.

The men chatted for another few minutes and then said goodbye. Books promised to call back later that night or first thing the next morning. He debated about sending flowers, but quickly dismissed the idea. Bernie wasn't a flowers kind of guy, never had been. Now dark chocolate caramels were another matter. He'd seen his father go through a two-pound box faster than a rabbit through a carrot patch.

He met Beth Tanner a few minutes later at the Ranch Inn
& Café for breakfast. He arrived ahead of her, taking a booth
in the back of the restaurant that would provide a modicum of
privacy while they discussed the case. Charley Sutter and Doug
Case were seated at a table by the front window engaged in what
Books thought was an animated discussion. Both men nodded as
he walked past, but neither asked him to join the conversation.

A waitress stopped at the booth. "Want the usual, J.D.?"

"I'll wait on the food order until my partner arrives, but I'll
have a cup of coffee."

"You got it." She moved on to another table.

Books had finished his first cup by the time Tanner scurried
into the restaurant. She was wearing blue jeans, cowboy boots,
and a long-sleeved gingham shirt. Her hair was still wet. "Sorry
I'm late."

"Long night?" Books said, smiling.

She returned the smile. "None of your business, Ranger
Books."

"Fair enough. Listen, there are a couple of things we need to
discuss."

"Sounds serious, but all right."

Before Books could begin, the waitress returned and placed
a cup of coffee in front of Tanner and topped off Books'.

"I know this young lady well enough to know she's a grouch
in the morning until she has that first cup of coffee. Now what
can I get you kids to eat?"

"You're a sweetheart, Marla," said Tanner, "and you sure got
me figured out."

Marla smiled, took their breakfast order and disappeared
into the kitchen.

"As I was about to say," said Books, "effective sometime later
today, Special Agent Randy Maldonado is going to arrive from
BLM headquarters in Salt Lake City. He's going to assume
control of the investigation."

"What do you mean? That's bullshit."

"No, it's not. I can understand how it's being seen at head-quarters. We're now eight days into this and we don't have it figured out yet. Headquarters probably thinks it's time for some fresh eyes to take a look, and maybe they're right. Besides, they've gotten wind that Becky Eddins is representing Begay, and they've been told that she and I have been a bit more than casual friends."

"How would they have found out about that?"

"It's hard to say, but I think our local newspaper editor, Lamont Christensen, may have tipped them off. They obviously smell a conflict of interest."

"For the record, I don't think it's fair," said Tanner. "You've done a great job with this case, and besides, we're close—about ready to blow this thing wide open."

"That might be a stretch, but I love your optimism. And for the record, Beth, you've more than pulled your weight in this investigation. You're a good young cop with a bright future. And Charley knows it, too."

"Enough of the mutual admiration society. And speak of the devil, here he comes," she whispered.

Books glanced around in time to see Doug Case leave the restaurant. Sutter slid into the booth next to Tanner, spilling coffee on the table as he sat.

"Shit," said Sutter, mopping up the mess with a napkin. "What sort of mischief are you two up to this morning?"

"Just talking things over," replied Books.

"Don't let me stop you. I'll just drink my coffee, if I can avoid spilling it, and you just pretend I'm a fly on the wall."

That suited Books just fine. For some reason, the sheriff seemed upbeat, not his usual starched, brusque self.

"I was just about to tell Deputy Tanner that Wilma Harris picked Earl Buck out of a photo lineup as the mystery man who posted Benally's bail. He used false identification of the famous pot hunter, Earl Shumway. He and his son, James, also have their fingerprints plastered all over the stolen explorer."

"James is the one whose print we found on the trowel at the excavation site, right?" asked Sutter.

"That's right."

Sutter continued. "What about the note?"

"So far, we've drawn a blank on the note. Besides Benally's prints and those of Officer Harris, there is a third set, but we don't know whose they are."

"Huh," said Sutter. "You'd think they'd belong to one of the Bucks."

"That's what I would have guessed," replied Books. "But no such luck. I've even had them compare Bobby's prints. They're not his either."

"That must have been a relief," said Tanner.

"It was."

"What about the Benally kid?" asked Sutter.

"I hope to get a call from Becky sometime today telling us he's accepted the plea offer and is coherent enough to be interrogated. I'll be at that hospital in a flash as soon as I hear he's ready to talk."

"We need to find the Bucks," said Tanner.

"I was about to suggest the same thing," the sheriff said.

"Easier said than done," replied Books. "Apparently the old man is homeless and lives off the land by poaching, among other things."

"Great," huffed Sutter, "just what we need. Another outdoor survivalist who hates the government and is running around thinking he's Kit Carson."

"I wouldn't underestimate him or his son," said Books. "Their military training alone makes them extremely dangerous, in my opinion."

"Are you planning to get warrants for them?" asked Sutter.

"I think so, but I'm holding off for a few hours until Maldonado gets here."

"Didn't know he was coming," said Sutter, surprised. "What's that about?"

Books explained the decision by BLM brass to place Maldonado in charge of the investigation.

Sutter started to say something when Books' cell chirped. He glanced down hoping to see Becky Eddins' caller ID. Instead, he recognized the number of probation officer Roslyn Jones.

"Good morning, Agent Jones. Have you found our mutual friend?"

"No, and I'm concerned about it. After we talked last night, I called the Buck residence in Blanding several times. Nobody ever answered. This morning I got up early and drove to Blanding. After pounding on the front door for ten minutes, I managed to roust Jason Buck."

"Who's that?"

"Jason is James' younger brother. He claimed he hadn't seen his brother for a couple of days and didn't know where he was or what he was up to."

"You think he was telling you the truth?"

"Hard to say, but I doubt it. I thought he sounded evasive. I pushed him pretty hard but he stuck to his story."

"What happens now?"

"Unless you can give me some reason to seek a warrant, I'm not sure there's much I can do. If he doesn't show up for his scheduled appointment next week, I can get a warrant for a technical violation of his probation."

"Maybe we can save you the trouble. I think there's a better than fifty-fifty chance we'll file state charges against both James and his father, Earl. Their prints were found all over the stolen Ford Explorer used in the hit-and-run on Joe Benally."

"Keep me in the loop," said Jones, "and I'll let you know if he turns up here."

They disconnected.

"Wait a minute," muttered Books to himself.

"What...." said Tanner.

Books held up a hand as he redialed Jones' cell.

"That was fast," said Jones.

"Got a question for you."

"Shoot."

"You mentioned this Jason Buck. How old did you say he was?"

"I didn't, and I'm not sure. I'd guess eighteen or nineteen. Why do you ask?"

Books ignored her question. "Does he have a criminal history?"

"Hmm, if memory serves me correctly, I think he had several referrals to juvenile court—couldn't tell you what for unless I look it up."

"Would you do that for me?"

"Sure. I'll call you back in a few minutes."

"What was that about?" asked Sutter, after Books disconnected.

Books filled him in on the work he'd been doing with the Four Corners Task Force and probation agent Roslyn Jones.

Sutter listened carefully and without interruption. When Books finished, he said, "You're really convinced that the disappearance of Rolly and Abby is part of some larger criminal enterprise?"

"Convinced might be too strong a word. Let's just say that I'm curious and I wouldn't rule it out, at least not yet."

Sutter shrugged. "Sure hope you're wrong."

"Me too, Charley, me too."

The conversation lapsed as Tanner and Books went to work on their breakfast. Sutter pushed his coffee aside and slid out of the booth. "Gotta go, children. Thanks for the coffee."

Between mouthfuls, Books said, "He does that every chance he gets, the cheapskate."

"Lucky for you it was just coffee. He's gotten me for lunch," said Tanner. "By the way, are you buying?"

Chapter Twenty-nine

Books didn't wait for the criminal history information from Agent Jones on Jason Buck. He had a hunch and decided to chase it. After breakfast, he drove to the Kanab Hospital, hoping Benally's mother, Ruby Grant, was with her son. In the parking lot, he spotted Becky Eddins SUV. That was a good sign. Maybe now he would be able to interrogate Joe Benally, assuming the kid accepted the plea deal offered by the DA's office. He suspected DA Virgil Bell was growing short on patience. Nothing prevented him from yanking the plea agreement off the table and Books hoped Eddins was feeling the heat.

He found Ruby Grant in the hospital's waiting room reading a magazine and drinking a can of diet coke. Books wouldn't describe her greeting as exactly friendly, but at least it was devoid of the anger and hostility she'd greeted him with the past couple of days.

"How's Joey doing this morning, Mrs. Grant?"

"Better, I think. They kept him in intensive care for several hours after the surgery, but moved him to a regular room around eight last night. He's in some pain, but they tell me, that's to be expected."

"Glad to hear he's getting better. I noticed Becky's SUV in the lot when I pulled in. Is she with him now?"

"Yes. She asked to speak to him alone. He's so drowsy from all the medicines they've been giving him. I wouldn't be a bit surprised if he doesn't fall asleep on her."

"Mrs. Grant, are you familiar with a young man who might be a friend of your son by the name of Jason Buck?"

Grant hesitated. "Why do you ask?"

"Jason is about the same age as your son, and I just thought…."

"A lot of young men are about my son's age, so what are you trying to say, Ranger Books?"

Now it was Books' turn to hesitate. "It's possible, Mrs. Grant, that some members of the Buck family, not necessarily Jason, might have been involved in the attempt on your son's life. Your cooperation might bring me closer to catching the people responsible. And you do want that, don't you?"

"Of course."

There was a long pause and Books wondered whether Grant was going to answer him. Finally, she said, "Jason has been to our home several times."

"How long have they known each other?"

"I'm not sure, several months, I think. Ruthie would probably know."

The Ruthie she was talking about was Ruthie Todd, Benally's girlfriend. Books thanked her and hurried out to the Tahoe. He fumbled through the case file until he located the phone number. Ruthie Todd lived in Escalante with her parents. He called and she answered.

"Ruthie, this is J.D. Books. I'm the BLM ranger handling the investigation involving your boyfriend, Joe Benally."

"So."

"I'm at the hospital and I just spoke with Joey's mother. Joey's showing improvement today by the way."

Silence.

"Ruby told me that Joey's become friends in recent months with a kid named Jason Buck. Is that true?"

"Why should I answer your questions? You're the cop who busted Joey."

She had a point.

"Wouldn't you be interested in finding out who almost killed him?"

Silence.

"Look, I have reason to believe that some members of the Buck family may have been involved in the assault on Joey."

"Jason wouldn't have nothin' to do with anything like that."

"I didn't say he did."

"So what exactly do you want to know?"

"When was the last time you saw Joey?"

"Last night at the hospital."

"Before that."

"Wednesday, last Wednesday."

"You're sure of the day?"

"Just a minute. Mom, what day did you take me to Grandma Brewster's house, Tuesday or Wednesday?"

Books heard a muffled female voice in the background shout, "Wednesday, why?"

"Never mind. Yeah, it was Wednesday. I spent two nights at my grandmother's house outside Kanab."

"So you stayed with your grandmother Wednesday and Thursday nights. Is that correct?'

"Yes."

"Was Jason hanging out with you and Joey?"

"Some of the time."

"What do you mean?"

"Like, Jason wasn't with us every minute, but we hung out together some."

"What about Friday? Did you hang out together on Friday?"

"Naw, I had to go home and Joey said he had stuff to do."

"What stuff? Did he say?"

"He just said he had business to take care of or words to that effect."

"Was Jason planning to stick around over the weekend with him?"

"I think so. I asked Joey to come see me in Escalante on Saturday, but he said he was too busy. We got into a fight about it. I told him that if he'd rather spend time hanging out with his buddies instead of me, we should just break up."

"And what did Joey say?"

"He got mad—told me to fuck off."

"So you don't know what he and Jason had planned for the weekend. Is that right?"

"Uh huh. The next thing I heard he was in the hospital."

"How did you find out about that?"

"Ruby called and told me."

"Have you heard anything from Jason in the last day or so?"

"Nope."

"Do you know how to reach him—cell phone number or something?"

"He's got a cell. I saw it, but I don't have the number."

Books thanked her and disconnected.

While he was talking with Ruthie Todd, a call had come in on his cell. The caller was Roslyn Jones. Books listened to the message.

"Hey, J.D. I checked the juvenile court database and found that Jason Buck has prior arrests for retail theft, vandalism, burglary of a vehicle, and possession of a controlled substance. These offenses were all misdemeanors. He was on probation for almost two years. It looks like he paid some fines, victim restitution, and worked about two hundred hours of community service. When he turned eighteen, the juvenile court terminated his probation. He's had no arrests since becoming an adult. Call me if you have any questions. Oh, and by the way, he just turned nineteen. His date of birth is 7-4-92."

Books' hunch that Jason Buck might somehow be involved, either unwittingly, or by design, seemed to be gaining traction. It was possible that he participated in the burglary of the Rogers home. The timing was right. He may also have written the note to Benally telling him to go to the city park when he left the jail.

Could Jason have been the driver of the Explorer that struck Benally? Possible, but highly unlikely, thought Books. The boys appeared to be friends, and there was nothing in Jason's history to suggest he might be violent.

If the authorities had a set of Jason's fingerprints, they could be compared to the as yet unidentified third set of prints left on the note and on the unidentified latents Tanner had pulled from the home of Rolly and Abby Rogers. Unfortunately, like most states, Utah law prohibited the police from taking the fingerprints of arrested juveniles. Hence, there were no fingerprints on record for Jason Buck.

For the first time, Books felt a note of optimism in what had otherwise been a frustrating case.

Chapter Thirty

When Books returned to the hospital waiting room, he found Becky Eddins seated on a couch next to Ruby Grant. She looked tired and drawn, he thought. The women were deep in conversation. He stood off to one side and waited until they finished. When they were done, Grant grabbed her purse, got up, gave Books a curt nod, and left the hospital. Becky motioned him over to the couch.

"Mrs. Grant headed home? She looks exhausted."

"Nope. She won't leave his side—been here round the clock since Joey was admitted. She just ran to the pharmacy to fill a couple of prescriptions."

"Have you spoken with him this morning?"

"I have, and so did Ruby."

"And how did it go?"

"Not the way I expected."

"What do you mean?"

"I mean my client has refused to accept the plea offer."

"I think that's incredible considering what's happened to him." Books shook his head in disbelief.

"That makes two of us."

"You think his decision is final?"

"For his sake, I hope not. Ruby was pretty hard on him and so was I. He was crying when I left the room. I think he's confused and really afraid. He's never been in this kind of trouble before.

When I explained the possible prison sentence he faces if we go to trial and lose, his eyes became the size of silver dollars."

"So you'll continue to try to get him to reconsider?"

"Absolutely. I think accepting the offer is clearly in his best interest."

"I think you're right."

She glanced at her watch. "And the clock's running."

Books gave her a puzzled look. "I don't understand."

"Virgil Bell called me at home last night. He told me I had until noon today for Joey to accept the offer. After twelve, the offer comes off the table."

Eddins had to walk a fine line in her representation of Benally. If she put too much pressure on him to accept the plea bargain, it might come back to bite her later on. In his Denver P.D. days, Books had seen more than one defendant march into court demanding a change of plea, or in some instances, a retrial based on what the offender claimed was coercion on the part of his lawyer to force him into accepting a plea agreement.

"Listen," said Books. "I want to apologize for how I acted yesterday. I've thought about it and come to the conclusion that I was being unreasonable. You were right. You've got your job to do and I've got mine. We're going to have to be patient with each other so we get through this with our relationship intact."

She leaned into him, kissing him lightly on the lips. "Thanks for saying that. It means a lot to me."

He walked her down the hall toward Benally's room. They parted with the understanding that Books would remain nearby, and that Eddins would call if Benally had a change of heart. As he turned to leave, Books heard the phone ring inside the room. The uniformed officer sitting outside the door was reading a newspaper and didn't react. Books was concerned because calls from outside were not allowed. Books reached the phone before Benally did. He handed it to Benally, but listened in.

"Hello"

"Joey, it's me…."

It sounded like Mrs. Grant, but Books wasn't sure. Abruptly, a male voice came on the line.

"If you ever want to see your mother alive again, you'll keep your fucking mouth shut," said the caller. "Do you understand?"

Books nodded at Benally, encouraging him to acknowledge the threat.

"Yeah, I understand. Let me talk to my…"

The line went dead, catching Benally in midsentence.

Books was already out of the room running to the Tahoe. As he drove out of the hospital parking lot, a disturbing thought occurred to him. What if this incident was a ruse designed to distract the police from their primary responsibility of protecting Benally? He radioed dispatch and requested that additional officers be sent to the hospital to increase security around the man.

Chapter Thirty-one

Books realized almost immediately that they'd gotten lucky. A witness had dialed 911and reported seeing two men force a struggling female into a van in the Kanab's drug store parking lot. The caller didn't see the license plate number but described the vehicle as an old, beige Volkswagen bus.

Books made a decision, a decision based solely on a hunch. The kidnappers could try to lie low somewhere in town until things quieted down, but he doubted they would. Instead, he figured they'd make a run for the place they felt safest, the desert wilderness of the Grand Staircase Escalante National Monument. If they could make the Monument, there were innumerable places to hide.

With his emergency lights and siren engaged, Books sped through Kanab and turned south toward Page on U.S. Highway 89. On the outskirts of town, he shut the siren off but left the emergency lights flashing. The Tahoe raced through open, rolling terrain with sage and stands of piñon and juniper passing in a blur.

Police radio traffic in Kanab had turned up nothing so far, Books noted. He radioed the dispatch center and informed the on-duty dispatcher where he was and what he was doing. He was told by the dispatcher that a Utah Highway Patrol trooper and a Kane County Sheriff's deputy were headed toward him on 89 from somewhere near the town of Big Water.

His hopes were dashed each time the Tahoe crested a hill and nothing but empty highway stretched out in the distance. If he'd guessed correctly, the kidnappers would make a dash for the Johnson Canyon Road exit. That road was about ten miles out of town and served as the gateway into a maze of Monument trails, byways, and slot canyons.

As Books approached a quarter-mile from the road, he eased off the gas. A sense of disappointment filled his gut. Either his hunch had been wrong or he had been too slow reaching the turnoff.

Disappointment turned to hope and adrenalin pumping energy when he glanced up the road and observed what looked like the rear of a van in the distance. Books made the turn and punched the Tahoe's accelerator. The road, he knew, was paved for about two miles and then became a washboard dirt affair that would worsen the deeper he drove into the Monument. An even greater worry was that after the road changed from asphalt to dirt it went another two miles before abruptly splitting. One fork, the Glendale Bench Road, headed west while the Skutumpah Road traversed the Monument in a northeasterly direction. If he didn't have the vehicle in sight before it made the fork, he'd have no way of knowing which direction it went.

This part of the road climbed gradually and was filled with twists and turns. Books kept the Tahoe moving as fast as the terrain would allow, all the time worrying that he would come around some blind corner and find the Bucks standing in the road ready to pepper him with automatic weapons fire. Nevertheless, he closed rapidly on the vehicle ahead until he could see it well enough to ascertain that it was a Volkswagen bus and that it was a dead ringer for the one described by the eyewitness.

Books gave dispatch the information as well as his location. He was told not to attempt to stop the vehicle until backup arrived. Good advice, he thought, but sometimes bad guys had been known to take that decision out of the cop's hands.

"BLM 1 to dispatch."

"Go ahead."

"ETA on back up?"

"Stand by."

The radio chatter that followed told Books two things. First, he had backup coming from two different directions. And second, both were at least ten to twenty minutes away. He was on his own for the next little while, and there was nothing he could do about it.

Books cursed his declining vision. Nearsightedness forced him to close on the bus before he could read the license plate number. He passed that information along to dispatch.

Flowered curtains covering the back window moved slightly. Seconds later, the Volkswagen's rear window was smashed and the barrel of a shotgun protruded from the broken window. Books hit the brakes and the Tahoe went into an immediate slide, forcing him to let up on the accelerator in order to regain control. In that instant, Books heard the explosion of the shotgun and saw flame dance from its barrel. The buckshot struck the grill and the front windshield on the Tahoe's passenger side. He slowed again, deliberately putting more distance between himself and the bus.

Considering the circumstances, his options were limited. Returning fire at a moving vehicle was almost never a good idea, and firing at one with a hostage inside was a major no-no. About all he could do was follow at a safe distance, keep dispatch informed, and wait for help.

What happened next came as no surprise. The driver ahead slammed on the brakes, and the bus ground to a sudden stop, spitting dirt and rocks everywhere. Books hit his brakes and slid to a stop, turning the front of the Tahoe at a forty-five-degree angle. He knew what was about to happen, and he wanted as much of the trucks' engine block in front of him as possible.

He jammed the Tahoe into park, threw open the door, and dove to the ground just as a second blast from the shotgun struck the front windshield where his upper torso had been moments before. He scrambled on all fours to the rear of the Tahoe and removed a Remington 870 pump-action shotgun from its gun rack. The shooter fired twice in rapid succession, and Books clearly heard the sound of one of his front tires explode. Buckshot struck the Tahoe's front-end. They were going for the tires and radiator in an attempt to disable the truck. Two could play that game. He dropped to the ground and returned fire from under the Tahoe. He blew out the Volkswagen's rear tires. While the Tahoe had been effectively disabled, so now had the Volkswagen bus. The suspects wouldn't be able to drive far on two flat tires.

Using his hand-held radio, Books called dispatch and reported that he was under fire. He looked for better cover and spotted a cluster of rock and sandstone boulders next to the Tahoe but off the road. If he could make it, that position offered better protection than remaining behind the Tahoe. He took a couple of deep breaths, jumped up, and ran for the safety of the rocks. He made it just before one of the suspects began a steady round of fire from a weapon that sounded like a semi-automatic. Then, as quickly as it started, the shooting stopped. Things went errily quiet save a muffled cry from Mrs. Grant inside the bus. Suddenly, the shooting resumed, and a sporadic volley of shots sprayed the area around him. A small piece of flying rock struck Books under his left eye, drawing blood.

He heard the engine start and then saw the bus lurch slowly forward. They were trying to drive away and Books wasn't going to let that happen. He spotted another rocky outcropping and ran for it, remaining parallel to the bus as he ran. He shouldered the shotgun, and fired one round at the driver's side window, hoping he didn't hit Mrs. Grant. The glass exploded and he heard the driver scream in pain. The bus abruptly shuddered to a stop.

"Stop your shooting right now, or so help me God, we'll blow this fuckin squaw to kingdom come," shouted a gravelly voice from inside the bus. "You'll need a spatula to scrape her off the walls."

"I hear you. What do you want?" shouted Books.

"We're leavin, and you're letting us go."

"Not with the woman, you're not."

"Then she's a dead cunt."

Books heard more crying, hysterical sobs this time.

"Tell you what," said Books. "I'll let you go, but the woman stays. I won't try to stop you. You'll probably have a ten- or fifteen-minute start, and then this place will be crawling with cops."

There was a short pause and Books could hear muffled voices. "Okay. It's a deal. You set that scatter gun down and walk over here unarmed. We'll give you the woman, and then we'll leave."

"Not happening. You leave her in the van unharmed. In return, I'll let you leave unmolested. That's the best I can do."

"All right. We'll do it your way, but understand this, if you open fire while we're trying to leave, we'll come back to the van, kill you and the woman, and then make our stand right here. Do we understand each other?"

"We do. I won't shoot. You're safe to leave—my word on it."

"Somehow, officer, that ain't too comforting."

"Best you boys get a move on it. You're burning time."

Books heard movement from inside the bus. He cautiously peeked over the rocks and saw the passenger door standing open, and two suspects dressed in military fatigues moving off to the northeast, one half-carrying the other.

"Mrs. Grant, can you hear me?"

"Yes," she said her voice barely audible.

"Are you hurt?"

"No."

"Are you alone?"

"I think so."

"Is anyone inside the bus with you?"

"No."

Books didn't like his options. Nothing prevented them from lying in wait somewhere near the bus and catching him in the open as he approached the Volkswagen. And what if the suspects had rigged the bus with explosives? There were no guarantees.

"Can you walk, Mrs. Grant? If you can, I want you to come out through the driver's side door."

"I can't. My hands are tied behind my back and my ankles are bound."

"Okay, sit tight. I'm coming for you. You're going to be all right."

Books calculated the distance at no more than twenty yards between himself and the Volkswagen. If he kept the bus between himself and where he'd last seen the suspects, he would have only momentary exposure. For at least a minute, he watched and listened. Everything seemed quiet. With shotgun in hand, he dashed for the bus, entered through the driver's door, and dove headfirst to the rear floor where Mrs. Grant lay. Books used a pocket knife and had her wrists and legs cut loose in seconds. He considered waiting for the cavalry to arrive, but the possibility that the suspects might possess armor-piercing bullets that could penetrate the skin of a VW bus made him decide otherwise.

"We've got to get away from the bus, Mrs. Grant. It's not safe here."

"Can't we just wait until help arrives?

"Not a good idea, I'm afraid. These guys could be lurking nearby, and this tin can would be a bad place to have to make a stand. We're safer in the rocks. Now here's what we're going to do."

As Books eased out of the driver's side door, he noticed copious amounts of blood splattered on the dashboard, instrument panel, and windshield. He'd definitely hit one of the suspects. That was a good thing. Mrs. Grant slid out beside him and waited for the signal to run. Books scanned the horizon for any sign of movement. Seeing none, he told her to go. He waited until she had reached the safety of the rocks and then he followed.

The sound of approaching sirens in the distance convinced Books that reinforcements were closing fast and that he and Grant were going to get out of this predicament alive, and for the most part, unhurt.

Books remained vigilant while waiting for help to arrive. He notified dispatch that the suspects had fled on foot in a northeasterly direction with one man seriously wounded and both heavily armed.

He couldn't help but admire Mrs. Grant for her courage, toughness, and stoicism during her captivity. She had betrayed little emotion throughout the ordeal.

Books had several questions for her and decided he'd better ask them before the cavalry arrived or he might not get the chance.

"Mrs. Grant, which of the suspects was shot, the younger man or the older one?"

She glanced at him from her position crouched down behind a large sandstone rock.

"The older one."

"Where was he hit? Could you tell?"

"I tried not to look, but most of the blood was running down his face and neck. He was screaming and cursing. I started praying, certain that he was about to kill me."

"About how old would you say he was?"

"Late forties, early fifties."

"Did you recognize either of them?"

She shook her head. "I've never seen them before, but I think I heard the older one call the other guy Jimmy."

Chapter Thirty-two

Within an hour, the manhunt had begun. Sheriff Sutter was among the first to arrive, accompanied by Beth Tanner. Soon after, BLM Special Agent Randy Maldonado showed up, having finally made it from Salt Lake City. Books, who had previously been reticent about turning over control of the investigation to Maldonado, was now almost giddy at seeing the man. Giddy because somebody was going to have to take control of what probably would be an exhaustive search, and it was a job Books had little experience at and even less interest in. He had a different agenda in mind for himself.

Sutter and Maldonado assumed command of the crime scene and began marshaling resources for the search. Books didn't see how the Bucks could make it very far or travel very fast considering the old man's injuries. But it didn't mean that they were any less dangerous or without options. They might choose to stand together and make a fight of it, or they could choose to separate, giving Jimmy Buck a greater chance of escape.

Ruby Grant, although badly shaken, had come away from the incident with only minor bruising. She was driven in a fire department vehicle back to the hospital in Kanab, where emergency room staff would examine her. And Books knew the FBI would also be waiting to swarm this case. He had been surprised that the FBI hadn't been sniffing around the investigation before now. From the information Mrs. Grant had provided about her assailants, Books was now convinced more than ever that her abductors had been the father-and-son duo of Earl and James Buck.

After providing as much information as he could about the chase and subsequent shootout, Books caught a ride back to Kanab with a Utah Highway Patrol trooper who dropped him at his office. Beth Tanner came with him. He hoped the events of the past several hours would convince Benally that it was time to cooperate. Considering what had just happened to his mother, along with his own brush with death the day before, it was impossible for Books to imagine that the kid might still refuse to give up his co-conspirators.

At headquarters, Books found a set of keys to another BLM vehicle. The Tahoe was going to be out of commission for some time. He also picked up a tape recorder and the list of questions he planned to use in Benally's interrogation. He found two voice messages had been left on his office phone. One was from fingerprint examiner Greg Jasper while the other was from his boss, Alexis Runyon.

"You're never going to ask me to do anything for you again," said Jasper. "Those prints you had me look at belonging to Brett Gentry do not match anything we lifted from the Ford Explorer or the note sent to Benally. Wish I had better news for you. Call me if you need anything else."

"Damn," said Books.

"What?" replied Tanner.

"That was Greg Jasper. He couldn't find any latent prints belonging to Brett Gentry on the stolen Explorer or the note sent to Benally."

"Doesn't mean he's not up to his neck in this thing."

"True, but we've got to find proof somewhere. All we have at the moment is theory and conjecture."

The second message from Runyon informed him that starting Monday, his holiday from normal patrol duties, was over. The BLM ranger who had covered his calls the past week was leaving for a week of in-service training. That meant he'd have to juggle the Rogers investigation with his normal duties, although, with Maldonado in town, some of that workload could be passed along to him.

Books leaned back in his faux leather chair pondering this latest development. He'd have bet hard cash that Brett Gentry's fingerprints would be found on either the note to Benally or the stolen Explorer. Maybe he had been wrong about Gentry all along. On the other hand, it was possible that he ran the operation, pulling the strings behind the scenes while keeping his own hands clean.

Even the information he'd recently learned about Jason Buck was largely speculative. It was true that the timeline for the burglary coincided with Buck's presence in Kanab. And there was little doubt that Benally and Buck were together in the hours preceding the break-in. Ruthie Todd had confirmed that. Yet so far there were no witnesses or physical evidence linking him to the burglary.

Books remained convinced that father and son, Earl and James Buck, along with Joe Benally, were deeply involved in the case and probably formed the nucleus of the rogue pot-hunting gang that worried Sergeant Walker of the Four Corners Task Force. The priority now was finding them. Their military training and outdoor survival skills made them more than capable of disappearing into the desert wilderness and living off the land indefinitely.

And finally there was the matter of his brother-in-law, Bobby Case. What was his relationship with Brett Gentry? Was he only peripherally involved in the crimes, as he had so adamantly insisted? For his own sake and that of their family, Books hoped so.

He got up and started for the door. "Come on, Deputy Tanner. Let's go see if Mr. Benally has had a change of heart about talking to us."

When Books and Tanner arrived at the hospital, they found a small cadre of people gathered outside Benally's room talking in hushed tones. There were a couple of uniforms present along with Becky Eddins and District Attorney Virgil Bell. Several other people, who Books surmised were Benally's family members, were also there, however, he didn't see Mrs. Grant anywhere.

As they approached, Eddins broke away from a conversation with Bell and rushed to him.

"Oh, my God, you're hurt." She touched his face where the cut on his face had already started to scab over.

"Nothing serious. It's just a scratch."

"How do you manage to get yourself into so much trouble?" asked Eddins, squeezing his hand.

"I was wondering that very thing myself. It seems like I've been dragged into more life-threatening situations here in less than two years than I did in more than eleven in Denver."

He nodded toward the small knot of people. "What's with the small mob?"

"Ruby's husband is here with their two children. I called Virgil and suggested he drop by. We're down to two cops now, but after you called in the warning, we had cops everywhere."

"I don't see Mrs. Grant anyplace."

"That's because she's in with Joey. They checked her out in emergency and then released her. She's been in with him for about ten minutes."

"So where do we stand? Is he going to cooperate or not?"

"Unless he has a last-minute change of heart, he's accepted the deal, and you can sit down with him as soon as his mother finishes up."

"Good. I'm ready to go. Do you plan to sit in?"

"I do."

"Can I ask you a favor?"

"Shoot."

"Could you keep Mrs. Grant out of the room while we do this?"

"I think so, but why?"

"I've learned that you get more information from young offenders when you keep their parents out of earshot."

"I'll see what I can do."

Books pulled Virgil Bell aside. "I guess he's accepted your offer and is going to cooperate."

Bell nodded. "About time. My patience has worn pretty damn thin. The deal was about to come off the table, and defense counsel was tearing her hair out."

"Can't say that I blame her. There's a lot at stake. Are you planning to join us?"

"As long as you're okay with it. I don't plan on asking him any questions. I'll leave that to you."

"I don't have a problem if you do."

"I do have a problem with it. I prefer not to end up being called as a witness in my own case."

"Gotcha."

The door to Benally's room opened and his mother emerged. She strode directly over to Books.

"He'll talk to you now, Ranger Books, and I'm confident he'll tell you everything he knows."

"Thank you, Mrs. Grant. I'm sorry to have dropped all this on your doorstep."

"You don't owe me an apology. You didn't bring this to my door step, my son did. And thanks for what you did for me out there today. If it hadn't been for you, I don't think I'd have gotten out of there alive."

Chapter Thirty-three

Books walked into Benally's room, nodding at the boy as he entered. "Afternoon, Joey."

Benally didn't respond, but followed Books with his eyes. He looked frightened and confused. No surprise there. Books plugged a tape recorder into a wall socket near the bed and placed the recorder on a small table between himself and Benally.

Beth Tanner, Virgil Bell, and Becky Eddins followed, taking seats off to one side, the lawyers with pens and legal pads at the ready.

Books began with the usual lengthy preamble that included the date, time, and location of the interview as well as those in attendance. When he got to the Miranda Warnings, Eddins interrupted.

"Ranger Books, my client will waive a reading of his Miranda rights. I've gone over them with him, he understands them, and is willing to give up his right to remain silent and answer all your questions truthfully, and to the best of his ability."

"Thank you, counsel. Joey, I'd like you to go back and start by explaining your relationship with Rolly and Abby Rogers. How do you know them?"

"Well, I knowed Mr. Rogers from high school—I took a couple of history classes from him."

"And Mrs. Rogers?"

"She helped me get a job where she works at the Jubilee Family Market."

"And what did you do at the market?"

"Bagged groceries and stocked shelves mostly."

"How long did you work there?"

He considered that. "Ah, a few months, I think."

"And why did you leave?"

"Mr. Ryback fired me."

"Mr. Ryback owns the store. Is that correct?"

"Yeah."

"And why did he fire you?"

"Missin' work and coming in late."

"Had you been in the Rogers' home prior to the burglary?"

"Yeah, a few times. When I was in Mr. Rogers' classes, he brought me home sometimes and gave me chores to do around the house for money, like a part time job."

"And is that how you met Mrs. Rogers?"

"Yes."

"Okay, let's go back a week to last Saturday, said Books. "Who did you spend the day with?"

"With my girlfriend, Ruthie Todd, and Jason Buck."

"Ruthie is your girlfriend. Who is Jason Buck?"

"A friend."

"How and where did you meet him?"

"I don't remember where I met him, but we was introduced by Jason's older brother, Jimmy."

"Have you ever met Jason's dad?"

"Yeah."

"What's his name?"

"Earl."

"Do you like Earl?"

"No, not really."

"Why not?"

Benally arched his eyebrows and shrugged. "I don't know. He's kinda creepy."

"What makes you say that?"

"Ah, I mean like he talks kinda crazy sometimes. And he can blow his stack over nothin, and then you better just stay out of his way, else he'll hurt ya."

"All right," said Books. "I want to come back to your relationship with the Buck family in a minute, but first I want to ask you about something else. You said you spent last Saturday with Jason and your girlfriend. What did you guys do during the day?"

"Um, we just hung out at Ruthie's grandma's house for a while listening to music and stuff. Then we went into town."

"By town, do you mean Kanab?"

"Uh huh."

"Where did you go in town and what did you do?"

"Hung out, mostly. We was at McDonald's for a while and then went over to city park."

"Did you go out with Jason on Saturday night?"

"Yeah."

"Was Ruthie with you?"

"Naw, we ditched her."

"How come?"

"Cuz we had business to do?"

"What business was that?"

He paused and looked down. "Robbin' and stealin'."

"Robbing and stealing what, exactly?"

"We busted into the Rogers house."

"By we, do you mean yourself and Jason Buck?"

"Yeah."

"What time was that?"

"About midnight, I think."

"How did you get in?"

"Jimmied a lock on a slider behind the house."

"Was that difficult?"

He smiled. "Not really."

"What did you do when you got inside?"

"Stole some shit."

"What did you steal?"

"Jewelry and stuff."

"Did the 'stuff' you're talking about include the Rogers' Anasazi artifacts collection?"

"Yeah."

"Did one of you also kill the family cat?"

"Yeah."

"Who?"

"Me."

"Why'd you do that?"

"Just look at my face, man. I didn't get these scratches from playin with Ruthie."

Books continued. "How did you know the Rogers weren't at home? What if they'd been in the house sleeping when you and Jason broke in? What then?"

Benally looked away nervously, his eyes darting from Bell to his lawyer. "They weren't home. We knew that."

"How did you know that?"

"Cuz we took 'em the night before."

"What do you mean, you took them?"

"We like, kidnapped them."

"Where were they when you kidnapped them?"

"I ain't sure of the exact spot, but they was camping along the Strip southwest of town."

"What were they doing out there?"

"They're diggers, so they was fixin to go grave robbin'."

"And you and some of your friends interrupted them?"

"Yeah, you could say that."

"What would you call it?"

He thought about it for a moment. "I guess you could say we stopped 'em and took over their site."

"So you followed them until they set up camp, and after they discovered the site, you confronted them. Is that right?"

"Yeah."

"How did you know to follow them in the first place?"

"Cuz Mrs. Rogers told me what they were doing and when they was going."

"She told you they were going pot-hunting. Why would she do that?"

"Not in so many words. She told me they was going campin' and gave me a sly wink."

"When and where did she tell you this?"

"Couple days before they left, Tuesday, I think. I talked to her for a few minutes in the Jubilee parking lot after she got off work."

"You keep mentioning 'we.' How many of you were present when you kidnapped them at the dig site?"

"Five of us."

"Who were they?"

"Me, Jason Buck, his brother Jimmy, and their old man."

"By 'old man,' do you mean Earl Buck?"

"Yeah, we call him Sarge. That's what he likes to be called."

"You mean like sergeant as in the military?"

"I guess. That's what everybody called him."

"Okay, that makes four. You said there were five of you. Who was the fifth?"

Again, the nervous eyes went flitting around the room before finally settling on his lawyer. Eddins nodded as if encouraging him to answer.

"Bobby, Bobby Case," said Benally. "He was the other one."

Books was stunned. He had been confident that the name he was going to hear was Brett Gentry, not his brother-in-law. He felt instantly sick to his stomach. If this was true, it was going to destroy his family.

Eddins and Virgil Bell appeared equally shocked. The look of confusion and distress on Books' face was almost unbearable to watch.

"Joey," interrupted Eddins. "Are you absolutely sure that the fifth man was Bobby Case and not somebody else."

"No, ma'am, it was him. It was Bobby."

Bell stood and spoke for the first time. "I think we need to take a short break. Would somebody shut off that damned tape recorder?"

From the hallway outside Benally's room, Becky Eddins and Virgil Bell conversed in hushed tones.

"Geez, I thought the guy was going to faint right where he stood," said Bell. "Did you know about this, I mean, the Bobby Case thing?"

"Not at all," replied Eddins. "I had a general idea what he was going to say, but I didn't know the identity of all the players involved. Had I known, I wouldn't have let it come out this way. What are the implications of all this for your office?"

"What do you mean?" said Bell, a look of mild indignation on his face. "Never mind, I know what you meant. I'm going to do my job, that's all I can do."

A few minutes later, a badly shaken Books returned to Benally's room, his features a mask of sad resignation and dogged resolve to see the interrogation through regardless.

Bell pulled him off to the side. "You gonna be able to make it through this?

"Absolutely, we can't stop now. We're almost there."

The questioning resumed. "Joey, once the Rogerses were taken hostage, what happened next?"

"Sarge and Jimmy tied them up and left Jason to watch over them. Me and Bobby was sent over to their camp looking for shit to steal."

"And what did you find?"

"Food to eat, mostly. Oh, and Mr. Rogers' Glock.

"What happened to the gun?"

"Bobby took it, told me not to say nothin' to Sarge—said he'd sell it and split the money with me."

"And is that what you did?"

"Yeah."

"Whose idea was it to break into the Rogers home?"

"Jimmy and Sarge. I'd told 'em about the collection, and they wanted it."

"So they sent you and Jason to get it."

"Yeah."

"At the time we arrested Bobby, he had some of the stolen property in his truck. How did that come about?"

"Him and me decided to skim a little off the top. Bobby said he knew where he could sell the stuff, and, like the gun, we agreed to split the money."

"So you and Bobby essentially decided to steal from Sarge and Jimmy Buck—is that right?"

"I guess so."

"Sounds a little risky. You might have gotten caught."

Benally shrugged, "They never paid us as much as they promised, so we figured, what the hell."

"What were you paid?"

"Whatever they felt like givin' us, mostly. Bobby always wanted cash. I took some of mine in weed and some in cash."

Books was anxious to find out who ran the operation. He already had a pretty good idea, but needed help from Benally to confirm it. It had to be someone with the money and connections to move stolen relics into the marketplace, where they could be sanitized and then sold to museums, art galleries, and individual collectors from around the world.

"Joey, we need to know who's running this operation. What happens to all the stolen artifacts?"

"I don't know. Jimmy and Sarge pay us off, take the stuff, and we never see it again."

"Who's the 'we' in this operation? How many people actually participate on a regular basis?"

"I'm not sure. I don't, and I'm pretty sure Bobby don't either. I think it's mostly Jimmy and Sarge—not really sure about Jason."

"And you have no idea who might be running this thing from behind the scenes?"

"Nope."

"If that's true, why did I find a phone number in your bedroom for Brett Gentry and Red Rock Touring? What business do you have with him?"

The question caught Benally off-guard and he asked to speak with Eddins. Books and Virgil Bell stepped into the hallway, but Eddins called them back seconds later.

"I've instructed Joey to answer your question as best he can," Eddins said. "However, it's an area that he has no direct knowledge about."

She returned to her chair next to Bell. "Go ahead, Joey. Tell Ranger Books what you just told me."

"Okay, well, I met Bobby at a Burger King in St. George to give him some of the stuff you found in his truck. When he went to take a leak, I snooped through this book he left on the table. It was like an appointment book of some kind. Anyway, inside I found a scrap of paper with that number written on it, so I took it."

Books looked puzzled. "But why?"

"Cuz I thought, based on some things he said, that Bobby knew who really ran things and just didn't want to tell me. It was like he was keeping a big secret."

"So what did you do with the phone number?"

"I dialed it one day and hung up when some woman answered. From there, I kinda put two-and-two together and figured it had to be Brett Gentry."

"Did you ever confront Bobby or Brett with your suspicions?"

"Naw, I was afraid to—afraid somebody might decide to come after me. I just kept my mouth shut."

"Do you believe the Rogers kidnapping was an isolated incident, or do you think Sarge and Jimmy Buck have been accosting other diggers?"

"I think it's what they do. I think they like it."

"Do you know how to contact these people—cell phone numbers, perhaps?"

"I got Jason's cell and Bobby's, but that's it. Jimmy and Sarge keep changing numbers regular like."

Books had Benally recite the cell numbers for Timmy and Bobby Case. He had them memorized.

Books continued. "Have you ever overheard them talking about other kidnappings involving pot hunters?"

"No…. well, maybe once. One time I heard Sarge and Jimmy laughing about taking some guy down over in Chaco Canyon."

Chaco Canyon, Books knew, was an archeologist's wet dream. Located in the Four Corners region of northwest New Mexico, it was filled with ancient Anasazi cliff dwellings and burial sites and contained a treasure trove of antiquities.

"How many of these of these little adventures have you personally participated in?"

Eddins interrupted before Benally could answer. "I'm sorry, Ranger Books, but our agreement with prosecutors was confined only to the disappearance of the Rogers and the burglary of their home. I've instructed my client not to answer that particular question."

"Fair enough," replied Books. "I'll move on. Do you know how often Bobby Case has taken part in these activities with the Bucks?"

Benally hesitated, glancing over at Becky Eddins. "Answer the question," she said.

"I'm not sure. It's not like I keep count or nothin. I ain't ever heard him talk about going out with 'em before."

"All right, Joey, here's the big question. We've been looking for Rolly and Abby Rogers for almost a week now. Where are they?"

"I don't know, and that's the truth. Sarge and Jimmy took them away someplace, but I don't know where. I overheard them talkin about driving to Page and forcing the Rogers to get cash from their bank account. That's all I know."

"Did you ever see the Rogers again after the kidnapping on Friday night?"

"No."

"You're sure about that."

"Yeah, I am."

"Do you think it's possible the Rogers have been killed?"

"I don't know. I hope not. They been kind to me."

Books wished Joe Benally had thought of that a little sooner and maybe none of this would have happened.

"Do you think Bobby might know what's happened to the Rogers?" Books asked.

"He might, but I'm not sure. He left by his self, and Jason and me left right after him."

Books ended the interview by asking Tanner if she had questions. She didn't. He told Benally to think about what they had discussed and if he remembered anything else, he should contact Becky Eddins.

Chapter Thirty-four

When Books emerged from Benally's room and walked into the hospital lobby, he was met by two suits. Their youth, clean-cut appearance, and dress reeked of FBI.

The taller of the two, a guy with a short crew-cut, stepped forward. "Ranger Books, I'm Special Agent Ed Freeman of the FBI, and this is Special Agent Alberto Sanchez." Books nodded and shook hands with both men and then introduced Beth Tanner.

"We'd like to talk to you."

Books had always wanted to ask an FBI agent just how "special" they were; however, good manners and interagency cooperation had always prevented him from doing so.

"Sure, but not here," said Books. "Why don't we meet at the sheriff's office? I'm sure we can borrow the conference room."

"That works," said Freeman. "How soon can you be there?"

"Give me ten minutes."

Books turned to Virgil Bell, who was walking behind him beside Becky Eddins. He introduced Eddins and Bell to the FBI Agents and then invited Bell to join him at the meeting. Bell agreed to attend.

As they left the hospital, a knot of media types was camped outside the front entrance to the hospital several doing live feeds.

"Holy crap," whispered Tanner.

"They're back," said Books.

Media interest in the case had subsided as the hours had turned into days and still the Rogers hadn't been found. With the events of the day, media interest had again peaked. Even Books, who normally disdained the media, thought it was a great story made all the better because of its positive outcome.

"We're going to have to say something to this crowd before long, Virgil. What do you think?"

"I agree." Bell glanced at his watch. "It's almost two-thirty. Why don't you tell them to assemble at the sheriff's office in an hour, and we'll have a statement for them. That'll give us time to contact Chief Spencer and Sheriff Sutter. Preferably both ought to attend, but if that can't happen we need at least one of them."

"Let's make it four o'clock," said Books. "That might give Sutter a better chance of making it back."

"Given how nervous Charley gets at the thought of a press conference," said Bell, "he might prefer to stay out there on a manhunt even if it turns into a shootout."

They announced the four o'clock press conference and then hurried on to their meeting with the FBI. On the drive to the sheriff's office, Books speed-dialed Sutter's cell number. When Sutter didn't answer, he left a message alerting the sheriff to the four o'clock press conference. He left the same message for Kanab Police Chief George Spencer.

Books, Tanner, and Bell sat on one side of the rectangular table, the FBI agents on the other. Books spoke first. "Well, gentlemen, this is your party, so how can we help you?"

Ed Freeman was the older of the two agents and acted as spokesperson.

"I think maybe we can help you," countered Freeman. "The Bureau has been watching this case with growing interest over the past week."

"And why is that?" asked Bell.

"As I'm sure you understand, the FBI cares deeply about federal lands and wants to do whatever it can to help preserve and protect its resources."

Never heard that one before, thought Books. Where are my hip waders?"

"The scope of this particular investigation seems to have grown beyond the limited resources of local agencies," continued Freeman. "And since the Bureau does hold primary jurisdiction in matters involving the transportation of kidnap victims across state lines, we are considering offering our considerable resources by entering the case."

Books had heard that one before. How do you spell pompous ass?

"For starters," said Books, "We have no evidence that the victims have been transported across state lines, although they may have. Our assumption from the get-go was that you have jurisdiction. The kidnapping occurred in Mohave County, Arizona, but it wasn't on state or county land, it was federal. And had you needed our permission, that decision would have to be made by somebody way above my pay grade.

"We are well aware of that, Ranger Books. Nonetheless, as the primary investigator in the case, your cooperation would be essential," said Freeman.

"And what might that entail?"

"We would expect to make you an important member of our team. We'd want to sit down with you for an extensive debriefing. And of course, we would require access to all investigatory and lab reports, as well as all physical evidence."

Condescending bastard.

"Of course," said Books. "I don't think I got where you gentlemen are from—I assumed the Salt Lake City field office. Am I right?"

"Sorry," said Freeman. I should have clarified that. I'm the resident agent-in-charge of the St. George office, and Agent Sanchez works with me."

"Then who makes this decision—you guys, or the brass in Salt Lake City?" said Bell, testily.

"Um, ultimately the decision will be made by the SAC of the Salt Lake office," replied Freeman.

SAC, Books knew, was Bureau jargon for special agent-in-charge of the field office.

"Then why don't you have them contact me directly," said Bell. "We hold primary jurisdiction in the burglary that occurred at the victim's home. I anticipate that we will file additional state charges for felony theft and possession of stolen property."

Freeman now looked decidedly uncomfortable and unsure where he should go next. "So I can report to my superiors that you would welcome the Bureau's participation," said Freeman.

"We'd be glad to consider it, yes," said Bell. "Let's talk."

For what Books had always assumed was nothing more than a small-town country bumpkin prosecutor, his opinion of Virgil Bell had just gone up a notch. He had acquitted himself quite nicely in their encounter with the feds.

"And of course, you can count on my full cooperation if directed to do so by my superiors," added Books.

It wasn't a ringing endorsement of FBI participation in the case, but it was the best Freeman was going to get, and he knew it. The agents left, undoubtedly to report that the local minions were less than enthusiastic about turning the investigation over to Big Brother.

◇◇◇

After they closed the door, Books sighed and learned back in his chair.

"So what the hell do you think that was all about?" asked Bell.

"Beats me. Maybe they'd been sent in to do a little reconnaissance—see if they could figure how much local resistance they might encounter if they bully their way in and take over the investigation."

"Maybe. It's not like they have to get anybody's permission. The state doesn't have jurisdiction on the kidnapping case anyway."

"True. It'll have to be prosecuted in federal district court. That said, it doesn't mean we don't need a strategy," said Books. "We should be proactive about deciding what state charges to bring and against whom."

"Bell nodded. "The feds are the feds, and they're going to do their own thing no matter what we think. I'd prefer being out in front of them rather than giving chase."

"Me too."

Books was prepared to give Bell a grade of "A" for courage. Charging the son of arguably the most powerful politician in Kane County was not to be taken lightly, nor would it come without Bell having to pay a political price. From everything Books had ever heard, Doug Case, while considered a fair man by most, was a ruthless adversary when crossed. Some people believed he was the kind of man to carry a grudge straight to the grave.

"So what do you suggest?" asked Bell.

"I think we ought to move quickly and get arrest warrants for the entire Buck family. Earl and Jimmy, for attempted murder in the assault on Benally, and Jason for one one count of residential burglary and felony theft."

"And what about Bobby Case?"

"Damn, Virgil, that's a tough one for me because Bobby's family, but I don't see that we have much choice."

"Neither do I," said Bell. "My inclination is to file a possession of stolen property charge against him. And that'll be the least of his problems once the feds come down on him for the kidnapping beef."

Books turned to Tanner. "You with us on this, Beth?"

"Sounds right to me. With Benally and Timmy Buck charged, that will allow us to close the burglary case. I'm real sorry about Bobby, J.D. Maybe you should let us deal with the family."

"Thanks, but I don't think so. I'll need to be the one to break it to Maggie. It's going to be damn hard on our family. It's Maggie and the boys I'm really worried about."

"While I've got to do my job, if there's anything I can do to help, please let me know," Bell said. "And I want you to know how sorry all of us feel that you had to hear about Bobby's involvement during an interrogation."

"Thanks for the kind words," replied Books, "but it's sure not your fault."

"I know that, but still. You should also know that Becky had no idea that Benally was going to name Bobby as one of the principals," said Bell.

"I was wondering about that."

"She was as shocked and upset as you were. If she'd known, she would have told you in advance. I'm sure of it."

"Good to know, I guess."

"Since we're talking about Becky, I should tell you that I probably made a mistake by not filing a motion with the court demanding that she recuse herself. Frankly, Charley convinced me that having her represent Benally might be something that could be turned to our advantage."

"It didn't though, did it?"

"Not in the slightest. The lady drives a hard bargain."

"Charley doesn't know Becky Eddins as well as he thinks he does."

"Apparently not. Can I offer you a piece of advice?"

"Sure."

"From now on, you need to step away from this case. You're too close to it and too personally involved. It's not your fault, but it's a problem, and one we don't want to have to face if the case ever comes to trial."

It was good advice and Books knew it.

"Once I start a case, it's damned hard for me to step away."

"I know, but it's the right thing to do. You need to turn this over to Charley, Beth, and Maldonado. When Bobby is arrested, you want to be as far away as possible, for your own sake, and for your family's as well."

At that moment, Chief Spencer of Kanab P.D. knocked on the door and walked in. "Anybody heard from Charley?"

"Not a word," replied Books. "We left him a voice message at the same time we left yours."

Spencer glanced at the wall clock. "We still got forty minutes. He might still show."

Virgil Bell smiled. "I wouldn't bet on it."

"Come to think of it, I wouldn't either," said Spencer. "Charley's never taken much to standing under those hot media lights."

"Speaking of bets, what's your take on the Jazz making it into the playoffs this season," said Books.

"Oh, I think they'll make by the skin of their teeth—a seven or eight seed and out in the first round," said Bell. "What do think, George?"

"Couldn't tell ya. I really don't pay much attention to them. This time of year I'm getting geared up for the baseball season."

"I think you may be right, Virgil," said Books. "I figure the Jazz will get in with a high seed and probably disappear after the first round. The only saving grace for me is I've got two teams in the west. My loyalty to the Nuggets is still pretty strong. Hopefully, if the Jazz can't get it done, the Nuggets will."

The men continued making small talk until it was fifteen minutes before the scheduled press conference.

"Well, what should we tell them?" asked Spencer, glancing at Books.

"Often, it's just as important to decide what you're not going to tell them," said Books. "But it's your show, chief. This abduction happened in Kanab, and the media will expect to hear from you."

"Okay then. What shouldn't we tell them?"

"I wouldn't discuss any physical evidence we've got, and I would avoid all questions about Joe Benally except his medical condition."

Books realized that Chief Spencer hadn't been briefed on Benally's confession and the damning new evidence broadening the suspect list to include Jason Buck and Bobby Case. So he and Bell explained what they'd learned from the Benally interview as well as the recent visit from the FBI.

"Holy moly," said Spencer. "Bobby Case involved in the kidnapping. I can hardly believe it. That isn't the Bobby Case I know."

"My sentiments, exactly," replied Bell.

"What about the manhunt for the Bucks?"

"Oh, I think we should supply that information. Let's get these guy's names and pictures on the wire. Hopefully, we'll find them soon, but if it doesn't happen, we might as well enlist the media's help. And, based on what we just learned from Benally, we should include Jason Buck on the list."

"They're going to ask questions about the attempt on Benally's life. I see no reason not to point the finger at the Buck clan for that as well," said Spencer. "I'll tell them the Bucks are wanted for questioning in the attempted murder of Joe Benally as well as the kidnapping of Rolly and Abby Rogers."

"I don't have a problem with any of that," said Books. "Do you, Virgil?"

Bell shook his head. "What if they ask questions about who posted Benally's bail?"

"Why not tell them?" countered Spencer. All eyes were fixed on Books.

"Hmm. Hadn't thought about that one. That discussion goes directly to our evidence, namely, the eyewitness identification of Earl Buck. On the other hand, it won't take some nosey reporter long to sniff that out, so I guess I'd tell them, although I wouldn't volunteer it. Wait and see if they ask."

Chapter Thirty-five

At precisely four o'clock, Chief Spencer walked to the podium to address the media while Books and Virgil Bell stood off to one side to help answer questions if it became necessary. As expected, Charley Sutter was a no-show. Tanner was seated in the back of the room near FBI Agents Sanchez and Freeman, who had apparently decided to take in the spectacle.

The press conference came off with only one awkward moment. A reporter from KSL Radio in Salt Lake City asked Spencer if there were others, besides Benally and the father/son duo of Earl and James Buck, involved in the Rogers' kidnapping. Spencer, caught off guard, hemmed and hawed before finally sputtering a vague answer. When pressed for more detail, he refused additional comment.

The press asked Spencer more questions about the current manhunt than they had anticipated. Even if Spencer wanted to answer those questions, details remained sketchy.

From radio chatter, they had learned that the Johnson Canyon Road had been closed at the turnoff to Highway 89 in the south. From the north, a similar road closure occurred near Sheep Creek on the Skutumpah Road. Units were canvassing trails and back roads inside the Monument with orders to evacuate everyone they came into contact with. The possibility that the Bucks might seize civilian hostages was on everybody's mind.

At the conclusion of the press conference, Books grabbed Tanner and left the building hurriedly, wanting to avoid an encounter with probing members of the media and particularly Lamont Christensen, editor of the *Kane County Citizen.*

Books' new ride was a GMC Sierra pickup with its best days behind it. The old rig shuddered with every undulation and pothole he drove through in the road, leaving him to wonder whether the aging wreck would stand up to daily use until the Tahoe made it back into service.

Before returning to BLM headquarters, they stopped at Tanner's apartment so that she could change into her uniform. The sheriff had ordered all sworn deputies back to work, cancelling all leave days until the present crisis was resolved.

Once settled in his office, Books did two things. First, he put Tanner to work preparing her first arrest warrant, this one for Jason Buck. Then he called the Four Corners task force, hoping he might reach Sergeant Dan Walker. It was Saturday and nobody answered. Books didn't bother leaving a message. He rummaged through the top drawer of his desk until he found Walker's business card with his office and cell number. Walker answered on the first ring.

"Thank God for caller ID. If it hadn't been you, I wouldn't have answered," said Walker.

"I'm glad to know I'm held in such high regard."

"Don't flatter yourself. I also answer if the caller is my mother-in-law."

"Well, go screw yourself then."

Walker chuckled. "What's up, J.D.?"

"Trouble by the boatload, I'm afraid." Books filled him in on the day's events.

"Wow, you have been busy. What can we do to help?"

"We need to get somebody out to the Buck residence in Blanding immediately, in case any of them show up at the house."

"I thought you said you had Earl and Jimmy cornered somewhere in the Monument."

"We think we do, but they're still at large. No guarantees, you know how it is. Besides, we have no idea whether Jason is somewhere out here or sitting at home. We want him as well."

"Are you getting warrants?"

"We should have arrest warrants entered into the system for all three members of the family, plus Bobby Case, within a couple of hours. That's assuming I can find a judge to sign them."

"Okay. It doesn't seem likely they'll show at the house. They'd have to know it's the first place we'd look."

"True, but these guys may not be the brightest bulbs in the box. I think it's possible that Jason might not be aware of what's going on. If anyone does show, I think it would be him."

Walker said, "Even if we were to capture them at the house, you're still going to need a search warrant."

"I know. As soon as we finish the arrest warrants, I'll go to work on the affidavit for a search warrant. That house might contain a treasure trove of stolen property. I'm anxious to have a look."

"Me, too," said Walker. "I assume most of your evidence is coming from the Benally kid."

"That's right. Benally participated in the kidnapping of the Rogers couple on Friday night, and then Saturday night, he burglarized their home in the company of Jason Buck."

"Busy young fellow," observed Walker.

"It's the truth, but the good news for us is that Benally can identify everybody involved."

"Including your brother-in-law, apparently."

"Yup."

"Sorry about that. It must be tough."

"It is what it is."

"I assume Benally's cooperation has come with a price," said Walker.

"Don't they all? He received a plea deal that will probably turn out to be overly generous, given how deeply involved I think he is in this mess. But I also understand where we'd be without his help."

"Do you think you've gotten everything out of him you're going to get?"

"That's hard to say. You can't discount the possibility that he can't recall everything or that he's deliberately withholding information. Time will tell."

"And of course, the defense will attack his veracity in court, claiming he's lying to save his own neck," said Walker.

"No doubt. I've seen it a hundred times before, but we'll worry about that later."

They agreed on a plan.

Walker would call the Blanding Police Department and have the Buck home placed under surveillance until he could make the hour-and-a-half drive from his home in Durango.

Meanwhile, Books and Tanner would obtain arrest warrants for the four men and a search warrant for the Buck residence in Blanding. The arrest warrants would then be entered into the National Crime Information Center data base as well as the Utah Crime Information system. Armed with the search warrant, Books would make the four-hour drive from Kanab to Blanding where he and Dan Walker would lead a police raid on the Buck home. Books realized the warrants for Earl and James Buck would turn out to be unnecessary if Sutter and Maldonado managed to capture them in the ongoing manhunt.

Tanner and Books worked until almost nine o'clock before completing all the paperwork. They stopped periodically to follow radio traffic at the site of the manhunt. The searchers appeared to be focused on a rugged section of the Monument off the Timber Mountain Road. Books knew the area as extremely inhospitable terrain containing a large number of potential hiding places and nearly as many spots from which to spring an ambush.

At nine-thirty, Books and Tanner arrived at the home of district court Judge Homer Wilkins. Wilkins led them into the home's spacious great room, inviting them to sit while he examined the warrants.

Wilkins sat in a leather chair under a bright floor lamp, a pair of reading glasses perched on the end of his nose as he carefully perused each affidavit. At one point, he looked over at Books and Tanner. "Looks you kids have been busy today."

"We sure have, judge," replied Books, "and will continue to be for quite a while, I'm afraid."

"Sure looks like it."

Finally, his reading finished, the judge looked at Tanner and Books over the top of his readers.

"Everything seems to be in order. Officer Tanner, please stand and raise your right hand."

The request caught Tanner by surprise. She stood tentatively and took the oath, swearing that everything contained in the affidavit was the truth and nothing but. Books did the same with the other warrants.

From experience, Books knew that Wilkins was a thorough judge who expected that all the t's be crossed and i's dotted before he would sign a warrant. He had little tolerance for sloppy police work, a trait that annoyed more than a few local cops.

Wilkins walked them to the front door, told them to be careful, and sent them away with one final admonishment.

"Be sure to get me a return of service on the search warrant as soon as you can and an inventory of everything you seize."

"Will do, judge," replied Books. "Sorry to have disturbed your evening."

"Not a problem. Good luck."

"Nice home," whispered Tanner as they walked to the Sierra.

"I'd love to have a home like that someday," said Books.

"Me, too."

"What happens now?" asked Tanner.

"We'll get the arrest warrants entered into the system, and then I'm on my way to Blanding with the search warrant."

"Can I tag along?"

"Sure, but you better get an okay from Charley. He might have other ideas."

They tried to raise Sutter on the radio but he didn't answer. Books tried his cell but that kicked directly into voice mail. He did finally reach Randy Maldonado for an update.

"What's going on out there?"

"We found a blood trail, but so far, no sign of either one of them. You must have got the old man pretty good. He's lost a lot of blood. I can't believe he can make it very far—hurt too bad, I think."

"They probably decided to lay low and lick their wounds."

"That's exactly what we're thinking. The problem now is that it's gotten so dark that you can't see a damn thing. We're got to hunker down for the night, get more manpower up here, and resume the search at first light."

"Anything we can do from this end?"

"Get those warrants ready, for starters."

"They're done. Signed, sealed, and delivered."

"That was fast—good work. We need to meet with you. Sit tight until we get there."

"How soon? I need to be on my way to Blanding ASAP."

"We'll be there shortly."

Maldonado explained that a team of FBI agents were on their way from the Las Vegas field office to provide assistance. Exactly what that assistance would entail, he didn't say.

Chapter Thirty-six

Every law enforcement agency in southwest Utah volunteered personnel for the manhunt. Within hours, more than sixty cops from federal, state, and local departments had assembled in Kanab. The FBI set up a mobile command center at the mouth of the Johnson Canyon Road. The location served as the gateway into the rugged Grand Staircase National Monument, and it was located only a few miles outside Kanab.

Books huddled in the sheriff's department conference room with Sutter, Maldonado, and an FBI supervisor from the Las Vegas field office. Sutter had refused Tanner's request to accompany Books to Blanding citing the local need for as many personnel as possible until the current crisis was resolved. Tanner understood, but disappointment was etched on her face when she received the news.

"Having warrants out on all the major players will only serve to shorten the duration of the manhunt," said Sutter. "Even if they slip through our net, we'll have these wackos in the crosshairs of every police agency in the southwest."

Maldonado said, "J.D., I got hold of BLM Ranger Florence Mendez out of our Monticello office. She'll hook up with you and this guy from the Four Corners task force in Blanding. Do you think you'll have enough help over there?"

"I think so. With Mendez, Dan Walker and me, plus help from the locals, we should be all right."

"I would be very careful about enlisting the help of local law enforcement in Blanding," warned FBI Tactical Supervisor Karl Heiner. "If you recall our 2009 raid on the pot hunters in that town, one thing we learned was that sympathetic local law enforcement officials would have leaked our operation ahead of time, and the raid would have been a bust."

The raid Heiner was referring to had netted federal indictments against twenty-three individuals, most of them Blanding residents. Local politicians and law enforcement administrators had criticized the raid as unnecessary and another example of heavy-handed intrusion by the federal government into the lives of local citizens.

"You may be right," said Books, "but I find it hard to believe that local law enforcement is going to view these characters as innocent victims of harassment by the federal government. These guys hardly qualify as Boy Scouts."

Worried that the disagreement might escalate, Sutter quickly changed the subject.

"So what's the plan when you get to Blanding?" asked Sutter.

"I'd like to sit on the house until at least dawn before we execute the search warrant—see if any of them show up."

"That seems highly unlikely," posited Heiner, skepticism in his tone.

"The best shot we've got," countered Books, "is if Jason surfaces. There's been no sign of him around Kanab since the burglary a week ago. What if he doesn't know what's going on with his dad and Jimmy? And even if he does, it's possible they told him to go back to the house and destroy any evidence hidden there."

Everybody agreed on the importance of remaining in close contact as the investigation continued to unfold. "Keep us apprised of what is happening in Blanding, J.D., and we'll do the same from our end."

◇◇◇

Books excused himself and left the meeting, anxious to be on his way. He drove home, parked the Sierra, and transferred the department-issued Remington shotgun to his own Ford pickup.

If he was going to engage in covert surveillance, it wouldn't do to show up in Blanding driving a marked BLM patrol vehicle. Inside the trailer, he removed a .25-caliber Smith from a small locked safe in his bedroom, and strapped it to his ankle. It was a weapon he didn't use often, but it always provided him with an extra measure of safety.

The two-hundred-forty mile drive took Books about four hours. When he arrived at the town limits, he glanced at his watch. It was just after two. He met Dan Walker in the parking lot of a closed convenience store.

"Anything going on?" Books asked.

"Quiet as a graveyard. I got here about eleven. The house was dark, no vehicles on the property. Been that way ever since."

"Was anybody watching the house before you got here?"

Walker nodded. "I spoke with a Blanding P.D. uniform as soon as I arrived. The guy had just pulled a swing shift and was going off duty. He told me that he'd done drive-bys every fifteen minutes starting at 2145 hours. Nothing going on—stone quiet."

"How about Mendez—she here?"

"Yeah, she got here before I did. She's on the house now."

Walker reached out his car window and handed Books a portable radio.

"Take one of these," he said. "I wanted to be sure we could all communicate with each other. Set it on channel two."

"Mendez has one?"

"Yeah. So how do you want to handle this?"

"Why don't we sit on the house until mid-morning at least? If nobody has shown by then, we go in."

"That makes sense."

They established a rotating schedule where one officer took a break from the surveillance while the other two covered the house. They shifted every half hour, enabling each of them to take a short break. They agreed to maintain radio silence unless there was activity at the house or it was time for the shift rotation.

Books had always hated stationary surveillance. The sheer boredom was almost unbearable. He couldn't sit still. He drank coffee to stay awake and the coffee made him hyper. During his breaks, he got out of the pickup and took short walks, always carrying the handheld with him.

The town started to come awake shortly before sunrise. A couple of mini-mart gas stations opened at six and traffic began moving shortly thereafter. There had been no activity around the house all night, and Books was beginning to think that nobody would come. That changed shortly before nine.

Books and Mendez were on the house with Walker on break. Mendez, who was parked on a side street behind the home, broke radio silence.

"J.D., I've got a solo male who just drove down the street on a motorcycle. I think he's checking things out. Stay out of sight."

"Roger that. Does he fit the physical description?"

"That's affirmative—appears to be the kid brother."

"What's he doing?"

"He's headed your way."

"Did you copy that, Dan?" said Books.

"Ten-four, I'm close by."

"Okay, I've got him," said Books. "He parked in the driveway and just walked into the house."

"Dan, why don't you join Mendez and come in from behind the house? I'll knock on the front door and see if I can spook him out the back right into your arms."

"Right," said Walker. "Give us a couple of minutes to get into position, and watch yourself."

No kidding thought Books. If only he'd known, staying in Denver might have made a lot more sense.

Books removed his department issue .357 magnum Smith & Wesson and stashed it under the front seat. He parked the pickup on the curb directly in front of the house and pulled on his Colorado Rockies ball cap. If the kid watched him approach, he'd see a guy in a long-sleeved denim shirt, no jacket, blue jeans, and wearing ratty looking hikers. Never mind the .25 caliber strapped to his ankle. With a little luck, the kid might assume the visitor was someone other than a cop. He could only hope.

Books followed a narrow sidewalk to the front door. The yard had long since gone to weeds, and what little grass remained, looked dead. Books knocked and waited. He heard the sound of movement from inside the house. The front door opened a couple of inches and a young man with a shock of red hair, a waxy, pale complexion, and enough pimples to make him the poster boy for every zit cleanser ever made, peeked out.

"What do you want?" he said.

"I'd like to speak to the lady of the house if I might," replied Books.

"She ain't here. Now go away."

Books removed a folded copy of the search warrant from a leather bound notebook he carried and handed it Buck. "Then would you mind taking a moment to answer several questions from our consumer products survey? It'll just take a minute."

He gave Books a confused, quizzical look as he unfolded the sheet of paper and started reading.

"What the...."

Books flashed his police creds and stepped into the home's entryway. "Police officer, please step back. We've got a search warrant for the house."

Buck tried to slam the door but Books was already inside.

"You can't..."

"Oh, yes we can, son. The house is surrounded. Stay calm and you won't be hurt."

Books spun Buck around, spread-eagled him against a wall, and patted him down for weapons. He cuffed him behind the back while telling him that he was under arrest for burglary."

The kid looked stunned. It had all happened so quickly and smoothly that he'd had almost no time to react. It wasn't until a few minutes later that Books realized that Jason Buck's lack of resistance had less to do with his own theatrics and more to do with the fact that the kid was stoned on something. Suffice to say that Buck hadn't been thinking too clearly, nor had he been able to move with any sense of urgency.

Moments after hearing the commotion at the front of the house, Walker followed Books through the front door, leaving Mendez to cover the rear. They sat Buck on the couch where he could easily be watched while they waited for a Blanding P.D. cruiser to arrive. When Books looked at Buck, he saw a frightened and confused kid. That created an advantage for them, an advantage that screamed for an interrogation as soon as possible.

In his haste to get out of Kanab, Books had forgotten to bring an evidence kit, an embarrassing but not fatal mistake. Fortunately, Walker and Mendez hadn't forgotten theirs. With Buck secure, Mendez stood guard while Walker and Books searched the house.

It was an old place, a two-story brick affair typical of homes constructed in the years after World War II. This one had a carport that had been cobbled together years after the house was built. The main floor had a small living room, a formal dining room, a kitchen, and what today would be called a mud room that lead from the back door down a narrow hallway into the kitchen. Upstairs were three bedrooms and a bath. One of the bedrooms contained an old metal desk and chair with a two-drawer wood file cabinet beside it.

To suggest the house lacked a woman's touch was an understatement of biblical proportions. This home lacked anyone's touch! The garbage and dirty dishes strewn about and the dust so thick on everything made Books wish he'd worn a hazmat suit.

A Blanding P.D. patrol officer transported Jason Buck to the police department, where he would be booked and held until Walker, Mendez, and Books finished up at the house.

"What a fuckin' mess," said Walker. "Where do you want to start?"

"Let's ask Mendez to grab the camcorder and shoot some footage of the overall conditions in this rat hole. Then we'll split up. Mendez and I will search the upstairs while you do the main floor. Afterwards, we'll switch."

"Fair enough."

Mendez and Books moved slowly from room to room. They found little of value in two of the bedrooms save small amounts of marijuana and assorted drug paraphernalia. From the metal desk in the third bedroom, however, they made an important and incriminating discovery.

The top drawer contained a black ledger book chronologically listing what appeared to be the details of numerous sales transactions involving ancient artifacts. The meticulously kept ledger showed the date of each transaction, a brief description of the item sold, who it was sold to, and the sales price. Penciled almost exclusively into the eight-page ledger was the name B. Gentry. On the inside cover of the last page was a list of names and telephone numbers, including that of Brett Gentry, that corresponded with the names of the individuals to whom items had been sold.

Finally they had made the connection linking Brett Gentry to an elaborate criminal enterprise in which artifacts were illegally dug or stolen from unsuspecting pot hunters like the Rogerses, and then resold. Books suspected that Gentry probably acted as a middle-man, employing people like the Bucks and his own brother-in-law to illegally acquire antiquities. He would buy them on the cheap, and then sell them directly to collectors, or more likely, to unscrupulous gallery owners, museum curators, and auction houses.

From downstairs, Books and Mendez heard Walker shout, "Bingo."

"What have you got?" hollered Books.

"Come down here and have a look-see."

Walker was standing in front of a six-foot-high walnut veneer bookshelf with two folding doors that had been padlocked using a cheap key lock. Inside, the shelves were full of every kind of Anasazi and Fremont Indian antiquity imaginable.

"Any of this look familiar?" asked Walker.

Books looked carefully at each artifact. "Yeah, I think several pieces came from the Rogers collection. When I get back to

Kanab, we'll compare them to the photos the family provided, but I'm pretty sure we've got some of it."

"How did you get that unlocked?" asked Mendez.

Smiling, Walker held up a small key.

"Some genius left it on the top shelf of the bookcase."

They photographed everything in the exact location where it had been found. Evidence tags and plastic bags were used to collect each item. Some of the more fragile pieces were carefully wrapped in paper and placed in cardboard boxes prior to removal.

Like Books and Mendez, Walker had found small amounts of marijuana on the main level of the home in sufficient quantity to have kept several people pleasantly intoxicated for a considerable period of time.

They loaded everything into Books' F-150 and then parted company. Mendez returned to Monticello while Walker and Books drove to the Blanding Police Department, eager to interrogate Jason Buck.

Chapter Thirty-seven

Sunday Noon—Day 10

Jason Buck was brought from a small holding cell in the basement of the police department to an office normally occupied by the police chief. Since it was Sunday, the chief was off-duty and Books had been given permission to use the office to question him

During the intervening hours between the time he was arrested and the interrogation, the kid had regained a measure of sobriety. Perhaps the gravity of the situation he faced contributed to that. The blank expression and glazed look in his eyes were gone. For nearly a minute, Books and Walker stared at Buck without speaking. Buck cast his eyes down avoiding eye contact.

"I wonder if you have any idea about the amount of trouble you're in," began Books. "The party's over, Jason. Benally has given us a statement implicating you in numerous crimes sufficient to keep you behind bars for the rest of your life. Do you understand what I'm telling you?"

He nodded, "Yeah."

"So here's what we're going to do. Sergeant Walker here is going to advise you of your constitutional rights. When he's finished, we'd like to ask you some questions. My advice to you, and it's the same advice I gave Joe Benally, is that you cooperate.

At least we'll be able to tell the court that despite your involvement in some horrific crimes, you at least assumed responsibility for what you did, and cooperated with us to make things right. Hopefully, the court will take that into consideration when you're sentenced."

Walker read him the Miranda warnings, and asked if he was willing to waive his rights and answer questions without the presence of an attorney.

To their relief, Buck agreed to talk. Maybe the long-winded speeches had resonated with him on some level and he realized that his cooperation was the one card he could play that would work in his favor. Or perhaps the sheer guilt of what he had done was tearing him apart like a malignant tumor eating away at his insides. In the end, the motive for Buck's cooperation didn't really matter anyway. What mattered to Books was getting him to help solve the puzzle.

Books covered much of the same ground with Buck that he had the day before with Joe Benally. Buck's statement corroborated virtually everything Benally had told them. What Books hoped for, however, was that Buck could shed additional light on the whereabouts of the Rogers couple as well as the involvement of Brett Gentry.

"Have you ever meant a gentleman by the name of Brett Gentry?" Books asked.

"Yeah, a time or two."

"How did you meet him?"

"My dad gave me stuff to take to him."

"What kind of stuff?"

"Stolen shit, mostly."

"Would this stuff typically include stolen pots and other artifacts?"

"Yeah."

"Where did you meet Mr. Gentry?"

"Different places, St. George sometimes, and Page."

"Did you ever meet him in Kanab?"

Buck had to think about that for a moment before answering. "Only once that I can remember. He never wanted to meet in Kanab."

"How come?"

"I don't know—probably afraid somebody would see him."

"Did he pay you for the artifacts you brought to him?"

"Sure."

"Did you negotiate prices with Gentry for the artifacts?"

"Naw, my dad or Jimmy always did that. I just delivered the stuff."

Books decided to shift the interrogation in a new direction.

"You participated in the kidnapping of Rolly and Abby Rogers. Correct?"

"Yeah."

"What did you do with them after the kidnapping?"

"Man, I don't know and that's the God's honest truth. They were okay when me and Joey split. I mean they was tied up and everything, but they weren't hurt."

"So when you and Joey left, who stayed behind with the Rogers couple?"

"My dad and Jimmy."

"What about Bobby Case? Was he still there?'

"Nope. He split before me and Joey did."

"And you'd like us to believe that you have no idea where your father and brother took them. Is that right?"

"I'm telling you, I don't know. That's the truth."

"You think they're still alive?"

"I'm not sure. Maybe."

"What makes you think they might be alive?"

"Cuz Jimmy and my dad wouldn't hurt anybody, that's why."

Books thought the youngster sounded almost indignant—like he didn't think it was possible that the Rogerses might have been killed and their bodies dumped in some God forsaken part of the desert. Buck was either lying or extremely naïve. Books wasn't sure which.

As the interview wound down, the one area where the statements of Benally and Buck didn't jibe had to do with the possibility that the Bucks had preyed on other unsuspecting souls much like the Rogers. Jason Buck vehemently denied that his family had engaged in any prior kidnappings. Benally, however, had at least intimated that the Bucks were no strangers to kidnapping other pot hunters and hijacking their artifacts. Benally had even mentioned overhearing a conversation between Earl and Jimmy Buck in which a reference was made to their having taken down another digger in Chaco Canyon.

Books arranged for Jason Buck to be transported to Kanab by the Utah Highway Patrol. He would be booked into the Kane County jail pending the filing of formal criminal charges by the DA. Walker and Books prepared to part company with promises of continued cooperation.

"What do you think the chances really are that the Rogers kidnapping was a first for the Buck clan?" Books asked.

"Quite small, I'm afraid," said Walker. "If you recall, we've got a missing persons case from a year-and-a-half ago from Chaco Canyon."

"Do you have a body to go with it?"

"We do—a known pot hunter from Shiprock. We'll reinvestigate that case and go over everything with a fine tooth comb."

"You might need to exhume the body," noted Books.

"Very possible. I'll keep you in the loop."

"Likewise."

Chapter Thirty-eight

The return drive to Kanab became an exercise in trying to stay awake. Books had been up for more than thirty straight hours, and his increased coffee consumption had done little to keep him alert. It did, however, necessitate numerous, unscheduled stops to relieve his overstressed bladder.

He hadn't checked his cell for messages in several hours. When he finally did, he discovered two—one from Becky Eddins and the other from Beth Tanner. The messages were nearly identical. An FBI swat team had closed in on the Bucks early Sunday morning. Shots had been exchanged, and when the dust cleared, the body of Earl Buck was found concealed in a rocky outcropping from which he'd made his last stand. The only question remaining was whether he'd taken his own life or succumbed from the wounds Books had inflicted the day before.

That was the good news.

The bad news was that his son, Jimmy, had disappeared without a trace. The search would continue of course, but Books somehow doubted that it would culminate in the arrest of the last member of the of the Buck family.

Despite his fatigue, Books was summoned to meet with Sutter and Maldonado to discuss the case against Brett Gentry. What concerned him most was that unless they could prove conspiracy on Gentry's part, he might end up charged with only some lightweight offense like receiving stolen property. To

Books, it didn't feel like justice for the man he believed was the brain trust behind this hideous criminal enterprise.

It was nearly two a.m. when Books reached the outskirts of Kanab. He stopped at BLM headquarters to secure the evidence seized at the Buck home. Prior to his appointment as Kanab's first law enforcement ranger, there had been no need for a secure place to store evidence. Shortly after his arrival, he'd set up a makeshift storage room near his office where evidence could be held pending court. Only he and Monument Manager Alexis Runyon had a key. It was nothing fancy, but it served to maintain the chain of custody of evidence prior to trial. After he finished logging each item, he headed over to the sheriff's department.

The duty officer informed Books that Charley Sutter and Randy Maldonado were napping on cots in the sheriff's office but had left word to awaken them immediately upon his arrival. Books was ushered into the conference room and told that Sutter and Maldonado would join him momentarily. The room looked like it had been used as a cafeteria. Empty pizza boxes, pop cans, paper plates, and napkins were scattered everywhere. The lingering smell of pizza did little to assuage Books' hunger. To his way of thinking, nothing tasted better than cold pizza and an even colder beer, except maybe hot pizza and a cold beer.

Books found an unopened bottle of water in the refrigerator and had about finished it when Sutter and Maldonado entered the room. Like Books, neither man had slept much during the past twenty-four hours. They were haggard-looking and unshaven, with dark circles under their eyes, the stress of the current crisis obviously weighing on them.

"Well, J.D., we got one of the bastards," said Sutter, trying to stifle a yawn. "How did things go in Blanding?"

It was difficult for Books to contain his excitement. "It really couldn't have gone much better. Besides apprehending Jason Buck, we found a stash of antiquities in the house."

"Any of it from the Rogers' home?"

"Some pieces, for sure, but lots of other stuff too. We're exploring a possible connection between a dead pot hunter discovered in Chaco Canyon and the Buck crew. The Four Corners Task Force is working with us on that."

"We'll take all the help we can get," said Sutter.

"How do you want to handle things with Brett Gentry?" asked Books.

"We probably ought to consult our FBI friends," said Maldonado, "but I recommend we place Gentry under surveillance in case he decides to hightail it. While we're doing that, J.D. can prepare search warrants for the Gentrys' home and office and an arrest warrant for Brett."

Sutter nodded in agreement. "You okay with that, J.D.?"

"It's a good plan," replied Books.

"I agree. Randy and I will sit down with the FBI and get them to buy in. I don't see any reason why they would object."

The conversation waned momentarily until Maldonado broke the silence. "This is a little awkward, J.D., but we also need to discuss how to handle the situation with your brother-in-law."

Books had been expecting this, so it came as no surprise. "What do you suggest?"

"Charley and I have talked it over, and we think it would be best for all concerned, if you stayed as far away as possible from the legal proceedings against Bobby," said Maldonado.

"Meaning what, exactly?" said Books.

"Meaning you're not to be involved in that part of the investigation any longer. We'll get the arrest warrant, and we'll pick him up," said Maldonado.

"We think this is for your own good," noted Sutter. "After all, Bobby is family. You'll have enough problems on your hands without having to deal with this."

Books knew it made sense, and he also realized that he didn't have a choice in the matter. For the moment, Randy Maldonado was as much his boss as Monument Manager Alexis Runyon was, and he undoubtedly spoke for the BLM brass in Salt Lake City.

"I understand," replied Books, "one favor, though."

"If we can," said Maldonado.

"Can I have your permission to sit down with my sister, Maggie, and explain to her what's going on before you come for Bobby?"

Maldonado looked skeptical.

"Sorry, J.D.—can't do that," said Sutter, without hesitation. "It's not a good idea. I'm sure you understand why. Go on home now and get a few hours' sleep. You won't be any good to anybody until you do."

Books didn't try to argue the point. "Fair enough. I'll plan to be back in my office by seven. Will there be anything else?"

Sutter and Maldonado glanced at each other. "Yeah, there is one more thing," said Maldonado.

Books watched as Sutter fumbled through a folder on the table in front of him. He removed a zip-lock baggie with a note scrawled on it in nearly illegible handwriting.

"We found this on the body of Earl Buck," said Sutter.

The note read, *"You killed my father. We have unfinished business."*

It was not difficult to figure out who the unsigned note was from and who it was intended for. The thought gave Books the creeps. He had little doubt that Jimmy Buck was potentially the most dangerous member of the family, given his military training, combat experience, and youth. What's more, he now had a powerful motive to seek vengeance—the death of his father.

"Are you telling me this for any particular reason other than you thought I should know?" said Books.

"Well," said Sutter, "our FBI colleagues suggested we might consider, oh, how should I say this….?"

"Using me as a tethered goat."

"Uh, I wouldn't put it that way," said Sutter, "but I suppose that's what it comes down to."

"Tell 'em thanks, but I'm not interested."

The meeting ended and Books headed home. As exhausted as he was, he drove past the trailer twice, looking around carefully for anything that appeared out of place. In the morning he would talk to Ned Hunsaker and ask him to keep his eyes open and report anything unusual.

At home Books lay down on the bed without bothering to undress and fell immediately to sleep. He had always been a light sleeper, and shortly before dawn, noise from outside the trailer awakened him with a start. He remained motionless on the bed, listening intently. Nothing. He was about to drift back to sleep when he heard the sound again. This time he rolled out of bed onto the cold trailer floor, and reached for the .25 caliber he'd left holstered on the nightstand next to his bed. Whatever he'd heard had come from behind the trailer in an area where Hunsaker temporarily stored anything he wanted to get rid of. The old man was a pack rat, and whenever he had accumulated enough trash, he'd light it up using a rusty old oil drum as an incinerator.

Books crept slowly to the trailer's front door, carefully looking around before stepping outside. Gun in hand he stepped quickly to one end of the trailer closest to where he'd heard the noises. When he peeked around the corner, he saw the poorest excuse for a pit bull he'd ever seen. The dog was filthy and looked like it hadn't had a meal in a long time. She was so skinny Books could count her ribs.

It was impossible not to feel sorry for her. Books debated about what to do. She was obviously a stray. He could call animal control. The county operated a small, underfunded shelter outside town.

Then he had another idea. He went back inside, opened his frig, and removed a take-home box of Mexican food from Escobars. It was mostly rice and beans. He put it in a plastic cereal bowl and brought it outside along with a second bowl filled with water. When the stray noticed him, she acted skittish and trotted a short distance away. She regarded him warily as he set the food and water down. He called her, but she wouldn't come, so he left the food and water and returned to the trailer. He showered, put on his uniform, and left for work thirty minutes later. On his way out, he noticed the dog was gone, as was the food and most of the water.

He stopped at Ned Hunsaker's home for coffee on his way into the office. So far, Books had failed to convince him that a French press was the best way to prepare coffee, but the old man enjoyed his cup and didn't buy cheap beans either. Books tried to keep him supplied with whatever coffee he was roasting at the time.

"Sit yourself down, young fella. I must say you keep odd hours."

"You heard me come in last night. Sorry if I disturbed you."

"Not last night, this morning, and no, you didn't disturb me. Can't sleep worth a damn anymore, no matter what I do."

"That's what I've got to look forward too, huh."

"Afraid so. What's up?"

"I was drawn to your doorstep by the smell of fresh coffee and cinnamon rolls—figured I'd stop by and pig out before heading in this morning."

"Come right in and help yourself. You've been so busy lately I haven't seen much of you."

While drinking coffee and munching on one of Ned's decadent hot cinnamon rolls, Books spent the next few minutes bringing him up to speed on the latest developments in the case.

"Well, I'm glad to hear you're finally making some headway. I know you've been feeling frustrated," said Hunsaker.

"Trying to get anybody to talk has really held us up. I used to think following a drug trail from street pusher to the major supplier was hard, but this has been even more difficult."

"I'm not surprised," said Hunsaker. "Often, the diggers don't know, nor do they care, who the middleman is so long as they get paid, and they never ever meet the end buyer."

"You mean the actual collector?"

"Well, yeah, that too, but you're missing a link in the chain."

"I'm confused," said Books.

"It works like this. Somebody like Brett Gentry pays his diggers, and then he sells the relic to a middleman, who in turns sells the item to a wealthy collector."

"So who exactly would the middleman be?" asked Books.

"Could be anybody in the art business—it might be a gallery owner, a museum curator, or even somebody in an auction house. Hell, a five-hundred-dollar pot sold in Utah or Arizona might bring several hundred thousand dollars when it's resold to, say, an international collector. All I'm telling you is that the diggers don't know who the middleman is, and they certainly never find out who the actual collector is."

"But Brett Gentry will know?"

"Gentry won't know who the end buyer is, but he has to know who the middleman is—that's how he makes his money and moves the product along."

"Hell, Ned, the BLM ought to hire you as a consultant for this antiquities business."

"They don't need me when they got people like Randy Maldonado around. From what I hear, he's the foremost authority on the subject."

Books stood up to leave. He placed his coffee cup and plate in the kitchen sink on his way out the door. "Thanks, Ned. Talking to you is always an education."

"Don't worry about things around here. I'll keep my eyes peeled and if I see anything funny, I'll call it in.

As Books stepped out the back door, he heard Hunsaker shout, "Keep your head down out there, son, and watch your back."

Sound wisdom, thought Books.

Chapter Thirty-nine

Monday Morning—Day 11

When Books arrived at the office he found a voice message from Alexis Runyon, reminding him that effective immediately, he was back on patrol duty and would have to be available to respond to calls for service. If that happened, Sutter and Maldonado would have to find someone else to prepare the search warrant for Red Rock Touring as well as Brett Gentry's home.

Books checked with dispatch and found there were no pending calls requiring him in the field immediately. If his luck held for a while longer, he'd have time to get the warrant ready. He would then turn the investigation over to Sutter, Maldonado, and the FBI.

It didn't take long for Books to finish preparing the warrant. Lately, he had been getting plenty of practice. He called Sutter and Maldonado, but neither man answered. They were probably in the Monument directing the continuing search for Jimmy Buck. Phone reception in the Grand Staircase was always tenuous. Books left each of them a message explaining that the search warrant for Red Rock Touring and the Gentry home should be ready by noon, assuming he could get Judge Wilkins to approve it.

Just before noon, as Books sat outside the office of District Court Judge Homer Wilkins, Randy Maldonado called.

"Any luck with the search?" asked Books

"Afraid not. I'm starting to think he's slipped right through our fingers, but we'll hang on for a while longer and hope our luck changes. We got your message. Have you got the warrant ready?"

"It's written. I'm waiting for the judge to finish his morning court docket. His secretary told me he'd see me as soon as he gets out of court."

"Let me know when you've got it. We have teams standing by to execute the warrant as soon as you give us the green light."

"Will do." He disconnected as Judge Wilkins entered his chambers.

"Come in and have a seat," said Wilkins, as he removed his robe.

"Thanks for squeezing me in, judge. I know you're very busy today."

"You're keeping me rather busy, Ranger Books. Now let me take a look at what you've got." He reached across his desk for the paper work.

He studied it for several minutes. "Huh, quite the bunch of crackpots, I'd say."

He administered the oath to Books and signed the warrant. "Here you go. You know the drill."

"Yes, your honor."

"Where are you on the other warrants I signed?"

"I just gave the return of service and inventory to your secretary. We arrested Jason Buck earlier this morning at his home in Blanding. Bobby Case hasn't been picked up yet."

He found it interesting that Judge Wilkins didn't show the slightest indication that he recognized the Case name. Many people in Kanab knew Bobby, but everybody knew his powerful father, Doug.

When Books left the courthouse, he called Maldonado to inform him that Judge Wilkins had approved the warrant. Sutter and Maldonado had returned to the sheriff's office and were huddled with their FBI counterparts, planning the raid. On impulse, he changed course and drove past Red Rock Touring. While it was still early, Books thought it a little odd that the business was closed. The inside lights were off, and there were no vehicles behind the office where employees typically parked. No sign of the Gentry's black Cadillac Escalade, either.

Curious, he drove west across Kanab Creek into a neighborhood close to where Becky Eddins resided. Brett and his wife, Emily, owned a large log home with a 360-degree wrap-around deck and a second-story loft that led outside through French doors to a second, smaller deck, with magnificent south-facing views. The attached garage included two normal-sized spaces plus a large third bay, big enough to hold an oversized recreation vehicle.

It looked like nobody was home. There were no vehicles parked outside, the living room drapes were closed, and there were no interior lights on as far as Books could tell.

The Gentrys appeared to be living high and well, mused Books.

On his drive to the sheriff's office, Books noticed a nondescript four-door sedan, a Chevrolet probably, following several cars behind him. He was certain it was the same vehicle he'd noticed as he left Red Rock Touring. He thought he could make out the silhouette of at least two individuals in the car. It smelled of FBI.

It was possible, perhaps even likely, that they had been conducting stationary surveillance of Red Rock Touring, or it may have been that some bureaucrat decided to have him followed, hoping Jimmy Buck might surface. Rather than driving straight to the sheriff's office, Books chose a more circuitous route. Every time Books turned, the sedan eventually followed, the driver doing her best to maintain a discreet distance in an attempt to avoid detection.

Because he was curious, but mostly for fun, Books accelerated the Sierra along Highway 89 until he came to the local Subway restaurant. He pulled into the parking lot and drove around behind the building and then into an alley which led to a cleaner's next door. He hopped out and walked around the front of the cleaners and came up behind the sedan as it idled in the Subway lot, its occupants wondering how he'd managed to elude them. He approached on the passenger side and tapped lightly on the side window. The two occupants, one male and one female, glanced at each other and then the passenger powered the window down giving Books a sheepish smile.

"Good morning folks. I'm J.D. Books, but I imagine you already know that. Who are you?"

"I'm Special Agent Robert Dupont and this is my partner, Special Agent Mia Barnett."

"Pleasure to meet you both," Books said. "I know you're just following orders so I don't have a problem if you continue following me, but I doubt it's going to lead you to Jimmy Buck."

"We doubt it too, and thanks for being so understanding," replied Barnett.

"Not a problem. I'll be in the sheriff's office for a while and then in the field serving a warrant. If you get tired of sittin' in your car, come on inside and we'll get you something to drink."

With that, Books was gone.

The plan called for two teams of officers to simultaneously raid the office of Red Rock Touring and the home of Brett Gentry. The FBI brass had requested that Beth Tanner and Books participate in the raids, since they knew more about the case than anyone else and because they would have an easier time recognizing artifacts stolen from the Rogers' home.

All personnel assembled at 1500 hours in the sheriff's department conference room and were quickly divided into two teams. An FBI supervisor Books didn't recognize gave everybody their final instructions. On his way out the door, Sutter pulled him aside.

"Just wanted you to know that I'll be the one going out to Bobby's place. You don't need to worry that the house is going to be raided by a SWAT team from the FBI. That's not going happen."

"Thanks, Charley. I appreciate that. When do you anticipate making the arrest?"

"Depends on when we get the warrant but probably sometime tomorrow morning."

When Books arrived at Red Rock Touring, he spotted Randy Maldonado's BLM vehicle, a marked car from the Kanab Police Department, and an unmarked sedan, probably belonging to the FBI, parked in front of the office. A white Subaru Forester owned by Emily Gentry was parked out back. Members of the media had been corralled far enough away that they could take pictures, but not interfere with the search.

From the look of things, the search appeared to be focused more on business records than on artifacts. Office computers were being loaded into the back of an SUV as Books entered. A sullen Emily Gentry stood stoically off to one side scribbling notes on a legal pad, presumably about items being removed from the office. Books heard her complain to one of the suits that they should expect to hear from the family attorney before this was over—a lame threat that was probably heard by FBI agents every time they walked out of a business packing a computer or a box of records.

Maldonado spotted Books and motioned him outside.

"No sign of Mr. Gentry," Maldonado said.

"How about at the house?"

"We checked. He's not there either."

"What does Mrs. Gentry say?"

"Not much, I'm afraid. She's being deliberately vague about his whereabouts. She did say that Brett has become so distraught about the false finger pointing and trying to implicate him and Red Rock Touring in the Rogers disappearance, that he'd mentioned possibly going away for a few days."

"Sounds like a crock to me," said Books.

"Ditto."

"But I must say, there sure doesn't appear to be any treasure trove of artifacts stashed here," said Books.

"We really didn't expect it. From what I'm hearing on the radio, they have found a sizable collection at the house. Whether we can prove any of it is stolen is a whole other question. Tanner is with them now trying to identify specific artifacts that may have come from the Rogers collection."

Ned Hunsaker had been right, thought Books, when he described the antiquities trade as a murky business, some of it on the up-and-up and some of it not. Illegal traffickers like Brett Gentry frequently claimed that the origin of a particular artifact was from private land, not public or tribal, where removal was a violation of law.

"We don't really need you here," said Maldonado, "so if you've got other things to do, feel free to go."

Books took that as a signal to leave.

When Books arrived home, he did the same drive-by he had done the night before. Nothing seemed out of the ordinary. He called Hunsaker and the old man told him that everything had been quiet all day. He parked the Sierra in front of the trailer next to his own truck. When he got out, he spotted his new pit bull friend who had visited the night before, watching him from one end of the trailer.

"Sit tight a minute fella, and I'll see if I can find you something to eat."

Books went into the kitchen and removed a can of mushroom soup from the pantry. He poured the contents into a bowl and nuked it. He added some bread and then carried the concoction outside along with a pan of water. He approached the dog, but it nervously backed away, afraid. He set it down and returned to the trailer. A few minutes later, he stuck his head outside. The food was gone and so was the dog.

With the dog taken care of, Books changed out of his uniform and settled down with a cold beer, listening to the music of Neil Young. This would be his first night home at a halfway decent hour in almost two weeks. He settled into the leather recliner enjoying the brew.

As a kid, he could hardly stand his parents' choice in music, yet as an adult, his own eclectic taste included performers from his parent's generation like Seals and Crofts, Gordon Lightfoot, the Eagles, Neil Young, and others. He'd been a longtime fan of country legends like Brooks and Dunn, Willie Nelson, Randy Travis, and the Dixie Chicks. Recently, he had even begun acquiring a taste for contemporary Caribbean and Latin instrumental sounds. That worried him a little. Maybe it was an age thing, he thought, like a case of early onset gomerhood.

Chapter Forty

The next morning, Books got up early, went into the kitchen and made coffee. He was working on his second cup when he decided to call his father at the university hospital. He knew if this day became as busy as recent ones, it might be his only opportunity to speak with him. After several unanswered rings, Books began to worry. He hung up and called back, asking that the call be directed to the nurse's station. An aid answered and informed him that Bernie was already up and away from his room engaged in a daily exercise regimen. If he continued to improve, the aid said, the treatment plan called for his release sometime on Thursday.

It sounded like the old man was well on his way to recovery from the surgery. The question now was whether outpatient treatment would put the cancer in permanent remission.

Books prepared a breakfast of toast and a cheese omelet in sufficient quantity for himself and the stray. By the time he left for work, the dog hadn't put in an appearance. He refilled the water bowl and left the eggs and toast outside.

When he arrived at his office, he found a message from Alexis Runyon asking him to stop by her office before he left.

Runyon had left a stack of boxes in his office, tourist brochures probably, intended for the new BLM Visitor's Center in

Escalante. Books had apparently been appointed FedEx driver
for the day.

When he tapped on her door, Runyon was on the phone
but motioned him to come in and have a seat. A minute later
she was off the phone and reaching for a message buried in the
clutter on her desk.

"You look tired, J.D. You ought to be home in bed."

"No rest for the wicked, but it looks like the worst is over. I
actually managed seven hours of sleep last night, so I'm feeling
pretty good this morning. Any news on the search for Jimmy
Buck?"

She shook her head. "Nothing I'm aware of. I spoke with the
sheriff a few minutes ago. He sounded discouraged. He said they
would continue the search today but call it off tonight unless
they come up with something new."

"I'm not surprised," said Books. "Jimmy Buck has disappeared into the desert wilderness and may be gone for good."

"Let's hope so."

Runyon expressed her concern about Bernie's recent cancer
surgery as well as Bobby's legal difficulties.

"How is Maggie doing?"

"She's holding on. Some days are better than others."

"I'm sure. Is it okay if I give her a call?"

"Sure, I think she'd like that. Also, thanks for your concern
about Bernie. The surgery went well, and he should be coming
home in the next day or two."

"Great news! Is somebody going to stay with him for a while?"

Books hadn't thought about that. "Probably me for a few
nights. Maggie has arranged home health nurses to see him every
day for the first week at least."

"Good." She handed Books a note. "We've had two calls,
one late yesterday afternoon and the other this morning—a
complaint about illegal timber harvesting off the Hell's Backbone Road north of Boulder. We need you to check it out, and
while you're at it, drop those boxes I left in your office at the
visitor's center."

"Okay. Did the complainant give us any specifics about where along the road to look? It's a pretty long stretch."

"I think it's on the note."

Books reread the note. "Says it's off an access road about halfway in. That helps a little but not much. I'll see what I can do. Do we know who the complainant is?"

"Not unless it's on the note. You can call dispatch, though. They probably have something."

◇◇◇

From his office, Books called Maggie and asked if he could stop by the house. Although he felt genuine concern for his brother-in-law, if he was honest with himself, what he mostly felt toward Bobby was anger. What he was far more concerned about was how well Maggie and his two nephews were holding up under all the stress.

"Sure. Come on out, J.D. The kids are out the door to school and I just brewed a fresh pot of coffee."

Ten minutes later, Books parked the Sierra in the gravel driveway of the Case Cattle Company. Maggie met him at the side door and ushered him into the kitchen.

"Bobby's still asleep. We can talk in here."

She poured them both a cup of coffee then reached into the family liquor cabinet for a bottle of Bailey's Irish Cream. She poured a double shot into her mug and offered some to Books.

Books shook his head. "Rain check—can't do it while I'm on duty."

"Of course you can't, I'm sorry."

Books glanced at his watch. "It's a little early in the day for that, isn't it?"

"With things going like they are around here, it's not even slightly too early."

"I can't even imagine. I'm so sorry, Mags."

"Me, too, J.D. But as you sometimes like to say, 'it is what it is.' I don't mean for that to sound like I'm indifferent or uncaring. It's all so out of my control that I feel helpless to do much of anything. My emotions run the gamut from fear to frustration to intense anger, all of it directed at Bobby for being so damned stupid." She sighed. "Anyway, what brings you by this morning? A social call I hope? I've had about all the bad news I can stand for a while."

Books felt instantly guilty realizing that he couldn't tell her the truth, but knowing that more bad news was about to come knocking on her door.

"Just wanted to check in on you—see how everybody's doing. How are the boys holding up?"

"They seem pretty oblivious to the whole thing, but it's hard to imagine how."

"What makes you say that?" said Books.

"Bobby's stress level is off the charts. He's withdrawn, depressed, and when he does interact with us, he's usually abrupt and irritable. He seems to sleep forever—can't get him up in the morning. He never used to be like that."

No wonder, thought Books. Bobby had a lot to be stressed about, far more than Maggie realized.

"I called the hospital this morning—didn't talk to Bernie—he was busy doing exercises," said Books, changing the subject. "They're pleased with his progress. He's scheduled for release day after tomorrow, unless something unexpected occurs."

"That's good. I spoke with him last night. He's starting to sound like himself again. Unless you can get away, I'll plan to go get him and bring him home."

"I still can't get away, at least not for a few more days, but I know it's not a good time for you, either. I could ask Ned to get Bernie. I'm sure he'd be willing to do it."

"I don't think so, but let me think about it. I'll give you a call. How's your investigation going, by the way?"

"Maybe you haven't heard, but we finally broke the case wide open."

"Afraid I haven't heard much of anything. We heard what you did to save that woman's life. It took a lot of courage. I'm so proud of you, J.D."

"Thanks, sis—just doing my job. Yesterday, an FBI swat team cornered the man I wounded the day before in the Monument. His name was Earl Buck and we believe he was the ringleader of the group that kidnapped Rolly and Abby. He died in a shootout with the officers. We aren't sure whether he killed himself or was hit by a member of the swat team. We'll have to wait until we get an autopsy report to find that out."

"What about the others?" she said.

"Earl Buck has two sons. We believe both of them took part in the kidnapping. The eldest is still at large. He seems to have slipped away from the search party and is probably holed up somewhere in the Monument. Yesterday in Blanding, we arrested the youngest son, a boy named Jason."

"So, other than the one who's still at large, you've got everyone else in custody."

"That's about it," Books lied.

"But you still have no idea what's become of Rolly and Abby."

"Unfortunately, no."

Books finished his coffee and stood to leave. "Better get myself going. Runyon's placed me back on regular patrol duty, and I'm off today chasing an anonymous tip about some yokel illegally harvesting timber on Hell's Backbone Road."

Chapter Forty-one

As Books gassed the Sierra, his cell chirped. He reached into the truck cab and grabbed the phone.

"Hi Maggie, what's going on?"

"It's Bobby. He's disappeared, J.D.

"What makes you say that?"

"He left a note apologizing for the pain and humiliation his actions have caused the family and telling me how much he loves the boys and me. God, J.D., I think he's saying goodbye to us. I'm afraid he going to kill himself."

"What is he driving and when did he leave?"

"He's in his truck, the white Silverado. After you left, I ran into town for a few minutes to do a couple of errands, and when I got back, he was gone. I couldn't have been gone for more than forty or forty-five minutes."

Books looked at his watch. It was nine-thirty. That meant Bobby had an hour plus head start. "His guns, Maggie, does he have any firearms with him?"

"Hold on." She dropped the phone but was back on the line a minute later. "He must have taken his .40 caliber Taurus with him. It's gone."

"You're sure."

"Positive. His shotgun and hunting rifles are all here."

"Okay, stay calm and sit tight. I'll be right along," said Books.

He called dispatch and placed an APB for Bobby in Kane, Garfield, and Washington Counties. He provided a physical description as well as a description of the Silverado. As painful as it felt, he told the dispatcher that Bobby was wanted for kidnapping and that he should be considered armed and dangerous, and possibly suicidal.

Books drove the Sierra straight to the sheriff's office where he pulled Maldonado and Sutter out of a meeting with a team of FBI agents. He explained what had happened.

"Ah, shit," sighed Maldonado. "I had a bad feeling about this. We should have picked him up last night."

"Water under the bridge now," said Sutter. "He'll turn up sooner or later."

Books learned that Beth Tanner had prepared the arrest warrant for Bobby under the sheriff's careful supervision and was, at this moment, at the courthouse getting it approved.

Turning to Maldonado, Sutter said, "Why don't you and Books head over to the Case ranch, and I'll be right along as soon as Tanner gets here."

Maldonado followed Books to the home of Maggie and Bobby Case. Books knew they would search the home regardless of her insistence that Bobby had fled. When they arrived, they found her pacing back and forth in the kitchen. She had been crying. Her mascara had streaked the left side of her face and she dabbed at puffy eyes with Kleenex tissue. Books made the introductions.

"Show me the note, sis."

She pointed behind him. "It's behind you on the countertop."

Books read it while Maldonado read over his shoulder. "Is this where you found it?"

"Yes. I haven't touched it."

Books explained to her what was about to happen. "In a few minutes, Sheriff Sutter is going to show up here with an arrest warrant for Bobby."

"Oh, my God, what for?"

"There's evidence, Mags, that Bobby took part in the abduction of Rolly and Abby. They're going to look around to make sure he's not hiding somewhere here on the ranch. They're legally entitled to search the premises for him. They will probably ask you some questions about his possible whereabouts. Answer them as truthfully as you can."

"Okay," she muttered. Clutching a tissue in one hand and with tears streaming down her face, Books had never seen his sister look so distraught, so utterly defeated, as she did in this moment. Maggie had always been the upbeat, optimistic member of the family. Given his own moody nature, Books had always admired and at times even envied that quality in her. That was all gone now.

"Once they're satisfied that Bobby isn't here, they will probably ask your permission to search the house for evidence of Bobby's involvement in the abduction," said Books.

"Do I have to let them?"

Before he could answer, Books heard the sound of tires on the circular gravel driveway at the front of the house. Car doors slammed and Charley Sutter and Beth Tanner approached the front door.

"The answer to your question, sis, is that you don't have to give them consent, but understand that if you don't, they'll get a search warrant and come back. I suggest that you let them and get it over with."

She nodded, "All right."

"They could be here a while," whispered Books. "You don't have to stay if you don't want to."

She shook her head. "No, I'll stay."

Maldonado had been listening quietly throughout this exchange, looking decidedly uncomfortable. His posture suggested that he wished he could be somewhere else. For that matter, so did Books.

Books turned things over to Sutter and left, feeling guilty that he was abandoning his sister in a time of crisis but realizing that Sutter and Maldonado wanted him out of the way.

Chapter Forty-two

It was a hundred-and-twenty-mile drive to the town of Escalante and the remote area known as the Hell's Backbone Road, where Books would search for the illegal timber cutting operation. The drive gave him ample time to think.

Why had Bobby run? Had someone tipped him off that he was about to be arrested again, this time for a much more serious crime? Books was under no illusion that he would escape scrutiny as the source of a possible leak. They hadn't talked to him yet, but they would.

And where would Bobby hide? Certainly not with family or friends. It wouldn't take long for a team of police, probably FBI, to begin contacting anybody whom Bobby might seek shelter or assistance from. Books knew that Bobby enjoyed his creature comforts too much to remain on the lam for any length of time. His decision to flee would only postpone the inevitable, and make his legal difficulties exponentially more serious.

Even more disturbing, was Bobby suicidal? Would he really kill himself? Was he in so deep, he couldn't see other alternatives? J.D. shuddered at the thought of what that would do to Maggie and the boys.

The route to Escalante traversed an area with Zion National Park to his west, Bryce Canyon National Park and the Grand Staircase to the east. He passed through several small towns, including Mt. Carmel, home for a time to famous poet and painter Maynard Dixon, as well as the tourist enclaves of Tropic, Cannonville, and Henrieville.

Along the way, he passed through a network of deep, brightly colored Navajo sandstone canyons, textured in muted tones of reddish-brown, tan, and ivory. Rock formations of every size and shape dotted the landscape, reaching high into a crystal blue sky. Juniper, sagebrush, and yellow-flowered snakeweed colored the canyon floor as far as the eye could see. Springtime in the high desert had ushered in blossoming prickly pear cactus in bright hues of pink and orange.

Since his return to Kanab, Books had come to view the nearly two-million-acre Grand Staircase Escalante Monument as his personal playground. Its solitary beauty provided him with a sense of inner peace and serenity.

He dropped the boxes Runyon had given him at the BLM Visitor's Center on the west edge of Escalante. He then stopped for lunch at a small diner in town before starting the arduous journey over Hell's Backbone Road. With Jimmy Buck still at large, Books knew that he had to remain alert and focused. The likelihood that the anonymous call was a ruse designed to lure him into the wilderness seemed remote, but he'd be foolish to disregard the possibility.

Hell's Backbone Road was a high-altitude, thirty-five-mile stretch that overlooked the Box Death Hollow Wilderness area and connected the towns of Escalante and Boulder. It had been built by the Conservation Corps as a public works project during the Great Depression.

Narrow and dangerous, it was little more than a one-lane road, built without guardrails or shoulders and climbing to more than nine thousand feet above sea level. Inattention or a careless mistake going up or down the narrow switchbacks could send a driver careening over the edge and down a two-thousand-foot drop to the canyon floor. Books had driven it before, often without ever seeing another vehicle.

It was a time-consuming, laborious drive, but one so beautiful it took Books' breath away every time he saw it. At lower elevation, juniper pine dominated the landscape. As Books climbed the switchbacks up the mountainside, the green became predominately piñon pine and then ponderosa at the highest elevation.

The area was replete with spur roads that frequently went nowhere. A handful ended at marked trailheads, but most were old dead-end ranch roads. He would have to stop and check each one.

Books drove slowly with his window down and stopped often to listen. If anybody was cutting wood, the sound of chainsaws would carry a long way. Eventually, Books reached a plateau where the terrain flattened out for about ten miles, winding across a mountain range before beginning the long descent down the other side. He stopped several times, shut off the Sierra's engine and walked short distances into the woods until he ran out of road. Finally, about halfway across the plateau, Books came upon a double-track spur where he spotted a freshly cut pile of firewood tossed by the side of the road.

He shut the Sierra down and listened. At first, everything was quiet, but then he heard it—the whine of a chainsaw as it roared to life. The sound came from deep in the woods. Moving as quietly as possible, Books removed a Remington .12-gauge from its rack inside the Sierra and started walking down a barely visible two-track dirt road. He moved slowly, stopping every few feet to listen. The whine of the chainsaw grew louder as he headed deeper into the forest.

Two hundred yards in, Books stepped into a clearing. A man standing with his back to J.D. was cutting a downed tree into two-foot lengths. A large axe leaned against a nearby tree stump.

There was something vaguely familiar about him. When he hollered at him to turn off the saw, the man half turned, and Books knew instantly that he was in serious trouble. The man was Bobby Case.

"Hi, J.D., glad you could join us," said Case.

From behind him came a second voice. "I told you we had unfinished business. Now drop the shotgun and step away from it."

Books complied.

"I want you to very carefully reach across your body and remove the sidearm, and I want you to do it with only two fingers—your thumb and forefinger. Got that? If I see anything else, this .45 I'm holding will blow a hole in you big enough to drive an eighteen-wheeler through."

Again Books did as he was told.

"That's good, now turn around."

Books turned to see Jimmy Buck whose face was colored in streaks of camouflage green to match his clothing. The boots looked like standard combat military issue. The gun in his hand, however, was not. It might have been the biggest damned handgun Books had ever seen—a .45 caliber Colt or Smith revolver, with at least a seven-inch barrel.

"Step over to the fire pit yonder, and have yourself a seat on one of those tree stumps." Buck motioned to an area next to where his brother-in-law had been cutting firewood.

"What the hell are you doing here, Bobby? This isn't your kind of party."

Before Case could answer, Buck said, "Shut the fuck up. I didn't give you permission to talk. Boy, are you ever one dumb son-of-a-bitch walkin' in here like you did."

"You never gave me much choice, J.D.," said Case. "If you and that little shave-tail deputy had let me go, none of this would have happened."

"Oh, it would have happened anyway, Bobby. You were going down regardless, just like the rest of this gang of thugs," Books said, nodding at Buck.

"Now I don't recall givin' you permission to speak," said Buck, stepping in front of Books, and slapping him across the face with the back of his hand. The blow stung and knocked Books off the tree stump. He righted himself, tasting blood on the inside of his mouth.

"Well, it don't matter much anymore, J.D.," said Case. "It's going to end right here and now, and we'll bury you right next to Abby and Rolly."

"Next to 'um. I was thinkin we'd let Officer Books here dig 'em up, then we'll shoot him, and bury them all together. That would give a whole new meaning to the term 'a threesome,'" said Buck, laughing.

"Geez, Bobby, so you did kill them. These are people we'd grown up around."

"Heell, no," interrupted Buck. "Your brother-in-law is a bit on the squeamish side when it comes to killin' folks, so Daddy and I did it. Unfortunately, this .45 makes a godawful mess, so it's probably best that you all get buried here. That way nobody has to look at what was once a face and now ain't nothing more than a pile of goo."

Books was frightened but also seething with anger. "Speaking of your daddy, from what I heard, he died like the cowardly dog he was," Books said.

Buck stepped in front of him shaking with rage. He pressed the barrel of the cannon he was holding to the center of Books' forehead and said, "You ought to know 'cuz you killed him."

"I didn't have to kill him," replied Books, "because the dumb bastard shot himself." Books didn't know that for sure, but all indications were that in the end, Earl Buck had taken his own life.

"You'd best not say one more word about my daddy, because if you do, I'll blow your fuckin brains out right where you sit."

A calm seemed to settle over him then, and he added, "Besides, I wouldn't want to deprive you of the opportunity to dig your own grave and get one last chance to say hello to the Rogerses." He smiled showing a mouthful of crooked, yellow teeth.

Buck ordered Books to his feet and pointed to a grove of aspen trees thirty yards away. "I picked a nice, quiet spot under them trees. It's even got a nice view."

As he marched Books in the direction of the grave, Case, who had been listening attentively, but without any sign of emotion, fell in behind Buck. As they approached the grave, Case drew his .40 caliber Taurus from under his sweatshirt.

"That'll be far enough, Jimmy."

Buck made a half-turn, a quizzical look on his face. "What the hell you think you're doing?" he said.

"Like I said, it ends right here, today. You and I are going to surrender to J.D. and take our chances in court. The killing's over."

Buck grunted as he spun, aiming the cannon at the center of Case's chest. A momentary look of surprise registered on Case's face as both men fired. Books dove to his right trying to get out of the line of fire, reaching as he did so for his ankle holster. He couldn't recall, even later, how many shots were exchanged. As quickly as it started, it was over. When the smoke cleared, a wounded Jimmy Buck stood holding his right side looking down in a state of shock at the still figure of Bobby Case staring into the sky with vacant, dead eyes. In that instant, Buck seemed to realize that he was still in danger. He turned just as Books cut loose with the .25 caliber, firing continuously until the chamber clicked on empty. Buck fell, the .45 still clutched in his hand. Books immediately disarmed the semi-conscious man, rolled him on his stomach and cuffed his hands behind his back. He died minutes later.

There was nothing he could do for his brother-in-law. Case was bleeding profusely from two gaping chest wounds that Books suspected had left even larger exit wounds out his back. He bled out in a matter of seconds.

Books radioed for emergency assistance. The first to arrive was the Escalante town marshal, followed by a Grand County Sheriff's Department sergeant, who had been patrolling in the area. Within two hours, Charley Sutter, Randy Maldonado, and a team of FBI agents, including crime scene technicians, had converged on the area.

The decaying bodies of Rolly and Abby Rogers were discovered buried together in a shallow grave exactly where Jimmy Buck said they were, and had it not been for the actions of Bobby Case, it might well have been Books' grave as well. A medical examiner was flown by helicopter to the site. Four bodies were subsequently air-lifted to St. George where autopsies would be performed.

Books spent hours being interviewed and interviewed again by local authorities as well as the FBI. He spent the night at the home of his sister trying desperately to make her understand that in the end, Bobby had done the right thing, and it had cost him his life. Though he would never know, Books wondered whether Bobby's actions had been planned all along or came about spontaneously when he realized the horror that was about to unfold.

What brought Bobby Case and Jimmy Buck together on that day and in that place would remain a mystery. Perhaps Bobby had overheard his conversation with Maggie when he had mentioned going to Hell's Backbone Road. Maybe he knew where the Rogerses were buried and suspected a trap, or maybe he helped Buck plan the trap and had a change of heart at the last instant.

The dead always kept their secrets.

Chapter Forty-three

Afterword

It was a beautiful Saturday morning and Books had joined three of his colleagues for a round of golf at Kanab's Coral Cliffs Golf Course. Instead of playing with his fellow cops as he had in Denver, he was joined today by a geologist, a botanist, and a career bureaucrat.

He'd taken up golf on a regular basis during his years with the Denver Police Department, primarily as a means of coping with stress, although sometimes he wondered if golf caused more stress than it relieved. As a kid, he had played golf only sporadically, focusing instead on high-school football and basketball.

"I hope everybody brought their wallets," said Alexis Runyon. "I intend to go home today with my round covered by your losses."

The remark brought grins to the faces of her male playing partners, Books included.

"You gotta love her attitude," said geologist Frank Cartchner, trying not to sound condescending.

Looking almost as confident was botanist Glen Hale, who, rumor had it, sported a ten handicap.

Books, however, was wary. He'd never played golf with Runyon before, but she'd always looked fit and athletic. He knew from experience that she was competitive as hell when it came to playing poker.

They settled on a wager of fifty cents per hole per player. That meant that whoever won a particular hole collected fifty cents from each of the other players. Holes in which they tied would automatically carry over to the next one. In the unlikely event that someone managed to sweep all nine holes, that person would collect a modest $13.50.

When they got to the first hole, Cartchner asked Runyon if she wanted to lead off from the women's tee box.

"Sure," she said, "but in the name of fairness, I thought I'd give you guys a better chance by teeing off with you from the men's tees." This time the cackling was audible. Even Books was smiling.

The grins disappeared in a hurry when she launched a drive on the first tee that sailed twenty yards past Books and his male cohorts. It was like that for the rest of the round. When it was over, Runyon hadn't lost a hole. Mercifully, she didn't rub it in afterward, insisting on using her winnings to buy a round of drinks for all. The closest thing to a dig came when she offered a toast. "Here's to male gender stereotyping and bruised egos—may they all heal quickly."

As they walked to the parking lot, Runyon said, "I probably forgot to mention this when we started, but I attended the University of Texas on a golf scholarship."

"Now she tells us," moaned Books. Later, he would learn that she not only played golf for the University of Texas for four years but had been named to the All-Big Twelve Conference team three of those years. The lady could flat play.

◇◇◇

When the dust finally settled, only Jason Buck, Joe Benally, and Brett Gentry were left to face criminal prosecution. For Books, the victory was bittersweet at best. His sister had lost her husband, and Bobby's sons, their father.

The funeral service for Bobby took place at the Mormon ward in Kanab six days after his death. It seemed to Books like half of Kane County showed up. Old friends attended, like Rusty and Dixie Steed, Becky Eddins and her family, Ned Hunsaker, Alexis

Runyon, and every manner of politician from town councilmen to state legislators, all paying homage to the family led by patriarch, Doug Case. Even Books'father, Bernie, insisted on going, despite feeling less than one hundred percent.

While Maggie and the boys were devastated, the family took some comfort in the story that emerged in the aftermath of the bloody showdown. Despite many mistakes and lapses in judgment, in the end, Bobby Case had made a heroic decision that saved Books' life and cost him his own. Perhaps that final selfless act was the one way he could atone for his own misdeeds.

Follow-up by the Four Corners Task Force failed to definitively link the Buck gang to any other cases involving missing persons in the Four Corners area. Perhaps their enthusiasm was dampened by the fact that both ringleaders were dead. And the Native American group calling itself the Society for the Preservation of the Ancients turned out to be in no way connected to the Rogerses' disappearance. They were, however, a group that might bear future scrutiny by Four Corners area law enforcement agencies.

Thanks to the legal wizardry of Becky Eddins in negotiating a generous plea bargain for her client, Joe Benally was sentenced to serve up to fifteen years in prison on one count of burglary. With time off for good behavior, and considering his youth, he'd probably parole in five.

Ten days after the raid on his home and business, Brett Gentry was arrested on a fugitive warrant as he attempted to cross the border into Mexico from Nogales, Arizona. In the absence of sufficient evidence linking him to the kidnapping and murder of Abby and Rolly Rogers, he would eventually plead to one count of receiving stolen property. He'd receive a prison sentence of up to five years, a $5,000 fine, and three years of parole supervision upon release.

His wife, Emily, was never charged criminally, but both she and Brett would face a massive wrongful death civil suit filed by the Rogers children. Mrs. Gentry loudly proclaimed her husband's innocence to anyone who would listen, while continuing to operate a struggling Red Rock Touring company in his absence.

The only person left to face the wrath of an angry public seeking retribution for the senseless crimes, was Jason Buck. When a federal grand jury indicted him for kidnapping and conspiracy to commit murder, local prosecutor Virgil Bell wasn't far behind. Buck would face three state charges including burglary, felony theft, and possession of stolen property. If convicted on the federal offenses alone, he faced the prospect of a life sentence.

Sheriff Sutter had managed to avoid much of the public acrimony. However, prosecutor Virgil Bell had not. In conservative Tea Party Kane County, the only chance Bell would have had of quelling community rage would have been to somehow have Buck sentenced to twelve days in the electric chair. Books figured the best thing Bell had going for himself was that his term of office wasn't set to expire for more than two years. With the passage of time, public anger would diminish.

It was Sunday morning and Ned Hunsaker and Books were settled in Ned's living room. They had already consumed an artery-clogging breakfast of *huevos*, hash browns, sausage, and toast and were working their way through a second pot of coffee while reading the newspaper. Their mostly left-leaning political views were largely compatible, enabling them to discuss *ad nauseam* local and national issues without drawing blood.

Books' father was steadily improving from his recent cancer surgery, and his prospects for a complete recovery looked promising. Bernie's brush with his own mortality had somehow opened the door to conversation that had not been possible in their otherwise tumultuous relationship.

Happily, his relationship with Becky Eddins had weathered the stressful times and was still intact. And he had made a new friend in Beth Tanner, two new friends actually, the other being a scraggly looking pit bull he'd decided to name Hootch, after the movie *Turner and Hootch*.

Books was slowly recovering from the physical and mental fatigue of a nearly two-week investigation that, by most accounts, had ended badly. Five people had died, two of them innocent victims, summarily executed in the aftermath of a murder/kidnapping scheme. There was little solace to be had in the prosecution of three surviving perpetrators and the recovery of most of the stolen property.

For Books, the emotional toll on himself and members of his family was incalculable. Only time would heal the loss of a husband and father. Without Bobby, the viability of continuing to operate the cattle ranch would surely come under scrutiny. Books was already thinking about offering to move in with Maggie and the boys. His BLM salary more than sufficient to pay the bills.

In the days since the investigation ended, Books had had ample time to ponder the propriety of the federal government's role in trying to suppress the illegal antiquities trade. In his mind, the issue was analogous to the government's long-standing and largely failed effort to control drug trafficking. So long as consumer demand remained high, whether for drugs or artifacts, the trafficking would continue regardless of the existence of harsh laws or rigorous enforcement.

Pot hunters, Books had learned, often engaged in the practice for several reasons. Clearly, one was profit, but it was more complicated than that. In the end, some people did it because they believed they possessed an inherent right to—an entitlement of sorts. And some participated in skeleton picnics for adventure, or because their ancestors had done it, the practice having been handed down from one generation to the next.

For Books and cops like him, perhaps it didn't matter. He knew from long years of experience that enforcing criminal law was often filled with shades of gray. He could worry about it some other time, or not.

To receive a free catalog of Poisoned Pen Press titles, please contact us in one of the following ways:

Phone: 1-800-421-3976
Facsimile: 1-480-949-1707
Email: info@poisonedpenpress.com
Website: www.poisonedpenpress.com

Poisoned Pen Press
6962 E. First Ave. Ste 103
Scottsdale, AZ 85251